JUNO'S SWANS

Tamsen Wolff

JUNO'S SWANS

Europa
editions

Europa Editions
214 West 29th Street
New York, N.Y. 10001
www.europaeditions.com
info@europaeditions.com

Library of Congress Cataloging in Publication Data is available
ISBN 978-1-60945-466-1

Wolff, Tamsen
Juno's Swans

Book design by Emanuele Ragnisco
www.mekkanografici.com

Cover photo: Pexels

Prepress by Grafica Punto Print – Rome

Printed in the USA

for Kate,
FITYΛPWAW
then, now, and always

and

for Heidi,
alchemist, co-conspirator, lifesaver

JUNO'S SWANS

PART 1
THE HEARTBREAK

S arah says she's in love with someone else. The idea is so hard to hold in my head that it keeps flipping over again like a bath toy you try to invert in the water. *I'm in love with her*, she said (or rather, she says every day, every hour on the hour, every four minutes and twenty-three seconds, like a hateful, erratic cuckoo clock). *I'm in love with her* (in a solicitous stranger's voice that makes me feel newly wild, broken open, vicious, sick).

You can't be, I said (glossy-eyed, disbelieving, glazed, cracked), *you're for me.*

Listen, I like a love story. And this would be a love story except that Sarah wrecked it, just came on in and jumped on its head casually in cleats, so instead I'm rooting around, but I'm not even finding the punctured remains. I know there are countless ways to make an exit, family who leave and friends who turn into strangers. But this. I could not have imagined it. If she hadn't loved me once maybe she wouldn't have left me to the dogs, to the wilderness, to my own devices, which as it turns out, all seem to amount to the same thing. Even with everything else that's happened, I keep circling the loss of her like an animal worrying a wound. I need one of those huge cones they put around dogs' necks to keep them from doing this, from licking the painful place again and again.

(*I'm in love with her.*)

I want her cleaned out of all the wispy misty corners where she's hiding. I want her cleaned out of all the places where I tucked her, deep in my pockets, close to my heart, under my entrails for safekeeping. I am going to have to cut her out like an infection, scoop her out, with a cherry pitter or a grapefruit spoon, the way they used any crude metal implement on the fields of the Civil War to dig out a rotting bullet wound. Clean it out from the beginning, from the start. That's my plan.

I know this much:

It started at a party in Wellfleet on Cape Cod last spring, not long after my seventeenth birthday.

(And right then, every time, the deafening tidal wave of her voice rears up. *I'm in love with her.* And the surge of despair pulls me under. *You can't be. You're for me.*)

Round and round it goes, a maniacal broken record. I don't know how to look at it and I don't know how to look away.

How many times can one person break your heart?

CHAPTER 1

I keep replaying the conversation in my head," I say out loud to Titch, louder than I mean to.

"Don't," she responds. Then, "I'm sorry."

"I couldn't speak, I didn't know what to say."

"Well that's a rarity," Titch says. Which is fair.

I look over at her.

We are sprawled on beanbag chairs in the basement in her mother's house where we once watched *Lady Chatterley's Lover* on the VCR, back when the VCR was a really big deal. Titch's mom had to drive us all the way to the video store in Lebanon because there certainly wasn't one in Etna, New Hampshire, the backass end of nowhere. The video store had rows of shelved black plastic cases that seemed to advertise something illicit, like the adult area of the magazine store, or beer bottles in brown paper bags, so it didn't seem that surprising when we got back to Titch's house and discovered *Lady Chatterley's Lover* in the case that claimed to hold *The Great Muppet Caper*. We managed to get through all the good bits before anyone upstairs noticed.

I wonder if Titch ever thinks about this. At the moment she has her right index finger in her book and is squinting out the sliding glass doors at the blurry world of October, frowning. It is raining lightly, spattering on the glass. We haven't said anything out loud for probably an hour.

(*I'm in love with her. You can't be.*)

I think, *Titch does not want to talk to me, she does not want to hear about Sarah, she does not want to hear about any of it.* I wonder if she will tell me that I can't stay. If she does, where am I going to go?

Titch and I used to be best friends. Her real name is Harmony, which is a terrible joke because she's maybe the least harmonious person around. She's an artist and a kind of prickly, lackadaisical hypochondriac with an excellent, very dry sense of humor. Before this summer, we'd been best friends since fourth grade. But right now, Titch isn't looking at me. She's reading again, her left hand clamped under her right armpit for warmth. Her hands are slender and long-fingered and nearly always blue from cold. She's one of the coldest people I've ever known. In the middle of summer, her mom, Lois, will seize both her hands and rub them together murmuring, *cold hands, warm heart.*

Lois teaches special ed in elementary school and volunteers at the hospital. She has a soft nest of dark hair and eyes that look amazed and gentle at the same time. I always want to perform tricks around her to get her to look at me the way she looks at Titch. Her face gets all kind of suffused, like she's blushing, but with helplessness and love. Sometimes not having my mother around all the time has seemed like an advantage, but whenever I see Lois look at Titch, it gives me pause.

When Lois was first diagnosed with breast cancer we were in sixth grade. That time she smoked pot medicinally for a while, which we thought was very cool, but which made her throw up. We sat around in the basement after she smoked, pretending we could breathe in the fumes from the air, laughing ourselves sick with the imagined high, and rolling about on the floor cushions deliriously, like demented puppies. We are sitting in that room now, that pretend pot room, that room of ridiculous juvenile giddy idiocy. It's right where we are now and in some other dimension.

Titch has never actually smoked anything to the best of my knowledge. She has a formidable list of real ailments, asthma, allergies that used to require special shots at the hospital once a week, diabetes that required insulin injections. She has a lot of paraphernalia to deal with all the contingencies, the dangers of low blood sugar, the wheezing, the bee stings. She's like her own walking hospital and she jingles when she moves because of all the various dog tags with information about how to treat her if she stops breathing. We used to practice for emergencies and I know how to administer her shots and even how to resuscitate her, if necessary. This always gave me a great sense of importance, and besides, it was fun. By the time we were faced with the plastic mannequin in CPR in high school—*"Annie, Annie are you okay?"*—we were old hands.

Titch looks up at me sharply right then.
"Nina?"
"What?"
"Did you just say *Annie, Annie are you okay?*"
I can't see any way out of it. "I was thinking about CPR with Mr. Honeywell."
Her eyes are flitting meanly from side to side without comprehension, as though I am speaking a foreign language. Her face is closed and furious. My throat cramps.
When she doesn't say anything else, I think *what am I doing here, I should get up and go, she doesn't want me here.* My heart is staggering in my chest, actually lurching from left to right.
I think: *I am going to lose her too.*
I think: *I already have.*
A band of pain clamps around my skull like a vise. It makes my eyes close, until I force myself to open them again and see Titch, scowling downward.
Part of me really wants to ask her something, like how I got here. Or even *how did we get here?* We used to be the ones

who knew that grown-ups disappoint and disappear, and that was part of what drove us so firmly together. But now that we've disappointed each other, disappeared on each other?

These are not the kinds of questions Titch likes much. If I asked her anything like this, she would be completely jumpy.

We have been silent in the basement for so long that the air in the room is starting to sit heavy on my chest like a wrestler. (*I'm in love with her.*) I know there's a way to get out from under this. (*You can't be.*) I keep thinking if I can get any kind of grip on what led up to this moment, or if I could focus on what was true, maybe I wouldn't have to be trapped forever, I could roll out from under, I could breathe again.

When we first came down to the basement this afternoon Titch had asked right away whether I was going to go back to school. I'd driven by the high school on the way to her house, trying not to look and see who was horsing around on the grass out front. I held my breath, like I was driving by the cemetery. I could hear laughter floating up, a girl's warning helpless giggle. I thought I could hear the sound of sneaker rubber squeaking on the linoleum floors inside and I imagined a random pair of disembodied Tretorns or Adidas running up the front staircase to where the wobbly glass of the victory case loomed, filled with photographs—the faded grinning lines of faces, ancient boys kneeling on the soccer field—alongside unpolished trophies with illegible writing.

To Titch I said, "If I go back I might as well have a hunchback or a third eye, because everyone knows. You might as well paint a big red X between my shoulder blades."

That shut her up.

I didn't say it, but actually you could paint two big X's for that matter, front and back, because I am doubly marked. I am branded twice over. And Titch knows it. She is partly to blame.

In our grade, starting in elementary school, there were

three kids who were visibly marked. Lucas Mitchell's head was too long for his body and he had seams on his neck from brain cancer surgeries. Ginny Schramm mostly looked normal, but she was tiny and had teeth that made me squeamish, child teeth in a grown-up head, baby teeth, small smooth mouse teeth. Lucas was shy and kept to himself, but Ginny and I were friends for a while in third grade because it was easy to make her laugh and she had that kind of breathless laugh that would make her laugh again harder and harder until she wheezed silently, just *phht phht*, like a bellows. That laugh would make me want to say whatever it was over and over again. She was a ludicrously easy audience, the best to be had in 3G. And I could overlook the teeth too—or at least rationalize my fear—because everyone knew Ginny had a defective heart and wasn't supposed to grow like the rest of us. So I figured her heart was the reason she still had baby teeth and I tried not to let that drive a wedge between us. She died the summer before the first year of high school I think or even earlier when they moved away, I don't remember which. One fall she just didn't come back to school.

Then there was Marcia Rabinowitz. She had been some freak victim of polio after there was never supposed to be polio anymore. She walked the way you do after you've sat on the toilet for too long reading a book and your feet have fallen asleep all the way up your shins: kind of splayed and unsteady, grabbing onto stuff. Her fingers were stretched apart and rigid, the skin on the knuckles yellow. Ginny, Lucas, and Marcia were like constant reminders of things we thought we were safe from. You had to be nice—although some boys used to trip Marcia on the bus and everyone tried hard not to sit next to her. She had a strange smell, the smell maybe of too many hospitals, but absolutely of the weak animal in the herd. No one wanted to touch her, or Lucas, or even Ginny. You just wanted to leave some offering at their altars under the cover of night, open a beer or something and pour it into the ground like our crazy Latin teacher Mrs. Herrera had us do with red wine for the Greeks & Romans Unit. *Libations!* she'd cry and empty a bottle of red onto the ground. This was outside by the flagpole, before some parents complained. Since we couldn't get our paws on the stuff it seemed like an awful waste and we'd stand around in our white sheet togas mournfully watching it seep away.

When I pointed this out to Titch, the super sad marked lineup I'd be joining if I go back to school, she considered it without speaking for a minute.

"You'd be more like Jessica Myers," she offered then, tentatively.

Jessica Myers had become an overnight sensation sophomore year because she was supposed to have tried to kill herself over the lone exchange student, Dmitry Petrov, who had come to our high school for the year as part of some do-good Cold War outreach effort. There was a lot of whispering about it and she did appear to have faint scars on her wrists. If you looked really hard when she was changing in gym class you might see them. She wore a lot of those braided embroidery thread bracelets though, so it was kind of hard to tell. At the time, Titch had said flatly, "What an excellent idea for us to be friends with the Russians. They don't even have to bomb us; they can just send over their teenage boys and get American girls to off *themselves*. Crafty Commie pinko bastards."

"Like Jessica Myers with a twist," Titch added. "Jessica Myers on *crack*." She said it like that commercial where the voice says, *This is your brain*—image of an intact egg—*This is your brain on drugs*—a smashed, splattered, fried egg.

This is my brain on crack.

Thanks, I said. Or meant to say. Nothing actually came out. I tried to smile at Titch, but that didn't work so well either. My face seemed to be kind of paralyzed. I knew that she was trying but I was not rallying well. She looked around uneasily and bit the side of her middle finger.

She had asked me if I wanted to talk about anything. When we first came into the house, she asked me. She wasn't looking at me when she said it, but she didn't seem exactly mad or upset. Careful. But we were both being careful, like wary, uncomfortable strangers.

"I don't know where to start," I said dully. The backs of my calves were sticking to the vinyl of the beanbag. This wasn't entirely true. I didn't know whether to start telling her.

I know when it started.

It started at the party in Wellfleet on Cape Cod not long after my seventeenth birthday, or four months and eight centuries ago. Titch was there, but she didn't know. She knew and she didn't know too, the way people who are close to you do.

(*I'm in love with her. You can't be. I'm in love with her. You can't be.*)

Please. Make. It. Stop.

When I didn't say anything else, Titch had picked up the book beside her on the floor.

"If you want to talk," she said, her head in the book.

Chapter 2

I don't want to talk.
Driving on Route 6 heading off of Cape Cod about nine hours ago, I heard something over the insistent jabber on the car radio. It was right before I reached Eastham, around seven A.M. In the middle of the toothless forced hilarity of the morning DJs—the obligatory useless female DJ was saying over and over, "Oh you *guys*"—I heard a terrible sound. It sounded like somewhere in the car there was a yowling animal that had given up on being saved from death. Then I saw in the rearview mirror that my face was appallingly contorted. It looked like there was a frantic bird trapped and flapping behind my eyes. I pulled over into the greasy puddled parking lot of the Dunkin' Donuts kitty-corner with Nickerson's gas station, forgot to cut the engine, and stalled. I was actually writhing in the seat, wrestling with the snaking grief in my gut. It slithered up and wrapped around my throat, cutting off my windpipe. It's amazing what can live in your belly and what can come out of your mouth. I mean apart from how awful I felt, even right then I was amazed. It was like I was ventriloquizing the entire sick house at the zoo, making the whole car resound with feline caterwauling, and that eerie otherworldly mewling that marine animals make. I had to slap myself hard in the face a bunch of times just to stop the sounds. Then I sat for a long blubbering snotty stretch of time.

Kate Bush was singing on the radio when I finally pulled

out of the parking lot. It sounded sort of like a sympathetic backup chorus, a muted and prettier animal lament.

Maybe this is what people mean when they say you have *a growing pain*. You sprout new limbs, monstrous organs right there on the spot—you feel the flailing, the impossibility of coordinated movement, your belly distended, pushing out your rib cage, and you hear the groaning, creaking, roaring fury of your cavernous bones. It didn't much make me want to talk. It didn't much make me want to open my mouth ever again.

So instead I am sitting here in silence with Titch reading and me on my lumpy seat, lumpy with grief, just stupid with it. There's the back of Titch's impenetrable neck. Over her bent head a poster is hanging partly off the wall. Under the curl of paper it says, *ACE: The New Frontier.*

SPACE. Of course: *SPACE. SPACE: The New Frontier.* It's from before the Space Shuttle Challenger exploded sophomore year and Christa McAuliffe blew up on national television along with those six other astronauts nobody can ever remember. We watched it happen, with most of the rest of the country, in our case in the school auditorium on a big television screen. A lot of people had posters and hats and the like. Our school and the whole state had a kind of proprietary interest since Christa was from New Hampshire, *picked from 11,000 teachers nationwide*, people liked to boast. She taught at Concord. Our football team had lost to Concord twice the season before the Shuttle launch. (We lost to everybody. We were a joke.) When the explosion happened seventy-three seconds after takeoff, people mostly looked around the auditorium, confused, as though an explanation would follow, but the faces of the teachers were as perplexed and stunned as ours. Then the television cameras zoomed in on the faces of her two kids, who were young, under ten anyway. That's when I understood what had happened, by watching their faces drain and shrink and pucker in shock. The way they were exposed, their skin peeled back right there in front of the world, was strange and terrible. Like slitting open the frogs in Bio, only worse because the frogs at least are already dead. Donna Henderson, our perpetually sweaty Music teacher, plowed forward like a giant damp cheese trapped in a polyester pantsuit, trying to get to the TV and turn it off. She was panting, and she trod hard on Trevor Sullivan's hand because Trevor was sitting on the floor in her path. He shrieked but she didn't even notice.

Listen, obviously it's not the same thing what I'm feeling now and what those McAuliffe kids were feeling. Obviously. But something has exploded. And anyone who really looks at me can see my chest is cracked open, my heart is visibly, senselessly banging away. Anyone who is looking at me can see that all I am is a collection of exposed organs, walking around.

It's dreadful being porous, the way everything and everyone gets in. There should be a plastic wrap for this grief and rage, or a way to lock me in my own phone booth so I can be left to stew alone.

(*I'm in love with her.*
You can't be. You're for me.)

This is not my only experience with heartbreak. I've had my heart broken. Not like this, but still. Broken. My heart broke when I was nine. My grandfather, who I loved more than anything—more even than my rabbit Milo, who was assertive, clean, and grouchy like most intelligent animals—my grandfather froze to death. My grandfather froze to death and I was not there to save him because I was away on a rare trip with my mother. (You get no say in these matters when you're a child. Your bag gets packed and you're told to get in the car this minute or else. Besides which, I liked traveling with my mother, she laughed more when we were away.) By the time we were back home, it was too late.

What I remember, what can't be true because I wasn't there, is my grandmother sitting in an armchair, wearing her blue velvet Christmas skirt that goes all the way down to the ankles. She has a grey cat on her lap, Potlatch, the cat of seven cats ago. (Cats don't last long on my grandparents' farm, coyotes get them or fisher cats, or we say only *they wandered too far into the woods*, like they are in their very own feline fairy tales.) Potlatch is shedding great clumps of grey and white hair, handfuls floating onto my grandmother's skirt and downward onto the carpet. My grandfather is freezing to death about a half a mile away from where we are. He has wandered too far into the woods. We don't know this but we can hear the police dogs, the sounds of men shouting. Snow the color of blue opal banks up above the window ledge.

(That bit is true. That winter the snow piled so high that I could climb out the upstairs window, and, taking care not to dislodge the slate tiles on the roof, slide right off into the snowdrift below.)

Inside, my grandmother is stroking the cat, slowly meditatively stroking and stroking. There are clouds of his hair everywhere. The cat's tail has a broken bone in its end and the tip twitches. I'm watching the tail twitch and I'm watching her. She doesn't have her teeth in. There's a hole in her face, a dark, irrevocable hole. I want to dive into it because it's inscrutable the way she is, it's like black water under ice, it's like something you have to flail against, something you have to ravage, something you have to destroy in order to get to the bottom of it.

Five days after we had returned from our trip, my mother took a walk. She found her father's orange hunting hat, a fluorescent bright, bright orange. It was supposed to make him visible so no one would accidentally shoot him with a hunting rifle. So he could walk through the world unharmed. She found the hat on a path. She walked a little farther. She found a pile of his clothes. He had folded them. There was a little fresh snowfall on them. All I could see when she described this to me was cat hair drifting like milkweed fluff on his clothes. He was naked. He was naked and he was blue like my grandmother's skirt all the way to the ankles so you can't see her legs. He was blue through his whiteness from his toes to his ears, the way that skim milk is blue.

I saw his death certificate. It said "exposure." Under "consequences of or due to" someone left-handed wrote in black ink "*lost in woods*" and then under "notes," right-handed blue ink added "*senile dementia.*" I was there when one of the policemen explained to my mother that in the end stages of severe hypothermia people often do something called terminal burrowing, when they try to dig themselves into a hiding place, a cave, a hole, a space under the bed, trying to make a small corner to crawl into, to hide in and die, as animals do. He said that people who are freezing to death also often undress—he called it "paradoxical undressing"—because when the muscles are exhausted from shivering to keep a person warm, they finally relax and the person who is freezing to death feels a sudden surge of blood and heat, especially in the extremities, a feeling of being so overheated that he or she will often tear off any clothing. My mother didn't say anything when the policeman told her this; she was stroking the sleeve of her father's worn brown corduroy jacket, which was draped over her arm. I wanted to say, but he folded his clothes, he *folded* them. He kissed my grandmother goodbye, he walked into the woods, he undressed, he folded his clothes, he laid them in a pile, and he stretched out on the snow on his back and looked up at the sky. He didn't burrow down into the snow or rip off his clothing. It wasn't paradoxical. It was intentional. I know it was.

Here's the thing: if I'd been home it never would have happened because even though they brought in police dogs they couldn't find him and I would have been able to sniff him out.

He had a very particular smell, a little sour, a little watery, like he never managed quite to wash the sleep dank off himself, but at the same time his whiskers could be as warm and delectable as brown sugar in oatmeal.

Sometimes he was sad. I cheered him up. We went for soft ice cream together, which would have been strictly verboten by my mother, or more accurately not recognized as being edible at all (it would be like saying *we went to eat Astroturf together*). But my grandfather and I would drive down Route 14 in the tan Hornet to a small place with one window that never ever looked open and always was even in the winter I think. We would go up to the hatch—he'd lift me up—and I'd ring the round bell, which I loved. It was like the bell that sat on Mrs. Harrison's desk that she rang when spelling speed tests were over. It made my heart race a little bit just to see a bell like that. This one looked rusty but when I hit it with the flat of my hand it would ping out clear and very slowly someone would emerge from the cross-hatched darkness and take our order, an old man in an apron in the off seasons and snippy teenage girls in the summer, all equally sullen. Then we'd sit and lick the cones, the vanishing empty sweetness, on the hood of the Hornet facing the White River, watching the light wink on the water or the ice or the muck of built-up leaves and old tires. It was a lovely leisurely silent glinting bubble we were bound up in. I don't remember speaking at all. Afterwards he would carefully clean his whiskers of the chocolate jimmies we always ordered. These reminded me of the dotting of mouse turds in the corners of my bedroom in their house. Even though he didn't say anything, I knew from the reflective, hard front of his belly, I knew from his thoughtfulness, from the silence, from the careful way he folded his handkerchief and returned it to his pocket, that we would never mention these outings. I never have until now, either.

Anyway he died, but that wasn't what broke my heart. I

mean it's not as if sad crap hadn't happened before this. My father had up and left, for one. But since his leaving led to my living with my grandparents, it always seemed to me that I came out ahead on that one. What finally broke my heart was at my grandfather's funeral when I realized that *he knew* I would have found him and that was why he'd waited until we were out of town. Because I could have prevented his death and he did not want me to. Even in his wandering state, his not-all-there state, he still knew me better than anyone else and well enough to know that I would have done anything to keep him with me.

I remember the words of the minister sliding back and forth over my head in a mindless seesaw. I was looking down into the grave and I felt my own chest yawn open so there was a gap and I made a kind of groan like trees make when the wind has pushed them too far or maybe something inside the trunk is giving way or rearranging. Someone, it must have been my mother, I don't remember, swept me up and away, although I was too big to be carried. My legs were all tangled up in the moving legs below, banging and bumping shins and feet and kneecaps. Over the moving shoulder—my cheeks slipping and jolting—I could see the grave receding. Then my shoes were being pulled off and a blanket tucked over me. I turned my face to the wall and slept and slept, trying to shut it out.

No one believes your heart can break so young, but why not? Why not worse? Just because your bottom is closer to the floor doesn't mean it doesn't hurt to fall. When my grandfather died, my grandmother started winding down very, very slowly, speaking less and less, like a balloon almost imperceptibly deflating. But I was promptly and completely floored by his loss. He was a big man and I counted on that bigness, it filled a space, it created ballast, it secured me. A lot of grown-ups seem to think that littler bodies have littler emotions, even sometimes that little means dumb when it's the god's honest truth that's their own stupidity shining through like the hangover day-light, every bit as harsh and blundering. Your body can capsize with grief whatever its size.

Now it happens with no warning, the ebb and swell, the grip and slither of grief. Mostly all I'm doing here, all I'm doing these days, is waiting grimly for the next wave. What I need is a certain kind of leverage, a foothold, to drag myself out of this stupid sad abyss. It's just like that too—a wet bog, a sandpit, something from the Brontës' world with craggy rocks all around—and I keep trying to pull myself up and out. It's sad in here. It's gloppy and messy and sad. Rage is about the only thing that helps. It's like a handhold or a skeletal structure, a backbone. Without it, I would be nothing but a pulsing blob, a pulp of sadness.

(*I'm in love with her. You can't be.*)

I want her to suffer in small pointed ways and in biblical plagues.

(*I'm in love with her.*) Don't think it won't happen.

(*You. Can't. Be.*) Don't think I can't make it happen.

For starters, I used to be a biter. I was biter right off in nursery school. I was living in London with my mother then, in Islington, by a park where all the tulips were planted aggressively according to color, vivid reds together, then yellows, then reds again. Sometimes when my mother carried me by the flower border, the bobbing of the colors over her shoulder would make me nauseated. That was the year my father left us. I believed for a long time that he was coming back, but I was pretty unhappy about it just the same. I bit in school because I was angry most of the time and it was extremely effective. I bit children who crossed me and they left me alone. Before long all I had to do was bare my teeth and other children would back away from me. Children are fast learners. I was no exception. That year, after I drew blood from the stringy forearm of the school matron for the second time, I was finally sent home to live with my grandparents on their sheep farm in Vermont. I still remember the sweetness of sleeping on that transatlantic flight, my head in my mother's lap, the muffled airplane drone in my ears, that stuffy sickly recycled airplane air coating the inside of my nose. I remember seeing my grandparents in the distance waiting to meet us at the gate at Boston's Logan Airport, and I ran toward them as fast as I could run, as fast as I had ever run, until I was enveloped in my grandfather's deliciously pipe-smoked rumpled coat, lightheaded with relief.

I never bit anyone in school again. But that doesn't mean that I'm not capable of inflicting pain. It doesn't mean I can't bite, or damage, devastate, or destroy.

Chapter 3

"D o you remember Billy Willenka?" I ask Titch abruptly. "Yeah, you clocked him," she says, not hesitating, totally straight-faced. She is speaking through her teeth, vigorously chewing a hangnail. She doesn't look up from her book. She is deeply intent.

"You cleaned his clock. You kicked his ass."

Cleaned his clock. Not true.

But true: in the seventh grade on the playground I hit Billy Willenka in the face as hard as I could and I broke his glasses. I mean I sent them spinning off his head in two pieces. We watched them arc up and out in horror. He looked so taken aback and terrified that I burst into tears. Blood leapt out of his nose. Mrs. Hanratty immediately seized Billy by the arm to drag him off to the principal's office because it was only possible that he had injured me, despite the bright red evidence to the contrary. Neither of us protested initially, from shock maybe or because in the larger scheme of things that was an accurate verdict. He, Billy, would do harm to the likes of me. Not that he had, not that he did much more than leer and harass, push too hard in touch tag, cheat on math tests, trip hapless students in the hall. Usually his targets were girls, especially if they had tender beginners' breasts. But he also went after those boys who could be counted on to cry, like Matthew Williamson, or boys who would let fly a useless flapping fist, flailing horribly at the slightest provocation, those poor boys who made you want to duck your head in shame so as not to be a witness to their lunchroom degradation.

Billy was only ever a low-level bully. His mother was Bunny
Willenka, the gray mean-eyed secretary in the principal's office
who spoke so forcefully that it seemed like her teeth would
come shooting out of her head. Everyone was afraid of her,
probably even Billy. In the moment when I hit him he had just
said something about being able to see blood on the back of
my pants—which was impossible at the time—but in saying it,
he conjured the single worst moment imaginable in school,
something that had actually happened to Heather Linney-
Proctor the year before. In French class when Heather stood
up to walk to the board, there was a bright blooming scarlet
rose across the seat of her white jeans. Shelly Adams jumped
up behind Heather, grabbed her elbow, and walked out of the
room with her. Chubby, smiley, previously completely unremarkable Shelly Adams who was forever pushing her thick
glasses up her nose. She planted herself behind Heather like
she was putting her body in front of a bullet. She was deaf to
the frenzied cries of Monsieur Hoover—*Où allez-vous?
Reviens immediatement s'il te plaît!*—even when he stood in
the doorway, calling down the hall after them. No one could
conjugate a verb for the rest of third period and Heather,
although tiny, blonde, generically appealing, and a superb field
hockey goalie, never really recovered.

The year after that, her father, who was a gynecologist, was
accused of sexual harassment and the whole family moved
away to San Diego. I remember Titch's musing with a certain
authority about the likelihood of being accused of sexual
harassment when your job was examining women with their
feet up in stirrups. The word *stirrups* in this context made me
deeply uneasy and I didn't pursue it, although under other circumstances I might have challenged her. At the time, what
happened to Heather and what her father did for a living possessed a sort of awful logical continuity, like the unfortunate
messy blot of female sex was stamped on the whole family, like

a paint line was slapped across their front door to indicate contamination from a plague.

When Billy invoked Heather Linney-Proctor's mythic nightmare moment, I wheeled around and hit him hard, square, closed fist in the face, with a glorious flowering of rage and power in my chest. My mother happened to be in town at this time so she was called into school and when I recounted what I had done she did not say, *We don't hit.* She did not say, *What's gotten into you, you've always been such a nice girl.* (That was the principal, who clearly did not know me well.) She said, *Nina has every right to defend herself and verbal harassment is an attack on her well-being.* And: *If this boy thinks twice about harassing someone else, you can thank her.* To me in the car she said, *Don't do that again.* Also: *We're not telling your grandmother.* But nothing she said later could change the fact that I have never loved her more than I did in that principal's office.

I didn't tell my mother that when I hit Billy I was flooded with the pleasure of the violence, the massive satisfaction of connecting knuckle to bone. It was like a dam burst in my chest. It was like the top of my head flew off. It scared the hell out of me.

I thought, *I could kill*, and it wasn't hypothetical. The certainty made hay of all the times I'd wept for dead things, my rabbit Milo whose cage sat out too long in the sun, or the moths that Danny Stern's older brother had pinioned with thumbtacks to the windowsill in Health. That person who had wept big fat baby tears was a fraudulent shell now. I felt myself step out of her, wearing the tighter, shinier skin of a killer, a person who caused pain and enjoyed the sensation. I had no idea it would be so thoroughly satisfying. It was the kick, the high as he collapsed in front of me that astonished and exhilarated me the most. It was unspeakable and magnificent and appalling all at once.

So you know what I would relish doing to Sarah now, given the chance? (*I'm in love with her*, she says). Okay. Given that moment again, I wouldn't say piteously *You can't be*, or, like a chump, like a fool, like prize freaking idiot, *You're for me*.

No. I'd say, *Just so you know, this is what I will do to you if I ever get the chance:*

I will bash you over the head with a tall, heavy, ornate, flowered Chinese vase, something from an Edith Wharton drawing room.

I will thwack you in the middle of the back, or behind the knees with a piece of lumber, hard, knock you sprawling, skinning your hands and legs.

I will trip you every so often, maybe once or twice a day, or shove you sideways, to keep you off balance, to make you fall hard, surprised, on your tailbone.

I will kick you when you are down.

I will jump on your head wearing motorcycle boots when you are down.

I will drop-kick you out of the stadium.

I will splinter your spine.

I will split you from stem to stern, cut you open like an apple with an axe.

I will reach into your chest, take out your wriggling heart, and wring it like a wet cloth.

I will take out your gut, tie it up in a bundle, and let it bob out to sea.

I will bite your neck open.

I will bite your head off.

I will show you the same care you have shown me.

Even if the pain doesn't come from me, it will come. (*Grief comes to us all, Mary Margaret.*) I'll be waiting, I'll be watching, and I won't be sorry, because whatever I say in the future, know this: I will never forgive you. Forgiveness is horseshit, forgiveness is hogwash, forgiveness is strictly for the birds.

I mean this.

I know it's not the thing to say you have regrets. It's customary to say two people are to blame for the end of any two-person situation. This is crap. One person can wreck another, one person can be shipwrecked, while the other person sails away. I think it happens that way all the time and to say *it takes two* is a total lie. Most of the time it takes one, the one dancing in clogs on the innards of the other. And there's no way that clog dancer can say, oh hey, sorry, I didn't know those were your innards I was dancing on, *sorry. Sorry about your innards.* That bastard clog dancer is to blame, I mean please, let's not kid ourselves.

So I might wish this weren't true—and I do, oh I do, I do in every single cell of my being—but right now all I have are regrets, a whole cross-country carload of them, and I don't care who knows it.

"I want to bite her heart out," I blurt, or something to that effect. My voice sounds kind of like I've retched up a hairball onto the carpet. Titch doesn't even blink.

"Mmmmmm," she says. She is trying to wedge a pen cap onto her pinky finger and doesn't look up from her book. I don't even know if she heard me. I can't see what she's reading, but she is completely lost in it. I wish I were too. I would give anything to be at sea in someone else's story right now.

When I arrived to live at my grandparents' I couldn't read yet, but I started almost immediately after that. In that house that's what everyone did. From early, my grandmother used to read me giant juicy classics like *Vanity Fair* (*you're going to be disappointed in Becky Sharp*, she said with resignation, and I was), *Pride and Prejudice* (*you're going to be disappointed in Charlotte Lucas*, she said, and I was), and *Lorna Doone* (*you're going to be disappointed in Gwenny Fairfax*, she said, and I

was). I don't know why she wanted to hurry up and acquaint
me with all the disappointment before there'd even been time
to think how lovely for Elizabeth to have someone clever like
Charlotte to talk to, or how fabulously wicked Becky Sharp is,
such a relief after the wet Amelia, or how loyal and fierce
Gwenny is to milky Lorna.

It wasn't just the tough women, the bold ones biting the
dust or letting you down that she warned me about either, it
was the sad bits of the story coming up. When Lorna's cousin
Charley, young and handsome and stupid, is about to be
crushed under the ruthless heel of Carver Doone, my grandmother took off her reading glasses with her left hand and
pinched the bridge of her nose with her left thumb and index
finger, a sure sign of distressing things to come. *Oh dear*, she
might say, clearing her throat, and then gear up and forge
ahead while I was lying in wait in my bed, weighted down by
quilts and foreboding. I've never seen her cry; I've never heard
her raise her voice. When she heard my grandfather's body had
been found, all she said was, "Well. We'll need a sheet." But
she always seemed to be visibly moved by the plights of these
characters, creaky with unease to encounter their sad fates
again.

We certainly read other books that were much less fraught,
much stranger, peculiar dusty books that I was sure could only
exist in my grandparents' house, not in the library with its offi-
cious warm date-stamp smells. One of those books was called
something like *Tales of a Brownie* and it concerned a small
puck-like figure, a kind of grumpy Scottish fairy who always
needed to be appeased. He was a troublemaker, a demon
really, the Brownie. I had him in my mind as part of a crew that
included the Wild Wooders, the ferrets and stoats in *The Wind
in the Willows*, and Puck in *Midsummer Night's Dream*. (My
grandmother set me to recitation on rainy days so I could jump
in anytime with *What? Jealous Oberon? Fairies skip hence, I*

have foresworn his bed and company, or *Over hill, over dale . . .*)
The Brownie liked any number of unusual acknowledgments
but the only one I remember was a bowl of milk set out, which
troubled me because I didn't see how you could prevent the
cat from getting it and consequently enrage the Brownie. It
was very easy to enrage the Brownie and difficult to placate
him. This was because he liked playing tricks and harassing
anyone who'd slighted him. I remember he would pinch people, painfully in unlikely places at irregular intervals, just *pinch
pinch* the day away. And his victims, who had often utterly
unwittingly irked him, would be in constant but erratic pain,
getting increasingly jumpy about when they would be pinched
again, like rats in some torture experiment with electric zaps.
The Brownie would chortle at all this misery. The Brownie
would hold his spirit sides and split himself laughing. It was
pretty sinister actually and I don't know why we read it. I
always liked the big bold love stories best.

*I'm in love with her. I'm in love with her. I'm in love with
her.*

And just like that without warning, I'm knee-deep in a river
of sadness. My boots are full and squelching, my feet are sodden. Just like that. *I can't make this stop.*

The grief is huge, stinging, saturating. Hearing the mental
loop of Sarah's voice is a lot like vomiting. I can feel her words
churning up again, unstoppable, wrenching.

I'minlovewithherI'minlovewithherI'minlovewithher.

If I thought it would help, I'd sic a Brownie on her, one
who hasn't been out of the forest in a long time, one with a
great deal of bad humor to dole out in hard twisting bruising
pinches, side stitches, in her heart, her intestine, her inter-
costals. *Did you feel that?* Did it hurt? Good. Breathe because
it won't happen again for a day or a minute, who knows
which, but it will happen again and again and again when you
don't expect it until the bruising is permanent—the purple

mementos, the lesions on your heart, your organs—those are gifts from me.

But this isn't helping. Not even anger is helping. (*I'm in love with her.*)

You can't be. Because how can that be true?

If anything I know is true, how can what she says also be true?

CHAPTER 4

T itch," I say, my voice dipping and sliding alarmingly up and down a crazy, uncontrolled, gulping scale.

"Titch, it happened right? I mean, I'm not crazy, right?"

She looks up at me, blankly, but not meanly. Perplexed.

"Well, a lot's happened," she says, slowly.

"I mean she loved me? And I was happy?"

She flinches slightly. "Yeah. You seemed happy."

"Really?" I am pleading, begging, unable to stop myself. I can't breathe for the sadness.

Titch's chin has dropped to her chest and her hands are clasped in front of her as though she is praying. I can't see her face.

Finally, in a low voice, not looking at me, she says, "When it started you were happier than I've ever seen anyone."

It's true. I was.

When it started we were at a party in Wellfleet on Cape Cod in June. Ruby, Titch's stepsister, had a party at the beginning of the season and we were invited. It was at Ruby's that everything began, right on our first weekend in town. Ruby was living in a tiny house on Whit's Lane in the center of Wellfleet. She shared the house with an older red-haired woman named Bess, who we had met briefly the day we stopped by when we arrived on the Cape. Ruby and Bess were both waitresses at Aesop's, a restaurant in town. The weather was cold and I was uncomfortable because I hadn't packed the right things and I didn't know anyone. I retreated into the bedroom with all the coats almost immediately after arriving, just to buy some time away, on the pretense of looking for something in my jacket. Not that I needed a pretense. Not that anyone was paying any attention to me.

The bedroom had a reproachful smell I couldn't place, a smell of sad, stale sex with an acrid vein like something had gotten caught in the toaster that shouldn't have—wool maybe, or hair. The smell rapidly made me uneasy and I stopped looking at the charcoal drawings tacked to the wall and rejoined the party.

But things didn't smell good there either. From the living room, yeasty smells of cumin, cilantro, and warm beer mingled, alongside the aggressive, revolting fragrance of a vanilla-scented candle. A man with a doleful jowly hound head was crouching down beside the chair of a woman I thought was named Brigitte. Everyone was clasping beers. I couldn't see Titch anywhere. Distantly but insistently, maybe from the kitchen radio, Madonna was suggesting that we take a holiday and some time to celebrate. I noticed that a serious Middle Eastern doctoral student I'd met that morning in the coffee shop was eyeing me speculatively from across the room. Feeling a little desperate and trying not to breathe through my nose, I made a break for the door.

There on the ledge, waiting calmly, was a dog, not big, not small, a well-proportioned brown and gold dog who looked like she had some beagle in her. I don't usually like dogs, but she seemed like an excellent diversion so I squatted beside her and she immediately offered up her belly for stroking, then sighed heavily and curled up in an impossibly small ball, her spine like butter.

"She's pretty worn out," someone said above me.

I struggled to get up and there was a girl looking at me. She had clear green eyes like glass on the beach, with a brown spot on the left one. She looked into me, frankly, amused. I was riveted. The dog lifted her head too, her muzzle a vertical line to the girl above. Together we gazed at the girl.

"I wore her out on the beach."

"Is she yours?" I said, stupid, dazzled.

She smiled, not a smile, brisk, dismissive, and I saw I was in the way, blocking the door. I lunged to the left, nearly falling over the dog, and the girl, carrying a six-pack of beer I saw now, walked past me into the party, her hair swinging. I spent the next two hours creeping around the edges of the room trying crabwise to get close to where she was, but kind of like the way something slips away from you in a dream, she kept receding to the horizon. Everyone seemed to know her.

Eventually Titch wanted to leave, grumpily, and I wheedled out of going. I said I would find a way home and she glared at me hard with total disgust, like she had really had it with me, and then she turned on her heel. The girl with the honey-colored hair was directly across the room with her back to me, looking out the window. I managed to sidle over, wobbly. She looked thoughtfully down at the handkerchief garden while I hovered for an alarming minute, all my neck hairs upright, prepared to bolt. Just then she lifted her head and had me in her sights.

"You're friends with Ruby's sister?" she said.

"Yes," I said and sank like a stone. Then, inspired: "We're here for the summer."

She smiled a little. "You're Nina."

Yes. Yes I am. Suddenly: I am. *Because she knows my name:* I am.

She didn't say anything else. I scrounged frantically, finally coming up with, "Do you live out here?"

"Sometimes," she said. "For the moment."

She had a small beauty mark on her left jawbone. The pulse in her neck was beating. She'd gone back to looking out the window. The silence seemed companionable and I stood very still, willing it never to end, for us to stay there forever with the weak sunlight reaching our knuckles and splashing our feet.

Ruby crashed into it, holding a large metal spoon and a potholder shaped like a lobster claw.

"Where's Titch," she said, not waiting for an answer. "Buggered off? Do you want dinner?" She asked my companion, not me. "The water's just boiling."

"No," she said, "I've got to get going."

"Just as well," said Ruby ruefully, as though there was more to be said on that score. But the girl just gazed through her, ignoring the opening, if it was one, and Ruby swung around, rallying the crowd towards the kitchen, her spoon held aloft in a Viking charge. The conversations followed after her.

"Do you need a ride?" the girl said to me, businesslike, and I said yes like I was the short person picked first for the volleyball team, then, mortified, downshifted to say *that would be great* so formally it sounded like my voice had cracked right there on the spot. Blissfully, she didn't seem to notice. She scooped up a grey windbreaker in one hand and headed to the door.

"Come on, Biscuit," she said and the dog bounced straight up like a ball.

She had a beautiful bright blue truck, the kind with rounded hubcaps and a hood curved like the tender benign snout of some loveable water mammal. Biscuit sat between us and I put my hand on her taut side feeling her sleep warmth and her full body breath. She kept her forelegs in perfect alignment with the edge of the seat. I was grateful to have something to touch.

We talked about the dog, how her name was going to be Basquiat until she turned out to be a bitch and how she'd come from the Animal Rescue in Brewster. She told me—Sarah told me, in the truck she finally said her name was Sarah, her name is Sarah, her name will always be Sarah—a little bit about what we were driving past. She never asked where to go, she seemed to know. She was an excellent driver. I made her laugh twice, which made me heady with power.

Two weeks later I slid my hand into hers one night at a crowded party when I was leaving and wanted her attention before I left, just to say goodbye I'm sure I told myself—although you know it's just as likely that I thought I would die if I went one more minute without touching her—but what I thought was *I'll just get her attention to say goodnight.* What I do know is that when I slid my hand into hers, the words *slid* and *hand*, *mine* and *hers* were blown open, just stretched to breaking like the skin of a balloon, as if I didn't know or had to relearn what sliding was, the ease the smoothness the grace the arms outstretched glee and terror of a foolhardy child hurtling down the chute at the playground. She held my hand. People around us were talking, but they were only so many silent movie mouths with oversized puppet heads. The world was between our palms, so discreetly and politely pressed, so heated and limitless, curious and fervent. The world contracted to that electric violet place. If we had opened our hands right then the light streaming out would have dazzled you blind. I didn't look at her; I couldn't look at her. I just held that pulsing jewel and marveled, brilliantly distracted. (*You know this to be true, deserter, betrayer, coward, liar, holocaust denier. You know who you are.*)

I don't know how this works, putting this together, because although I can pluck these details out, then they promptly smear and what I'm left with is a muddle of feeling sprinkled with the occasional crystallized moment, a shockingly defined image. Like walking down the beach with the enormity, the never-ending haze of moving water and floating sky on the one hand and then on the other, precise bits of whelk shell and that floppy green bean seaweed that unfurls its distinct fat fingers.

So here too: once, after she'd laughed and turned thoughtful, her pointy upper tooth third from center overlapped her lower lip like a cat's fang when they forget, as cats sometimes do, to tuck their canines in—this tooth jumps out even now from the general wash of truck sounds and conversation, the soft Cape colors in spring, brown, gold, and the breathtaking bleached blue. I can see that tooth, sharp as a needle, and the individual golden flat hairs on her forearm, set against a blur of happiness, a sun-filled golden draft like a warm bowl of clear broth. All at the same time, these pinpricks of clear wonder in a big terrible richness. I felt light as a bubble, giddy as a Ferris wheel, safe as houses.

If my grandmother were reading this story, she would take her reading glasses off at this moment, pinch the bridge of her nose, and clear her throat. *You are going to be disappointed in her.*

PART 2
THE GIRL

CHAPTER 5

That's one version of meeting Sarah. But this is also true: I didn't worry about her at all because it seemed ordained. Also because I thought it wasn't serious, couldn't be serious, didn't know what it would mean to be serious. She kind of snuck in and latched on like those puzzling skin tags that show up on your arms or belly or actually anywhere. Even if you're vigilant and you've been told repeatedly about the family history of skin cancer, you don't pay attention to a skin tag, or at least not if you're me. And then of course I had other things on my plate.

It was Titch's idea that we go to Cape Cod this summer. It was because of her that we got there, although we had some assistance from Ruby, who has been going to the Cape in the summer since before her father, Randy, married Lois. Now at twenty, she has a waitressing job she returns to in Wellfleet every summer and a circle of college friends who go back to work there too. Ruby is tall, curvy, and pretty, with lots of shiny wavy brown hair, but she has a bad-tempered expression on her face all the time, a mean mouth that I find completely offputting. Sometimes she's been friendly to Titch and to me—if nothing else was occupying her attention she would let us borrow her toenail polish, for example, or back before we had our licenses sometimes she could be persuaded to give us a ride into town—but she is unreliable at best. She barely acknowledged Titch in high school, when they overlapped there for a year. She's always acted like having a stepsister cramps her social style.

This past spring though, when Titch approached her mother with the idea that she and I spend the summer before our senior year out on the Cape, Ruby had grudgingly conceded that she could probably help us line up restaurant or catering work. We all knew she wouldn't concern herself with us more than she had to when we were out there, but I could tell that it made Lois feel better that she was around in any case. We were too old for camp, Titch argued, and we neither of us had any interest in being counselors. I had worked scooping ice cream at the Ice Cream Machine in town the summer before and Titch had worked as a library page, but we could hold the same kinds of jobs on the Cape and it would be much more fun.

Around the same time that Titch was hatching this plan, one of our teachers—Mrs. Habernathy, English Lit and Spanish—had talked to me about going to a summer drama workshop. I had taken three acting classes, two with her and another with Mr. Hall, and I had been in all nine of the high school's shows since I'd been there. She said it might be time for me to think about some serious acting classes outside of high school, because I had exhausted the offerings there. She said I needed more voice work and some proper training, and it would look good on college applications. She was keen on a program at Middlebury College, where she had gone as an undergraduate, but she had heard that there was a relatively new, promising summer acting program on the Cape that drew lots of good theatre people from New York out to teach. The two other possibilities she came up with—one in New York, one in London—seemed much less plausible and much more expensive. When these two pieces came together—what I might actually be able to do on the Cape and the possibility of employment for both of us—Titch and I had a momentary fit in the hall outside the cafeteria at school, throwing our hands up in the air, jumping up and down, shrieking with excitement.

Ruby couldn't help us with housing, though, which she said was very hard to come by in the summer season. She made it clear she was not going to stick her neck out for us even to ask around and she certainly wasn't going to invite us to live in her small, shared place (not that we would have wanted to do this anyway). Once we looked at what it cost to rent a place, I knew it would never happen. I didn't even bother asking my grandmother and I tried to forget about it. There was no way we could make that kind of money even if we were working full-time all summer.

But Titch, with the slippery, studied awareness of a child of divorce, moved on to her dad, Bob, as soon as she had gotten her mother to agree to the plan. I don't know how she put it to him, but undoubtedly she made him feel like we had this great dream and he was our last hope to make it come true. She's his only child and he's a sucker for her, which is part of his charm, at least for me. It turned out that he knows some people called the Davidsons who have a house in Truro, but who were spending their summer in some even more fancy remote beachy place in Nova Scotia. Somehow shell-game Bob finagled it so that Titch and I could housesit for the Davidsons for the summer. Titch spoke to Mrs. Davidson at length and obviously did a persuasive job of sounding extremely responsible. Which, to be fair, she is. In return for the house, all we had to do was agree to feed the birds, and take care of their two cats and many plants.

It seemed almost too good to be true, but by the middle of May everything was falling into place. My grandmother and my mother had agreed that I could go with Titch, and we had her old brown Toyota Tercel to get about in. I was signed up for the nine-week acting workshop and was planning to put in some hours every weekend for a catering outfit with the twee name of Jake's Edibles, where Ruby knew the manager. Titch was planning on focusing on her art, on painting and building sculpture and installation pieces, as well as working part-time for a sandwich shop in Wellfleet. We had big plans to go to the beach, and explore, and play. We could not get over the amazement of striking out like this together for the first time.

More than that: I was looking for a way out, a sanctuary, which Titch knew and only Titch knew. She never said anything to me about whether that was part of her thinking up the Cape Cod plan—I don't know if she knew how desperate I was to find a way to hide or to get out of town—and I never asked her about this. But I was grateful to her all the same. I felt like I had miraculously stumbled across the escape hatch.

The day after I met Sarah at Ruby's party was the first day of the drama program. Everyone gathered—about sixty or so of us—at a gallery overlooking the harbor in Wellfleet. The top floor was ours for the duration of the summer, but today as it turned out the last exhibit hadn't been entirely cleared. As we sat on the polished pine boards, called to order like kindergartners, large canvases of what looked like floating labia in angry orange or extraterrestrial blue frowned down at us from the walls. A middle-aged woman, balanced precariously on the balls of her feet, launched into a welcome speech. She had distracting white hair, a kind of dandelion fluff that seemed to float straight up and undulate gently above her scalp.

I didn't hear anything she was saying. I was busy hugging my knees, wrapped in a growing funk of certainty that signing up for this workshop was a ghastly error. I heard my grandmother talking once about a friend who had been a priest and then lost his faith and opened a brewery. The way she said *lost his faith* made me think he had set it down somewhere like a suitcase full of once valuable things he just couldn't bear to drag any further. Not like he had misplaced it, but much more like he'd sat down on it in a deserted railroad station, had a good cry, and thought, *I can't carry this one more step.* I had this feeling myself about acting, about being an actor, that it was a hugely valuable weight that I might be about ready to leave behind at the station. I could feel a lightness but also a terrifying emptiness about stepping away from it. What if it was a sign of fundamental weakness on my part? What if everything in the bag, my doctor's bag, my bag of tricks, could never be replaced once I put it down? I could not admit this to anyone. But I thought I might have lost my faith. Either that or I was anxious and afraid at having to prove myself at this moment in this place in front of these unknown people. Or both. It was hard to tell. Whatever the reason, I felt sick.

"—tremendous honor to have the remarkable director Bill McNeil with us to lead the workshop in its third year—so exciting—tradition of excellence here on the Cape—top theatre artists and professionals—Juilliard—voice—casting agents—movement—so excited—"

And then applause as a guy with small mean blue sunglasses slunk to the center of the far wall. The glasses, which sat on top of his head, looked permanently attached, like vestigial horns, or stunted antennae. (All through the workshop, all summer, when he'd pause and grimace, he always looked like he was waiting to pick up some frequency on his broken antennae. Wince—*where's the fucking signal?*—wince.) He had a gritty, hungover whisper and nursed a large paper cup of coffee. Although Introductory Woman clearly expected him to speak at this point, all Bill McNeil said was *cheers*, raising his cup to us in an unsmiling salute. Flustered, Introductory Woman began explaining that there would be six groups and that each group had an assistant or two, who were all talented actors coming to us from top schools and programs here and abroad.

"It's like camp with counselors," said the girl beside me, slightly disgusted. Her legs were stretched out straight on the floor and she was folded neatly over them, her chin on her frayed leg warmers. She looked like the bad seed, punked-out, pockmarked younger sister of Jennifer Beals. Her black hair

dye had seeped past her hairline and stained in front of her
ears. She had large breasts that gave off a hot, damp smell.
When the first group was listed, she unhinged herself in the
middle and got up. Her name, unexpectedly, turned out to be
Camille. "They're singing my song," she said glumly when
called and clumped away to join her people. I had a terrific
longing to grab her ankle as she went by and be dragged
along with her. I was seized by fear, convinced that my name
wouldn't be called, like in junior high before a game of soft-
ball, thinking *no team will pick me.*

But I was in Group 6, as it turned out, and eventually I
heard my name. I went over to the wall where Group 6 was
beginning to gather. A tall, beefy guy smiled nicely at me and
said his name was Geoffrey "with a G." Beside him, a small girl
with dark hair and a furrowed brow said, "I'm Ann," and held
out her hand, earnestly, and formally. I wanted to say, "Ann
with an A"? But I restrained myself. Eventually there were
eight of us altogether, five girls—me, Ann, Shisha, Nicky, and
Emily—and three guys—Geoffrey, Chris, and Doug. We were
one of the smaller groups.

The classes for the workshop were going to be held all over
town. We were given paper maps with arrows and crude drawings of the waterfront and buildings. It looked like we were
going on a second grade birthday party treasure hunt. The first
afternoon for Groups 5 and 6 was scheduled in the basement
of the First Congregational Church, Classical Monologues
with a tall skinny Englishman from LAMDA (the London
Academy of Music and Dramatic Art). These people only
speak in acronyms, like the federal government.) This
Englishman had clownish, flapping elbows and identified himself as Bertram Benbow, no kidding.

I had woken up that morning waterlogged with wretched-
ness. Titch dropped me off in town and it was all I could do
not to beg to go with her to the beach instead. It was worse

than being dropped off on the first day of school. The numbing dread made me very calm, almost sleepy, but completely out of it. By the time Bertie Benbow said brightly, *Group 6, here's your section leader!* that afternoon, I thought my head was going to be too heavy to lift off my knees. But then I heard her voice.

"So it won't take long for those of you who are new to the area to find your way around," Sarah was saying, poised, pleasant.

My chin flew off my chest and I sat straight up. Sarah's mouth kept moving, but I had no idea what she said because the actual fact of her in the room was so much more dazzling than whatever she was talking about; the whole room was shimmering with refracted light.

On break I went over to where she was collating pink schedules.

"I didn't know you were an actor," I said. She gave me the briefest of smiles, looked down at the pile of papers, stuck her tongue out of the corner of her mouth, and bit it. For some reason, this gave me courage.

"Do you want to go get coffee after," I said wildly, recklessly. I thought I'd better ask before I stood up to perform and forgot everything I knew in front of everyone. She looked surprised. Then she said yes.

On that first day she did a monologue from *The Two Noble Kinsmen*—I hadn't read the play but she played the Jailer's Daughter. She was strong on her feet, full of quick changes and *verve* Bertie Benbow said after and he was right. *Verve.* I was worried she wouldn't be good so I couldn't look fully at her, but I studied her calves, which appeared to be spring-loaded, and listened to her voice. She was good. Bertie applauded it afterward and then took the monologue apart beat by beat, lovingly, as though he were unfolding a complicated piece of origami.

One after another each person stood up to deliver an under-3-minute classical audition monologue. We had been allowed to use sonnets and one person in our group—Chris? I was pretty sure that was his name—had gone this route, but I thought listening to him that I was right not to because most sonnets answer their own questions so tidily that it's hard to find a foothold, an entryway. A tall, slightly overweight blonde girl with knee socks and plaid skirt got up next (what was this? Private school? Did she take the British thing too much to heart?). That was Emily. She was the first of two Juliets, possibly the world's most predictable choice.

I had struggled to find a monologue, precisely because I didn't want to jump in with Juliet, or Viola's ring speech from *Twelfth Night*, or anything from *As You Like It*. I love *As You Like It*, but I figured that there would be at least one Rosalind taker and maybe even one Phoebe. It looked like I was going to be right about this too: the pale dark-haired girl—Ann—had already stood up and held forth as Rosalind, sincerely if slightly woodenly, her wobbly ankles turned in and collapsing a little. Listening to her reminded me of when Titch and I played Rosalind and Celia in *As You Like It* in a scene for the Shakespeare Festival when we were in eighth grade. We had started to memorize poems in fourth grade that we recited at school assemblies. This was Titch's idea originally, but it turned out once we got started that I was the one with the insatiable hunger for performing. I liked the reliability of everyone's having to look at me, of their having to pay attention, even if restlessly and for a short stretch of time, even if only under the eagle eyes of our teachers. We had moved on to performing scenes and plays together in her backyard in middle school, and we read through a lot of Shakespeare together, skipping lightly over the histories and most of the tragedies the same way I skipped all of *War* when I read *War and Peace*. I have never had a problem skipping the bits that I don't like or that don't interest me.

But that day when we swept on the stage bantering as Rosalind (me) and Celia (Titch) something new happened. We were performing in heavy tapestry costumes borrowed from the Dartmouth College costume shop, which smelled like a combination of peppery undergraduate perspiration and mothballs. I remember being wrapped in that smell feeling maybe for the first time that all the pieces of myself—and I mean my unruly limbs and my haywire thoughts and my guts and my sweaty frantic incoherent ambition and my breasts, everything from my challenging hair to the bones in my feet— all these usually jostling warring pieces drew in and pulled together. It felt wonderful, for that moment, the ease of it. I couldn't remember ever feeling that way before, that all of me was in agreement and working together. The high in that moment was extraordinary and I chased it, in school plays, in classes, in local productions, in plays at the college, anywhere that offered the chance to feel that unity and lucidity again.

On a whim, three days before leaving for the Cape, I picked up *King Lear* and reread it. I've always loved *Lear*, despite its being a tragedy, and this time I latched onto a speech of Cordelia's, which was a short one but felt good to say. In the basement of the church while other people held forth, my attention spooling in and out, I mouthed the first lines of the monologue, trying to will myself into its story. The blonde girl was still earnestly declaiming in her knee socks. *It's nearly summertime, Emily*, I thought, staring at her dimpled knees with enormous antagonism. An Edmund from *Lear* followed, the squarely built guy named Doug who either had or was faking a decent Scottish accent. He raged on about being born a bastard. Spit flew out of his mouth and the front row recoiled under the spray.

I waited and waited through the others, miserably, and finally got up, the last to go. I always mean to volunteer early but can't manage it. Something about the way other people spring up enthusiastically always makes me feel glued to the floor with reluctance. Once up, I inhaled deeply and lunged through Cordelia's speech to her sleeping father, the reunion speech to Lear in the final act. This is post storm and devastation, long after her father has cast her out and then her sisters cast him out into the storm. It's when Cordelia finally sees her father again and breaks down.

O my dear father! Restoration hang /
Thy medicine on my lips, and let this kiss/
Repair those violent harms that my two sisters/
Have in thy reverence made!

(I had somehow decided to place the invisible Lear at the feet of Bertie Benbow. Why had I done this? Madness.)

Had you not been their father, these white flakes/
Did challenge pity of them. Was this a face/
To be oppos'd against the warring winds/
To stand against the deep dread-bolted thunder?

(Lear was unconscious; there was no moving him.)

In the most terrible and nimble stroke/
Of quick, cross lightning? To watch—poor perdu!—/
With this thin helm?

(A drop of sweat fell off my forehead and splashed onto my shoe. I saw it land, mesmerized, apparently utterly unable to lift my head.)

Mine enemy's dog,/
Though he had bit me, should have stood that night/
Against my fire. And wast thou fain, poor father,/

To hovel thee with swine and rogues forlorn,/
In short and musty straw? Alack, alack!

> (Bertie's socks did not match.
> Why in god's name did I have
> to notice this?)

'Tis wonder that thy life and wits at once/
Had not concluded all. He wakes; speak to him.

As soon as I finished, Bertie stood up heavily. I plopped down on the floor, filled with dark accusatory thoughts. *Oh well, I wasn't the worst*, I thought, unwilling to swivel around to check for confirmation on this, and, *It's his fault for wearing those socks.*

"Yes," he said, frowning down at me. "Yes, yes," he said again, this time shaking his head. He groaned a little and raked his fingers along his scalp from back to front. If he had had any hair it would have stood straight up.

"Yes. Nina, yes? You have great facility, Nina, facility with language. Great facility. Yes. Language comes easily to you, you have a feel in the mouth for the words. But there is too much here." (He clapped his hands on his head, elbows straight out to the sides, eyes bulging emphatically.)

"You have not connected here." (He hit himself in the stomach.)

"Knowing when to breathe" (shooting a fierce look around the room) "is not the same as being on the breath, using the breath. Knowing when to breathe is only the first step—you must be connected to the breath. Stand up, my love." (I did.)

"Now Lear has thrown you out, yes? He has broken your heart. He has forced you to leave your home with nothing, in total disgrace. You loved him, and he shamed you, he disowned you. And now here you are, you have come back to your father only to find him in this terrible state, at death's door. He is about to die, he may already be dead. He looks like death. Your father, whom you loved and who said such terrible things to you, such wounding, terrible, terrible things. The last time he saw you, he broke your heart, and now you are facing him again, in this terrible state. For what is very likely to be the last time. And you must be asking yourself, of course you must have to ask yourself, *How many times can one person break your heart?*" (He groaned a little to himself at this point, his eyes closed in a kind of reverie, then his eyelids flew open, he turned on me, and asked again, sternly:)

"How many times can one person break your heart?" (I stared at him blankly.)

"Okay. OOOOkay. I want you to breathe into your spine, yes, soft belly yes and let your knees go a little—not so much!—okay here is what we are after. As if you had droopy knickers. Droopy knickers! *Underpants.* Droopy drawers!" (I drooped.)

Bertie let out a squawk as though I had leapt full force on his foot.

"No, my love, no." Taking a hunk of my hair, he lifted it directly to the ceiling. I froze.

"We want a plumb line from the top of your head to the floor and another out from your shoulders. Good. Now just give the knees a little bend. Yes. So you are ready for action. So you can jump in any direction. There you are. That's my girl."

I tried to hold my stance obediently. I wished he would let go of my hair. He smelled, not unpleasantly, like sweaty doughnuts, a warm ripe oily smell.

"Now I want you to skip while saying the first line. After each skip, turn."

I began to skip away from the class.

Bertie roared after me, "Feel the heartbeat! I/am/bic. Iambic pentameter! Bb*boom*, bb*boom*. You need to feel the rhythm of the language in your heart; your heart needs to feel it. Break the lines down, my dear, into the sound of your heart beating. *Shakespeare is the sound of your heart beating.* Skip! Turn! Skip! Turn! Skip! Lines! Lines!"

I skipped, reciting, feeling enormously stupid, my arms swinging idiotically, stomping, a comic circus ape with no grace. It was ridiculously difficult. Soon everyone had to do it, which was worlds better. Before long, we were all cantering to the trochees, *beat beat beat, turn.* The rest of the morning we spent galloping the length of the basement chanting lines. This I could do. On one turn, as I bounded across the room I passed Sarah, airborne at the same moment, and we splashed wide open in a grin together.

Over coffee I learned that she had started in the acting program at Tisch at NYU the year before last, but then had taken the past year off. She did not say why. Her family was from the Midwest. She had never left the country. She hadn't seen the ocean until she was seventeen. While she told me these things, she either studied the rim of her paper cup closely or looked at me ardently, there was no in between. I stared off into middle spaces, at the roof of Uncle Nick's Café to the left of her head, or at the edge of her ear. Her face was shaped like a heart and I heard myself say so. She said she had never liked that and I heard myself say that she should, after which we both ducked our heads.

CHAPTER 6

I wasn't new to girls, strictly speaking. I wasn't new to the idea or the emotion. To begin with, I fell deeply in love with Genevieve James when we were seven. She had a totally mesmerizing Australian accent, and white blonde hair the color of unsalted butter that fell straight as rain, right as rain, past her shoulders. I would have followed her anywhere, to Australia even, if I'd had an independent income and been over four feet tall.

Her arrival coincided with second grade, and the romance slid over into a love affair with school. We raced to clean the chalkboard and to take the erasers out back and clap them on the brick walls to get rid of the dust. We were assigned farm duty in the spring along with permanently congested Eric Costello, which meant the three of us were released from fourth period every other Wednesday and carried a bucket of grain over to the lone bleating sheep staked out in back of the school building. We would sprint ahead of poor Eric, leaving him snorting in our wake. We read aloud to one another lying on the grass on our stomachs in her backyard or in the cemetery in town. We were working our way through the *Great American Poets*. I liked Walt Whitman. She liked Emily Dickinson, and any poem about death.

She said *chooks* for chickens and was not afraid of anything, not snakes or heights or even ski tow lifts, not the J-bar that grabbed you under the butt at Oak Hill and not the chairlift that swung up so terrifyingly high at Suicide Six. She played the cello seriously, her buttery cape of hair fanning out on both sides of the strings. I cried for two weeks very nearly when her father's sabbatical ended and she moved back to Sydney. We wrote letters for almost five years, in round and even script.

Later a senior girl in high school named Lindsey used to wrap me up in the heavy, dark, dusty red velvet curtain of the auditorium stage and kiss me, her cheek softer than pussy willow buds, her mouth tasting unfailingly like the delicious medicinal artificial sweetness of Dr. Pepper.

In the high school winter show, she played Ado Annie in *Oklahoma*, which is an unfair advantage. If you don't crush out on Ado Annie, something's wrong with that show. What does she sing? *I'm just a girl who cain't say no, I'm in a turrible fix.* Okay, then, you see what I mean. I mean that was me. I was the one in a fix. I couldn't say no. Happily I was in the chorus, so I got to flock around her picnic basket. I thought she was the bee's knees, as my grandmother might say, *the cat's pajamas.*

In our vocal warm-ups before rehearsals, I could see her sleek coppery head in the soprano section, ten people over from my sticky clump of freshman altos. One day she helped me with my hair before a dress rehearsal, twisting it up into what she called a *chignon.* When she was done, she paused, regarding me in the mirror. Taking the bobby pins out of her mouth, she said, "You have beautiful eyelashes." This made my insides collapse and I started sneezing violently, from happiness and all the hairspray.

She had a boyfriend named Mike, who played lacrosse. He had scary big knobs for shoulders like football pads only not, actual flesh and bone. Sometimes I would pass the senior lounge with my heart thudding, just racketing around in my chest like a rogue squash ball, waiting to see if she would be there. If she was, she'd be stretched out all summery on one of the beanbag chairs, fingers dripping like she was punting on a river and trailing her hand over the side of the boat, just tracing the water. She'd be laughing at the boys who lunked and wrestled, looking like overfed oxen bumping into one another. If she saw me in the hall she would lift her palm and smile in passing. Once she casually tucked my hair back behind my ear right in the hall outside Organic Chem with Mr. Hutchens, while I stood transfixed. I didn't love her, I didn't know her, but I knew she wanted to touch me and that was tremendous, that was stupefying information. I would never have followed up on this in any way, demanding or questioning or *doing* anything. All I did was to pocket every gesture, every moment, carrying them home to pore over as soon as I was alone.

I watched her graduate in a flurry of black robes before she went to the University of Vermont. She didn't introduce me to her parents, but when she was walking away with her friends after the ceremony, she turned back toward me for a minute, her hair tumbling down on her shoulders, the crumpled gown in one hand, the magical curve of her waist turning in her jeans, and she blew me a kiss. It was like being thrown a long silken rope of happiness and I caught the end of it gratefully.

Of course alongside the girls, by the time I was thirteen I was almost always in a couple with some boy or other. But boyfriend is not a word I've ever used much. It thrilled me exactly once in my life: in third grade when I was on the B4 bus going to school and Bruce Brickle mocked Sam Nicholson for sitting next to me, which Sam always did. Bruce lurched over the back of our seat with his enormous lumpy head looming over us and said, with all the sophistication of a mean over-sized moron, *you're her boyfriend.* He smelled like cough syrup and dirty damp scalp. There was some spit bubbling on his braces and suspended in a tiny triangle at the corner of his mouth. It made me think of *Charlotte's Web.* I thought, *Well, that's torn it* (my grandmother said that sometimes, *Well, that's torn it*). I pictured Sam and myself, so amicable and united today, torn in two like dismembered paper dolls, rent apart forever. We would never again be able to keep company on or off the bus, because what boy could withstand that kind of taunt? But before I finished mourning our end, Sam said, calmly, *Well I am a boy and I am her friend, so yes okay I am her boyfriend.* I looked at him with love for years because of that, no kidding. I doubt he'd remember. He got into fights later with his stepfather, wound up in juvenile court, and got shipped off somewhere. But he was loyal and he had a good heart. I would look at him with love today if I saw him.

By the time boyfriend was a desirable title, in the terms dictated from on high school high, I usually had one except for one strange four-month stretch in freshman year when they all seemed temporarily to dry up and evaporate.

The bigger difficulty was that I was bored out of my gourd. Usually I had trouble sticking to one boy and instead roved, trolled, overlapped with more than one. This got me in some hot water occasionally. But listen, I just wanted more information. I wanted the sex version of the *Big Book of How Things Work* in the children's section at the library, less on how steamships stay afloat or how electric currents run and more on the movements and vagaries of lips and hearts, skin and bones.

Mostly I wound up kissing boys who asked or seemed interested because it was worth the practice or I was indifferent, intrigued, wanted to educate myself. Usually this was a pretty unexciting pursuit but sometimes it had unexpected results. The first time I helped a guy masturbate, for example (it was Lewis Aronson if you want to know)—which is to say I held onto his dick while he showed me what to do—I worried the whole time that I would choke it somehow especially since it kept swallowing itself up in skin, which was incredibly disconcerting. Lewis's dick didn't smell like much to me surprisingly, inoffensive, unremarkable, kind of like butter that's been in the fridge too long and smells like the inside of the fridge. But, as

I said, inoffensive. The whole experience seemed unexceptional. Afterwards though, I had to sit down with my grandmother for dinner and I was really disturbed because the entire time my hand appeared to be glowing neon blue, like in those undercover TV specials when they use infrared detection or whatever to show you the traces of sperm left on the hotel sheets that only *look* clean. This had nothing to do with sperm (I tried to stay completely clear of that, even though it was a little like avoiding a blind man's sneeze). It had to do with me, but also with my grandmother.

In short flashes that suppertime—as I reached for the salt with my hand, or heard the familiar sound of my grandmother's voice, the scraping of her chair as she pushed it back from the table—I saw a fissure opening between us. It wasn't that my grandmother would disapprove of what I had done so much as she would not even recognize it and so could not necessarily recognize me.

I did not want the space between us magnified. Even as much as I wanted to know about how everything worked, there was also plenty that I didn't want to be forced to contemplate. Like for example, I did not want AIDS brought to my attention so damn much. Like it wasn't enough to be all the time horrified about pregnancy and what a total nightmare *that* would be.

The first time I heard the word AIDS was almost two years ago. I was sitting in the kitchen at the counter on a stool looking at the bird feeder in the sunshine and spooning up Cheerios while weighty National Public Radio voices were talking somberly about the gay cancer. The interviewer was explaining that some scientists, some experts, some people in the know—although not the president, apparently, or anyone in his administration—but a handful of other people thought it was possible that we could all get the gay cancer now, any one of us, from blood and kissing and sperm—bodily fluids, the first time I heard that said over and over, like an incantation, *bodily fluids, bodily fluids, bodily fluids.*

Before long we were hearing about this development in school too. There was even a special assembly for juniors and seniors, where, in the quiet, dark hush of the auditorium, the school nurse spoke to students gravely about safe sex. Some parents complained about this later, saying that this was over-reaching, that we were being told things we didn't need to know. But for most of us the bigger problem was that it was hard not to feel disgusted at yet another outrageous claim clearly designed to freak us out, this one smarter, more strategic because it was so sweeping and vague. *We don't know exactly what this is or how this happens or if you can protect against it* (except by locking yourself in a hermetic plastic box predictably). No matter what the alleged scientific discovery or medical advancement, the lesson always seemed to wind up being: *you will die if you touch someone.* Of course this wisdom came from the same people who had only recently realized apparently that *you won't go blind if you masturbate.* Mr. Hannigan, who had terrible dandruff and naturally picked the short straw to preside over eighth-grade sex ed, actually made Lisa Sullivan read the masturbation passage aloud from the book. It gave you a lot of faith in the experts. *We've been moronically wrong before about sex, but hey, we can tell you definitively that those bodily fluids are a* death trap.

I went out the very weekend after that sex ed class and wound up making out furiously with Michael North, much to his surprise, in the front seat of his ancient green Mustang, out by Wilder Dam. I had more fondness for the car than the boy who, eager with cherry Chapstick, was too clean to be really thrilling. Boys in my experience—the tall and short actors, lacrosse players, musicians, runners, brains, artists, soccer stars—were almost all tiresomely tender, terribly eager to be attached, devoted, floppy, needy, clutching at me in fact, or, occasionally and divertingly, brutally dismissive. But none of them could get properly sweaty—or that's all they could do, get *properly* sweaty running up and down the length of a jewel green athletic field—and I wanted some improper sweat. Bodily fluid, or, maybe better yet, a fluid body.

My last brush with trying to be in a couple had been the three months I hung around with Peter Salvato. He was okay, but eventually he had to spend nearly two hours in the front seat of his parents' Volvo before last Christmas break making a tortured effort to tell me that he loved me. He didn't really know anything about me, but he'd made up his mind anyway. I hate that. He was sweating with earnestness and if I'd been at all compassionate I might have helped him out, but as it was I could only summon up wild irritation. It was amazing to me that he couldn't see this irritation spray painted all over me, but it's true that he was only looking at his lap or—in moments of colossal bravery—at the dashboard.

We were parked up on Bragg Hill in Norwich, not far from his house. The tape playing in the car while Peter was rambling was Talking Heads' *Stop Making Sense*. We went through it twice. The motor was running the whole time because it was at least twenty degrees below zero outside. My feet were cold in my boots, and I curled and uncurled my toes. I distracted myself by thinking about David Byrne in his big white suit. I wondered what I would look like in a big white suit. I wanted to roll down the window, crawl out of the car into the towering snowdrift by the side of the road, and just lie there, preferably in a big white suit. By the time Peter had shyly stammered out his feelings, I was far along into a vision of my funeral, the cortege, white horses, the flowers, the music, the weeping mourners, me in my big white suit stretched out in the casket.

Somehow this exchange with Peter put me over some edge and sent me into a deep, cold rage. He was just another boy who seemed to require bottomless reserves of support and hand-holding and coaxing and care. I didn't think I was up to providing this kind of attention. Deep down I didn't feel anything for any of these boys. (Not even deep down. Right underneath the surface.) And the problem was that I didn't even want to be up to taking care of any of them. But if I wasn't up to it, if I didn't even want to be up to it, if I was filled with such casual loathing for them, what kind of person was I? Not a good one, clearly. I was angry all the time. It was so easy to get these boys and so hard to get rid of them that I desperately wanted a change, something I thought would be wild, something with teeth. I wanted to fast-forward through all these mind-numbing tender proceedings and get to something raw and real, a power surge in the heart, a jump start, a kick start, a running start—for god's sake already, a *start*.

Which doesn't mean I meant to start anything.

CHAPTER 7

It was illegal. I was underage. For starters. One day in early January this year I was working on a scene for the Woodstock High School Shakespeare Festival competition with a wet sack named Alan. I was eyeballing this Alan, my Macbeth, from my place as a hopelessly miscast, pissed off Lady Macbeth. It was 5 o'clock on a Wednesday afternoon, junior year. Snow was falling dark and cold and fast outside the second-floor classroom windows. The heat made a hissing sound and the air in the room was layered warm around the knees and chilly at chest level where the cold floated right into the room. The windowpanes were icy to the touch. I could see the headlights of cars, dappled and wobbly, progressing through the slush on Lebanon Street in front of the school.

I glared full on at Alan and he tottered a bit on his pins and broke the scene, saying, like the lame duck he was: "Look at her eyes, she's scaring me."

I was slipping in scorn at this point and snorted audibly (*read the script, you fucking crybaby*). That's when Roger Peters, director of the Shakespeare workshop and the most popular English teacher, maybe hands down the most popular teacher in high school, stepped forward with his bullet head and got in my sight line.

Here's what I thought, no kidding, this was really the line on the brain marquee: *I can take him.* Like it was going to be a wrestling match, a slow burn, touch football but I could sustain a full body blow. It was as if he had the words *Worthy Adversary* stamped on his forehead.

I directed the same even look of hatred at him that I had given Alan, now crumpled off to the side on his hapless haunches by the radiator. Mr. P, who was not British but had lived there for a time and was also known as the MP, looked back at me.

"I see what you mean," he said, levelly, and we neither of us blinked.

It's surprisingly easy in a small town to get it on with a teacher. (Anyone who's been there knows exactly what I am talking about.) It may be that after priests, teachers are the easiest mark around. Which doesn't make me proud and should make them less so.

Early on, driving me home from a rehearsal once, he said, "I'm not going to ask you up to see my etchings."

When I didn't say anything, he tapped his right fist lightly on the gearshift twice, glanced over, and said, "Do you know what I mean?"

I didn't but I thought he was embarrassing himself and so I didn't say anything. It was early evening and the world was all purple bruised shadows. Out of the car window, I saw Winnie Hastings, the elementary school art teacher, fiddling with the gas pump outside the Mini Mart on Main Street. I had a sudden longing for the smell of markers and those rich pigmented finger paints—what are they called?—for pungent glue and big hairy sheets of construction paper.

Etchings? What kind of talk was that? What movie was he in?

And anyway, of course, he lied.

He would come up behind me in the hallway. The MP. He stood at the door of the auditorium and held it open. *The Master Pretender*, Titch called him. He waited by his office. *The Maestro Player, the Manipulative Parasite, the Mixed-up*

Professor, the Mystery Partner, and then increasingly obscurely as time went on, *the Meal Pincher, the Milk Pusher*, and her final favorite, *the Mad Peanut*.

Once: *the Missing Parent*.

"What does *that* mean?"

She rolled her eyes at me.

"Well, you are missing one. And the MP is about that age."

"Gross," I said, lapsing into junior high. "Don't do that. Don't Spock me. You're not Dr. Spock." (Titch's name for the therapist her mother sent her to, following her parents' messy divorce and their remarriages. "Going to be Spocked now. Spock time," she would say, somehow acerbic and cheerful at the same time. "It's for the ears," she had told me, "not the detachment.")

She was silent for a minute, twisting her hair around her index finger, and frowning at the ends. We were sitting outside the public library waiting for her mom to pick us up and the breeze was spring cold.

"Well, what is it then? What are you doing?"

It was my turn to be silent.

"Because I mean, it's not like you have a shortage of boys," she said jokingly, trying to defuse the direct question.

I started to say something about how the MP's attention was a different kind of attention, but I pretty much stopped before I started.

"Seriously?" she said. "You want that? I mean I pay attention to you *and* I'm not trying to sleep with you. Double win."

Then, backing off when I went silent again, easily, good-humoredly, "Fine, don't tell me. I don't want to know."

At the beginning I had a fleeting new conviction, an unfamiliar power. I could feel the MP's watching me, which made everything heightened, and for a while everything at school was also in part a performance for him. I thought about what I was wearing, who he would see me with, where we might cross paths in school. I knew he did the same—especially once he learned my class schedule—so the entire school was a charged zone. At any moment, he might materialize, or I might, around any given corner, just spring into view like a jungle cat. When that happened, as it was bound to at least once a day, we would studiously or carelessly ignore one another. I would turn to the person I was walking with and a burst of bright white energy would flood my voice, or if I was alone I would clutch my notebooks tighter to my chest and herald someone down the hall, but I would always feel simultaneously a wave of heat down the side of my body where he walked by. I didn't have any sense of who was pursuing whom, just that we were on electrifying high alert all the time.

He left letters in my locker. Also shells, dried flowers, a pair of earrings shaped like loons, a turquoise pendant, and four small, wooden carved animals. I kept everything, carefully, in a box under my bed. Not for romance, not for saccharine memory, but thinking, *this is evidence*, Exhibit A, although of what I'm not sure.

The sight of his handwriting on those notes in my locker made my heart race uncontrollably at first. Sometimes they were unmarked; sometimes they came in an envelope with my first name written tantalizingly on the outside. He signed with his initial only, if he signed at all. I would take the folded sheet of paper and slip it inside my notebook to look at later. Sometimes I would unfold the paper right in the middle of another class, casually uncreasing it by running my thumbnail over the paper, folding the page back. When I looked down at the writing the thumping of my heart would actually make it impossible for me to focus; individual words would jump off the page at me, a single word bouncing upward with each heartbeat: "beautiful" "tonight" "meet" "wrong" "feelings"—

the words would levitate off the paper and explode in the air, like cartoon bombs.

I thought the set of his trunk-like body and the outcroppings of hair (who knew? on the *back*?) were pitiable but fascinating. He had greedy, blunt hands that were repellent and thrilling at the same time. He smelled like cold metal and bay rum. He had a smile that was knowing, cheeky, lopsided, and then, out of nowhere, surprisingly sweet. He believed that I understood poetry, which meant that I overcame my private fear of it and for the first time I thought I might understand it, and that was a strange unexpected gift.

I liked knowing how much he wanted to touch me and how hard he had to work not to most of the time. I liked that I could see his hands tremble from the effort. I liked that he asked me questions and listened to me intently, that he seemed so curious about and delighted by what I had to say. I liked the determined way he would lock the door and turn to me in a not untender way. I liked the fact that he wasn't clumsy and I liked the way he looked right in my face when he touched me.

I didn't like the fact that the MP's youngest son, Jason, was a grade behind me in school. I didn't like the rumor that this had happened once before with another girl. I didn't much like to think about what I didn't like.

The Middle-Aged Prick, Titch penned sweetly in my notebook in Latin class, but I scratched it out, furious, and wouldn't look at her. She was crossing a line there. She would also occasionally hum snatches of that outrageously pretentious teacher-student song by the Police—"Don't Stand So Close to Me"—like it was the *Jaws* theme, when she passed me in the hallway. This irritated me and was really, as I pointed out to her, at least as much about her obsession with Stewart Copeland as it was about me. She always thought she was especially clever for choosing Copeland over Sting, and that irritated me even more. But I was glad she knew even so. I was glad someone knew.

I had a class with the MP. *English 11: Shakespeare, the Histories and the Tragedies.* It didn't seem like there was a fat lot of difference between the two. Is there a history that isn't a tragedy? Because if there is, we didn't read it.

Some days I would look at him hard while he was talking in class. It was a great luxury for me that he had to stand up and speak in front of all these people. He had to stand up and speak but I could sit, smug and scary, crossing my legs, looking at him. Some days I would purposely not look at him at all, feign inattention, or carry on animated conversations with Nick Harrow, who sat next to me and had large, worshipful, bovine eyes. Then sometimes the MP would call on me, briskly—*please read Lady Anne starting at line 114 thank you*— and I would know what effect I had. This was like a drug. It was better than a drug. It was totally addictive, a great rush, with no discernible side effects.

Some days, though, the MP would say *I need to see the following people after class* and I would be on that rattled-off list, offhandedly lumped in toward the end of the group, like an afterthought, having no option, having no way to say, *No I don't think so I think I'll just go to lunch now, thanks, catch you later.* Or, *You know what, fuck you, actually.* And knowing too, with both slivers of dread and some anticipatory, hostile charge, that he would casually, thoughtfully talk to the others first and save me for last. The way he attended to other students, the way he angled his head, or laughed with another student, the way he would make me wait, made me quietly enraged. The happy ignorance of the other students, their pleasure in his attention, the secret sweat and roiling in my gut, the uncontrolled speed of my pulse, the high-wire tension of it all. It made me want to make him suffer.

For the class we had to write a sonnet. We had to perform

a monologue. We had to write a paper. I got A's on all of them. I deserved the grades, but it was galling just the same.

There was no way this was going to end well. But who thinks about the end at the beginning?

CHAPTER 8

When I sat opposite Sarah's heart-shaped face forgetting to drink my coffee after our first day of classes, I was possessed by a sense of immense lightness and agitation, as if I had shape-shifted into a hummingbird. When Titch picked me up that afternoon and drove me back to Truro, talking all the while about what she had done that day, I responded still occupied by this unfamiliar sensation of vibration, of anticipation, of hovering lightly in the air. She was busy with her discoveries—with having located a walking path behind the house, shopped, and reorganized the kitchen ("And wait until you see the bathroom!")—and she did not appear to notice. I followed her up the stairs to the house, carrying my satchel, her voice swimming past my head.

The Davidsons' house, the housesitting house, was wonderfully distracting, like finding ourselves let loose in an electric toy train museum after hours. I couldn't believe it was all ours. We shared it only with the two cats, an older, sedate fat white cat named Chester and a lean, black teenage cat named Jack, barely out of kittenhood and bored out of his mind with Chester. Jack was a recent addition, in anticipation of the demise of Chester, but it didn't seem to me that Chester was going anywhere anytime soon. He looked like a good thirty-year cat, a Guinness Book of Records cat, like he'd dug his claws into this life, settled, content. Jack was jumpy, cranky, likely to scratch. He spent his days complaining at doors, shredding furniture, and stalking Chester. They were a really poorly paired set of roommates. Also, they weren't allowed outside, which seemed like kind of a crime to me, because on the farm cats roam far and wide and conduct their private cat business in the hidden recesses of the barn and fields. These two were housebound. Since their dander made it difficult for her to breathe, Titch was happy to leave their general care to me. She took on the extensive detailed care of the many indoor and outdoor plants. The owners had left four pages of instructions for the plants on a legal pad by the phone.

The house, which we had been told the Davidsons had designed with a local architect four years earlier, was swanky and modern. Surrounded by Cape Cod National Seashore conservation land, in the middle of the woods, it spread out comfortably down a hill in three separate levels. There were a lot of photographs of blond smiling grandchildren in seashell-encrusted frames, but not so many of the home-owning grandparents, so my ideas about them came almost entirely from their library and the organization of the house, the smaller traces of evidence here and there. They had a *Solar Power!* sticker on the fridge and a sticker that read *Three Mile Island: Never Again*, for example, as well as Audubon bird magnets and an anti-Seabrook poster in the study. That seemed all of a piece. But most of their books were as unknown to me as Arabic. The complete works of Julia Child, cheap paperback mysteries, histories of the Cape, and books on religion and spirituality and what colors you were supposed to wear based on your blood type or astrological sign. These last were like reading binge candy, disgusting and delicious all at once. I wanted to gobble them up by the fistful.

One room, the second-level bathroom, was completely dominated by biographies of Elvis Presley. Titch immediately called it the "Elvis" room (as in, "does anyone need to visit Elvis?"). When we returned from the first day of the workshop, Titch dragged me in to see what magic she had wrought in this room. She had set up sculptures and bits and pieces of installations in and around photographs of the King. I could see that I was going to learn a lot about Priscilla Presley on this toilet, shadowed by a giant distorted cardboard cutout of Graceland that Titch had mounted behind the seat.

That night when we were finishing our dinner, the MP called. Titch answered and then held the phone out to me, mouthing, *it's the Mad Peanut.* I looked back at her uncomprehendingly, and she rolled her eyes at me and exaggeratedly mouthed *MP*, while drawing the letters in the air with her index finger in big swoops.

He was checking in, he said. He wanted to tell me that he had started seeing a therapist but *not to worry* because *he hadn't mentioned me.* I mentioned that mentioning me might be important, if not in fact critical to his therapy, and he got very quiet. I wished him luck and said I expected I would be too busy to talk much.

After that conversation, I went back into the kitchen where Titch was finishing her ice cream. I told her that I didn't think I wanted to talk to the MP anymore.

She pulled a slightly disbelieving face at me over her bowl. When I made a face right back at her she looked a little surprised and drank the melted ice cream from the bottom of her bowl for a minute.

"Okay," she said mildly, getting up to take the bowl to the sink, "Just Say No."

Her left eye was twitching.

Titch got her nickname because she used to twitch a lot—I don't know if she had a real tic or was just irritable—but mostly she'd twitch when she had to say her name out loud in school. This was not a small flinch, a scrunched-up face kind of thing; this was a full body jump like someone had thrown a hard rubber eraser with deadly accuracy at her side rib. This earned her the nickname *twitchy* from horrible Mr. Harrelly in second grade and by the time we joined forces in fourth grade homeroom everyone had resorted to Titch.

Harmony Carmody. Can you imagine? I mean, her parents are perfectly good people, but it's hard to respect them for giving Titch that handle. I like my own name because Nina's not common, but it's not objectionable either. Also my parents apparently had a moment of relative and rare agreement about it. My mother told me once that she would have liked to name me Virginia, with the nickname of Nina, because she's fond of Woolf and has rows and rows of her books and letters. But my father liked the simplicity of Nina better, and I don't mind because you can just hear the name-calling awfulness that will ensue from Virginia. The worst anyone could do with my name was to lump me in with the Pinta and the Santa Maria, which wasn't entertaining after about third grade and is nothing compared to the one-two punch of *virgin* and *vagina* that Virginia offers up so effortlessly. So I got off easy there. Titch did too, because no one ever thought to call Titch *bitch*, which says a lot about how she's regarded. She was one of those lucky few who leapfrog from being totally ignored to being really well liked. I would have envied that if she wasn't in my camp, but since at the time I was sure we had each other's numbers forever, it was okay.

When Titch stood at the sink, rinsing her bowl, I heard myself say again in a calm and oddly definite voice that I was done with the MP. I believed that I was. As I was speaking I believed suddenly that it was within my power to decide this. I was filled with relief to be far away from him, to be in this foreign, unreachable place. But also, sitting with Sarah that day— being in any kind of proximity with Sarah, the very existence of Sarah—had given me this strange lightened, almost effervescent confidence, a new humming certainty.

"Well, praise be," Titch said, neutrally. She began to refer to him as RIP MP, or *ripmip*. She has always been monumentally fond of acronyms and shorthand.

Listen, obviously I had my own doubts about the MP from early on and they weren't lingering, or what you might call subtle, sneaking kinds of doubts. Once I was sitting cross-legged on the unmade bed in the MP's apartment and I said to the MP, who had three sons, *You always wanted a daughter, didn't you?* And he stuck his head out from behind the bathroom door, toothbrush in hand, and said, *That's amazing, how did you know?* He really was amazed is the thing.

My father once told me—sometime in the year before he left—he told me that he had always thought he wanted a son till I came along, but then he couldn't imagine wanting anything more than a daughter because it was so great to be part of raising a strong girl. He raised his fist in the air when he said this in something like the Black Power salute. If I'd had any idea what that was back then, maybe I would have known enough to have been suspicious about the mixed messages. But I didn't. Whatever he wanted, it did not turn out to include Black Power or a strong girl as far as I know.

The MP's multiple sons were in pictures all over his apartment, boys with their arms draped around each other's shoulders, always outdoors, at the tops of mountains, standing triumphantly or sheepishly by canoes, or holding up fish they'd caught. Plaid barn jackets, goofy hats, backpacks, hiking boots. If you looked around, there wasn't anywhere for these boys to be except propped up in photos on the desk because the MP's apartment was just a sparse one-bedroom rental over the bike shop in Strafford. It smelled of old dog (a lame chocolate lab named Vincent who was a casualty of his divorce) as well as more generally of loss and dampness, moldy laundry around the edges. The toilet bowl was never really clean, which also depressed me. There wasn't room even to sit down and have dinner with more than two people. The two older sons were in their twenties with jobs and their own homes, although they were not far away; one was a policeman and one worked in a logging mill, both in New Hampshire. All three boys looked like dark-haired versions of one another and I had trouble keeping them straight.

(Okay, that's not true. I knew Jason perfectly well because he was in school with me. He was a star soccer and lacrosse player. He was tall and nice looking, with dark floppy hair and bright blue eyes. Once a few years ago I had been at one of his games and wound up talking to him on the bleachers afterwards while we were waiting for rides home. He had admitted, almost shyly, that he had always wanted to act but that he didn't have the time to try out for school plays. He told me this while we shared an unpleasant, mealy granola bar he dug out of the depths of his backpack and the last of the water from his water bottle. He had a lovely crooked smile. After things started with his father, though, I ignored his existence as much as possible. I had trouble looking at him, so I didn't.)

The MP was in some kind of complicated custody or ongoing divorce battle over Jason with his ex-wife, whom he occasionally referred to bitterly as *the missus*, but never by name. I knew who she was, of course, because she was the elementary school nurse. She had a pinched-looking mouth and a lot of gingery hair. She'd weighed me, measured me, tested me for scoliosis, and looked through my scalp for lice when Tammy Milliken had been sent home, crying, for infecting everyone. On one occasion, rather sternly, she demonstrated to my class how to brush our teeth and tongues, using a pinky beige plastic model of a jaw and a dry toothbrush. *Brush the upstairs and the downstairs and then brush the carpet*, she'd said. *Don't forget the carpet*. That annoyed me. (The carpet? What, were we morons? Why were they forever bribing us with lollipops and condescending to us? Why couldn't we call a tongue a tongue?). I could still conjure up her pink tongue sticking out after she said *carpet*, if I wanted to, which I didn't. It creeped me out.

But once when Titch had one of her panic attacks, I'd sat with her in the orange nursing cubicle while she breathed into a brown paper lunch bag and the nurse, *the missus*, had silently sat on her other side. She gave us ginger ale in plastic tumblers with red bendy straws before we went back to class. Her name was Lee. None of the sons looked anything like her except maybe Jason a little bit, in the blueness of his eyes.

The MP claimed that she was stalking him, that she had hired a private detective to follow him. That made me jumpy whether it was true or not. I had to hunker down on the floor of his car, out of sight, wedged down with the dog hair and big flakes of dried mud from the treads of his boots. And one time with my forehead jammed up to the glove compartment was one time too many.

Also, he started seeing a woman, a teacher, in fact a teacher I liked who had introduced me to Willa Cather two years earlier. Vanessa Hiller. She was the only teacher we'd had who wanted to be called *Mz*. Ms. Hiller. That was a first. She wrote her first name up on the board on the first day of class too, which was kind of unusual. Most teachers have no first names. Ms. Vanessa Hiller, with her bumpy nose, was all young-teacher skinny enthusiasm in her knee-length wool skirt. She had knobby knees, clunky sensible shoes, overeager teeth, and a really hopeful smile.

She once wrote *Excellent! 100%!* across the top of an exam paper of mine when I had failed entirely to answer the last two questions. This bothered me some, but not enough to point it out to her. She'd already made up her mind, the way teachers do, that I was an excellent student. This didn't have a lot to do with how smart I was—teachers just seem to decide one way or another about you, A student, B student, and then not give it a lot of thought again. I guess it's easier for them that way. Ms. Hiller decided I was *Excellent! 100%!* because I gave her a lot of support in the room, you know, when other students would rather die than respond, when they actually look like they are dying right there on the spot, like the book under discussion is sending them into a drooling coma. Maybe it is. But I loved Willa Cather. (I did want to know though, why *My Antonia?* Why not *Death Comes for the Archbishop*, Ms. Hiller, so much better, so much more fun?) Those were not the most pressing questions I wanted to ask. Higher on the list were, *What are you doing with this man? Do you know he wants a daughter?* And, *Can you tell me if I should tell you?*

I didn't. I didn't tell her. I felt a little bad about that, but I thought it was her lookout really. Even after everything that happened later.

Already a month or so into secretive meetings with the MP I had started feeling let down by what he wrote and said, which began to seem trite and repetitive. I fought this feeling at first—wasn't he an English teacher? He taught poetry, surely he could produce some. But the more besotted he seemed to become, the less interesting and legible the writing. Usually there were lengthy descriptions of nature—he liked hiking more than anything—(*Did you see the sunset tonight? Pink mare's tails scudding across the sky above the mountains. I was at the top of the Kancamagus heading home. I can't think when I've seen a prettier one. Then the moon—full or almost full, sitting like a gigantic spotlight in the sky, making the night seem almost like day. I walked around the green when I returned home just absorbing the beams and thinking of you*) and then repeated declarations of how beautiful I was (*No one, nothing, is more beautiful than you*).

My disappointment with the MP was confusing, disheartening, and hard to admit. I wanted to go head-to-head and toe-to-toe with someone, I wanted to run up against something hard, something and someone who had their own strength. I wanted someone to meet me and stand up to me. In fact I had gotten to the point where it felt not even like a desire but actually like a kind of necessity to go up against someone like this. But if the MP initially felt like something different, that feeling changed with astonishing rapidity. In the first place, it wasn't nearly as hard as I'd hoped it would be to start something. Also, much worse, very soon it started to seem like the entire affair had very little to do with me. It was the same thing that happened with everyone else, only worse because I'd hoped so for something new. I had a bad sinking feeling that this was all that romance was going to amount to: glazed, blind men, like sad Greek mythic figures, capsizing. Men latching on, like the proverbial monkey on the back, the albatross around the neck—not to me but to some idea of me that they held onto with a relentless grip. The disturbing new development was that they could be more than tiresome or burdensome or boring, they could be suffocating, they could drag me under with them. This made me panicky. I had always been able to outrun or abandon boys who weighed me down. It seemed like a good idea to be the one doing the leaving. But I wasn't sure the MP would be so easily unloaded. I thought I was going to require some help extricating myself, and somehow I was going to have to get that help without telling anyone what was going on.

CHAPTER 9

I did have a sort of a plan, a private plan. I never thought I was a pawn in this game. My plan was to draw the MP in close so that my mother could crush him.

Last April my mother decided it was time to move back home at least temporarily, or so my grandmother reported to me. My mother was worried about her mother (my grandmother said, dryly), worried that she was *starting to slip*. When my grandmother repeated this phrase to me she threw her hands in the air and did a startling little dance step in the kitchen, which made me laugh. I didn't know what prompted my mother's concern. I knew my grandmother had stopped reliably answering my mother's letters—although this might have been both a passive form of punishment and the result of the shakiness in her arthritic wrists. Any number of things that might have suggested slippage to the outside world were normal to us. The odd hours, for example, or the infrequent baths. She didn't go in for bathing much anymore. In warm weather she would still take a brisk dip in the pond where she transformed into a swimmer with a long reach and a graceful Australian crawl. I loved to watch this and I loved the way her bathing cap made her look a tiny bit like Katharine Hepburn. Sometimes she got her years mixed up on the phone, or she referred to me by the cat's name, or vice versa, I don't know. It wasn't unusual and it didn't worry me, but sometime in April my mother decided it was time to come home to Vermont, at least for a while, to deal with it.

My mother is a United Nations Refugee Resettlement expert which means she travels around the world wherever there are humanitarian crises or terrible conflicts, like Africa or the Balkans, and whenever there are people who need to be resettled, which as far as I can tell happens pretty much anywhere far away in the world all the time. She comes home about four or five times a year and stays for a week or two, occasionally as long as three, before she is off on another assignment. To my knowledge, my grandmother has only ever made three comments about my mother's comings and goings. The first remark was, "Kay always did have trouble sitting still." Since my grandmother would also say, *You have ants in your pants*, to me on occasion when I was younger, I was privately pleased by this evidence of a shared trait with my mother. The second and more baffling comment was, "Your mother always behaves as though she's on the lam." (It took me forever to crack this one. Of course as a small child I heard this as *she's on the lamb*, which led me to two possible but equally mystifying conclusions: either my grandmother meant that although my mother was a vegetarian she was somehow behaving as though she had eaten lamb meat, so that she was regrettably *on the lamb*, the way someone else might be *in the drink* who oughtn't to be; or, alternatively, the expression *she's on the lamb*, somehow disturbingly linked in my head with the phrase *high on the hog*, made me envision my mother as a miniature person, a midget's midget, a Tom Thumb, riding atop a lamb, although why she might be doing this, or rather behaving as though she was, I was hard-pressed to say.) The last thing my grandmother has said, more than once, is more oblique and doesn't immediately appear to connect to my mother, but by now I know what my grandmother is talking about most of the time and when she says this, she is talking about my mother. She likes to say, "Running away never solved anything." And we know what she is talking about when she says it.

Whenever my mother leaves, there's a day or two of empti-ness, of a strange weightlessness, but then my grandmother and I return to our rituals and all is well with the world until my mother returns to throw us off our game again. I like my mother well enough when she's around though. She used to want me to call her by her first name, which I did proudly when I was little, but lately I haven't wanted to—I might intro-duce her as "my mom, Kay" to cover all bases if I had to—but between the two of us, I don't call her anything. We don't look anything like each other, but she's very tough and she's funny, not at all sentimental. She gets really animated about her work, which I think she loves. And she's always been invested in treating me seriously, after a fashion. She's the kind of person who crouches down to speak to children at their level and does so genuinely and earnestly, as though they are fully cognizant adults, at the same time that with me she expects to be the absolute expert on everything. This didn't used to bother me, again because she's not around enough to enforce much authority. This past April I wanted her to come home, but I was deeply anxious about it. I wanted her to know about the MP but I certainly didn't want to be the one to tell her and I didn't even want to be in the same room when she found out, or really in the same hemisphere. Still, I hoped she might take up arms on my behalf, which I found privately reassuring.

She may not be present much, but she's been my only par-ent for the last twelve years. I didn't know what my father would have done about the MP, if anything—I couldn't even imagine the way I used to when I was littler—because I know almost nothing about him. I remember holding onto his thumb and trying to navigate a copper doorsill, and being lifted high into the air with the blur of his face and beard underneath me. I remember that he always sang on car trips even to the grocery store, union songs mostly, "Come All You Coal Miners", "Bread and Roses", "Which Side Are You On," occasionally a rousing chorus of "Hallelujah, I'm a Bum," that kind of thing. Before he left he imparted three pieces of information to me that stuck, although it's perfectly likely that I have mucked these up in my memory or confused them with something some indeterminate, unrelated person said. But if anyone asked me what my father taught me, I would say: one, that Henry Kissinger is responsible for a disproportionate number of the world's woes (Reagan will be Kissinger's *puppet* he said once, fiercely, while giving me a vigorous bath); two, that brushing my teeth with hot water will get them cleaner than brushing them with cold water; and three, that I should support the Sandinista revolution when I got old enough, or, at the very least, send my allowance to the cause. This last might have been a joke, but I thought of him a lot when the Contra war was gaining speed. He was long gone by then. But I kept track of the war and the Iran-Contra affair in the news for a while so he would know that I remembered what he said, that I was the kind of person who took these things seriously, and so I would be equipped to talk about them with him if he returned. When he left, he actually did go to Central America, to oversee something having to do with the Peace Corps, although my mother always snorted about this and said it wasn't the *real* Peace Corps. I still don't know what she meant by this.

When I was ten, my mother told me that she had heard that he had remarried, had two children, and now lived in Wyoming. She said he had *gotten religion*. She said this as though he had contracted an unspeakably revolting and terminal disease. At summer camp that year, I pretended that he had died in a fiery plane crash. I would trot him out on occasion, *my father who died*, for effect. I didn't know him enough to be affected even if he had died.

But I can remember how my stomach bottomed out when my mother said *two children*. The turbulence of hope and rage in equal measure.

"Brothers or sisters?"

She didn't say anything.

"Brothers or sisters?"

Her shoulders sagged.

"Three children," I said then, quavering, all but stamping my foot. "He has three children."

"Oh, bug," she said, helplessly. The baby name tipped me toward rage.

"I don't *care*." And I shot out of the house to go lie in the soft dirt in the garden, crying, with the asparagus ferning out over my head. The cat found me and sat heavily, comfortingly, on my chest. He dug his claws into my jersey and kneaded and I let him.

What my father's leaving meant to me in the moment was that it sent my mother pretty much out to lunch. We were living in London at the time he left, and every day when I came home from primary school she would be sitting in the darkened bedroom, chain-smoking and watching the children's television show *The Wombles*, which was about furry animated creatures who lived in burrows under Wimbledon Common and recycled trash. (*Underground, over ground, wombling free, the Wombles of Wimbledon Common are we . . . making good use of the things that we find, the things that most everyday folk leave behind.* Catchy. I could sing it to you in my sleep.)

That's when I took to biting people, which effectively drew my mother's attention so I got to come home. I was supposed to live at my grandparents' for a year or two, probably only until I started first grade and was in school full-time, but then my mother got her new traveling job, and no one mentioned changing anything, least of all me. I kept very quiet, because I was entirely happy where I was.

But now that my mother was coming home, temporarily or not, I developed my private plan. The plan was that my mother would shoot the MP between the eyes with a 12-gauge shotgun, which she would be holding across her knees in the rocking chair on the front porch. (We did not have a rocking chair, front porch, or 12-gauge shotgun to the best of my knowledge.)

It was not a perfect plan.

What happened instead was this. My mother came home in late April. Two days after she got back, I said I was going out to meet with a study group, and instead I met the MP in Strafford. When I came home after midnight, she was sitting waiting at the dining room table with its slightly rickety pull-out extensions. (You have to put the heavy pots in the center). The oval straw placemats were scrambled every which way, scratchy, unraveling. It was dark. My mother was sitting wait ing in that lonely light when I fell through the front door and caught myself mid-fall.

My mother spread her empty hands palms down on the table and did not look at me. She waited until I had righted myself. I could see her outline but her face was in shadow. It was always dark in the house because we replaced most of the bulbs with energy-saving fluorescents that give off less light than a dying firefly. The light seemed eerily reminiscent of both a B-movie interrogation room and a schoolroom, like I was standing under a lone humming bulb, tasting chalk dust and stale disinfectant on the back of my tongue, about to be given a test covered in questions no one could answer, just reams of them. Right then, waiting for the questioning, my scalp was electrified with fear and anticipation. In the silence, I could hear my heart and my grandmother's gentle sleeping emphysema wheeze from the downstairs bedroom.

"When you are lying to the people you love," my mother said then, quietly, without emphasis, "something is very wrong."

Then she cleared her throat, rose, and went upstairs.

I wanted nothing more than to throw something heavy at the back of her head, a wrench, a paperweight, the chair I was gripping.

Apparently without saying anything I'd lied—which was true, I was lying all the time like an addict about everything, cheerfully, or when not cheerfully, determinedly, bald-faced, as they say—but then again she didn't seem to have any interest in the truth, or whatever was happening that I might be lying about, which was confounding. She just wanted me to know she was onto the lying. Since I lied strenuously in order to be uncovered and relieved of the weight of all those lies, it was incredibly upsetting not to be questioned under that flickering light, not to be found wanting so that I could stop wanting to be found out.

I stood in the darkness, stunned, trembling, until I heard my grandmother sigh in her sleep, and I exhaled. I thought, *Okay, now I know.* She was home but she might as well have been in the Sudan. She wasn't going to help.

Worse, she was angry with me, as if I were the only one behaving reprehensibly or letting anyone down here. And if she was mad about being lied to, I had no idea how bad it would be if she knew what I had actually done. She might never speak to me again. I thought, *I have to get out of here.* I heard Titch's voice in my head say, *Abort, abort.*

I went to my mother later that week and said that I wanted to go away for the summer with Titch to the Cape, that we had a plan and a place to stay, that I wanted to do the drama workshop and I needed her help to pay for it, that I would do anything if I could go. And blessedly all my mother said was, *Okay, if that's what you want to do.* She was sitting at the kitchen table, frowning at a pile of electrical bills when she said this, but she never tried to go back on it.

So at least I had a Plan B and she didn't squash it.

CHAPTER 10

In the first week on the Cape I was going through the motions of the classes, settling in to the house in Truro and spending time with Titch, but running underground alongside and threaded through this, I was secretly, busily, and incessantly feeding my crush on Sarah.

She didn't seem even remotely acquirable, but that was beside the point. I had no end goal. I've never really connected crushes with outcomes. After all, my first crush was on Ingrid Bergman. She predates everyone else, because I was four when I was allowed to watch *Notorious* on my grandparents' fuzzy black-and-white television. I think I was supposed to be asleep on my grandfather's lap. I usually was because he emanated warmth from his front like a stove, so it was a cozy place to be. But I was awake. Actually, I was spellbound. Her autobiography was the occasion of my first theft from the public library at nine and I stole it mostly because I liked to look at her pictures so much, although her story was a good one too. But her face, that beautiful face: the irresistible soft bit at the end of her nose; the shape of her lips; the look in her eyes, dreamy or kind or full of delight; the way her jaw always looks a little swollen like she's a glamorous day away from having her wisdom teeth removed. Woody Guthrie wrote a song about Ingrid Bergman. He probably wasn't the only one, either.

If I could have, I would have written a song about Sarah, finding some way to spill out what I noticed about her in class in the first days: the sudden smile, exactly as shockingly bright as the sun when it springs out from behind unrelenting clouds; the way her hair fell and the futile, impatient gesture she made of pushing it back; her frown; the way she repeatedly touched her chin with her index finger and thumb, or the back of her hand; her stillness and the guarded way she sometimes held her shoulders; her radiant, controlled intelligence, like the blinding beam of a lighthouse bearing down on you. The softness of her cheek. The springy curl of her earlobe. The way she scowled and bit her lip in concentration. The alert, sometimes wary movements of her head and neck. The way she walked, game, boyish, and straight-ahead. All of it. It was a new variety of desire I was cultivating, just waiting for any opening, any invitation, to break out in wild Technicolor blossoms like some crazy mutant cross-pollinated tropical flower.

I didn't try to convey any of this to Titch.

Titch has never been what you might call a demonstrative person. Actually that might be the world's biggest understatement. I've seen her cry twice. Occasionally, grudgingly, under duress, she might hug someone, but she's like a cat whose whole body recoils even as it arches upward toward your palm. I can count on one hand the number of times I have hugged her. The last time was about two years ago. At dinner at her house, she got into a fight with her stepfather, Randy, after she stuck a fork into her hamburger, held it aloft, and began eating it delicately around the edges in a circle. He yelled at her about her table manners and sent her to her room without letting her finish her food. I left too in solidarity, found her on her top bunk, and climbed up.

"You don't know how lucky you are that your father left," she said, not looking at me, choked up. "It's a luxury."

"What do you mean a luxury?"

"The luxury to ignore his existence the way he ignores yours," she said. The beginnings of a smile crept into her voice. "Or to hunt him down and kill him. Either way."

I gave her a hug, which she tolerated, but barely. Because it was one of those astonishingly rare occasions that she let herself be touched, even as it happened I tried not to breathe, not to disturb her. Her ribs were sharp. She pulled away almost immediately and said, "I fucking hate him," and that was the end of that.

But when we arrived on the Cape this summer and climbed out into the glaring June sunshine in the parking lot of the Land Ho restaurant in Orleans, Titch linked her arm through mine and pulled me toward her. We were loopy from the long drive, the car littered with empty soda cans and wrappers and crumpled maps and mix tapes. In a moment of completely uncharacteristic affection, she started to sing the theme song from *Laverne and Shirley*, which we used to sing together on the playground in fourth grade. She sang boisterously, massacring the opening—*One two three four five six seven eight shlmiel schlmazel hoffentat incorporated . . . we're going to do it*—and then she spun me around in a circle, singing the ending at the top of her lungs, laughing, *And we'll do it our way yes our way make all our dreams come true (truuuuuue) and we'll do it our way yes our way make all our dreams come true for me and you.* I was so surprised by this that I couldn't even join in. I was laughing and protesting, fumbling and falling over my feet. With a big closing flourish, her whole face grinning widely at me, she said triumphantly, *Hey, look at us, here we are, we made it!*

Which is exactly how I felt, not just as it crystallized in that moment but more and more each day we were there.

Already in the first week the drama classes were beginning to fall into a rhythm, like the patter of our daily diction exercises. *What a to-do to die today at a minute or two to two, a thing distinctly hard to say but harder still to do.* Titch delighted in the tongue twisters and would croon, gobble, and chuckle them gently as she went about the house. *Rubber baby buggy bumper*, she might chant softly while folding laundry. *Tell me another!* she would cry. Oh, *What a to do-to die today. Red leather, yellow leather, red leather, yellow leather. How much wood would a woodchuck chuck? Toy boat, toy boat, toy boat.* And sometimes at breakfast, *mixed biscuits, mixed biscuits.*

After we had performed together in middle school, Titch had done several more plays with me—most of them in community theatre and one at Dartmouth, as two of the wide-eyed girls in *The Prime of Miss Jean Brodie.* But when we reached sophomore year, Titch had taken one class in painting with the pale, fanatic, hollow-eyed art teacher, Arthur Hill—he looked like my idea of Sherlock Holmes, but with ripped jeans and without the hat, tweed, or pipe—and she had promptly dropped everything extracurricular to join the slightly eccentric elusive cult of artheads who lived at the west end of the main second-floor corridor, behind the swinging orange door that led to the art room. "Do you wish you were doing the workshop with me?" I asked her one morning, in our kitchen, at the end of the first week. I was holding a Xerox of a script in one hand and trying not to drip honey on it from my toast.

"Not a chance," she said. "Acting used to make me break out in hives, remember? God, even thinking about it now is going to make me come all over in red bumps, just the thought of it. If I were still acting it would make me constipated and give me anxiety attacks. Why are we even talking about this? My heart rate is accelerating. Look at me." She lifted her chin high and yanked the top of her T-shirt down. Her clavicle was a little pink in splotches.

"Okay, I get it," I said, "but you were good at it. And sometimes I miss doing it with you. That's all I'm saying."

"It's not worth the suffering," she said, crossly. "Nobody's looking at me when I paint. And anyway. I'm right here." She stood up, cleared her throat, and walked to the counter, cracking the knuckles of both her hands efficiently. She stood with her neck erect, looking out at the bird feeders.

I used to badger Titch sometimes about why she wanted to be friends with me anyway or even about what she felt about anyone, because she was so staggeringly uncommunicative. Any teasing along these lines always made her clam up, frown, and say she didn't know, stubbornly.

If I kept pressing she might say she regretted having chosen me or she might flash all her mouth hardware at me in a grotesque face. It was like being bejesused by a truck horn or lots of shiny lights, like being dropped headfirst into Times Square at night like the giant apple on New Year's Eve.

Shut your maw, my grandmother used to say more or less affectionately when I chewed with my mouth open, so that's what I'd scream at Titch then, *Shut your maw!* Covering my eyes with my hands in mock horror, like the light from all that metal in her mouth might blind me. Sometimes, if she was in the right mood, she would chase me all around the house with her lower lip stuck way out, gnashing what was left of her teeth.

It was pretty spectacular in there, the crowning achievement of our infamous local orthodontist, Dr. Palientello, or Dr. Pal as he mirthlessly encouraged his patients to call him. Dr. Pal had taken one look at Titch's mouth and he'd seen a chance to build something really special, a kingdom all his own with a drawbridge in the form of tiny chains that dangled between her upper and lower teeth. Titch used to make small mournful doodles on notebooks about the horror, the metallic city, inside her head. We made up the names of the tiny people who lived there, their fiefdoms and thwarted romances (it was very Scottish, her mouth).

Titch used to sing all the time. She would sing her heart out in her damp basement, singing along with musical albums—*Annie, Oklahoma, Guys and Dolls, My Fair Lady.*

She loved everything about musicals. She even liked to reenact the musicals with me, whenever she could persuade me to do it. I'm not much of a singer, but I liked being on the makeshift stage of her back porch. We had a good time holding forth there together, and even brought in audiences, mostly family of course. But the dental work wrecked this for her. She stopped singing. She got a little more grudging, like some bitterness had gotten in with all that metal and she could always taste it. She would hide her mouth and duck her head.

Even just standing at the kitchen window in Truro, she had her right hand up to her mouth, her right index finger curled over her upper lip. Her hands always flutter up to cover her mouth when she smiles or talks or eats or laughs, like a person with a contagious disease who doesn't want to breathe on you, so that all those years of hard work have almost never been rewarded by the sight of her perfectly aligned teeth. It makes her seem more furtive and cagey than she already is, the way she hides her mouth—and that's saying something. I've never told her this, but her hands are beautiful and that gesture, that habit of shame, is surprisingly graceful.

"I'll run your lines with you though if you want," she offered then, making a face out the window at the bird feeder. "What's on this week? Is that still Cordelia?"

"I have to do the Cordelia monologue off and on all summer, but this is a scene from *Midsummer Night's Dream* with Helena and Hermia. I'm Hermia."

"Isn't Hermia the little one? Though she be little she is fierce?"

"Yes. But that's why they call it acting."

"Good luck with that," she said, laughing. "Now. I'm going to make some coffee because we're here and nobody can tell me not to and I don't care if it stunts my growth. Also, I really like it. Don't tell my mom. Do you want some? I think you have time before we head in. Besides if you're going to play Hermia, you could use a little stunting."

I crossed my eyes at her, and she laughed and grabbed two mugs from the cupboard that were cheerily monogrammed *Jennifer* and *Jeremy*. When she had filled *Jennifer* and presented it to me, she intoned, "Go forth, oh little one. Be fierce. And bring me home another tongue twister."

CHAPTER 11

Every morning we had movement and vocal warm-ups of various kinds led by a rotating set of characters, including Sarah in her capacity as our group's assistant. Then we spent the three hours before lunch with a visiting artist, usually a director, acting coach, or a movement or voice specialist. In the afternoons we worked primarily with the core group of resident teachers who circulated between the groups from week to week.

At the very end of the first week, which we in Group 6 had spent primarily with Bertie Benbow, all six groups gathered to meet the visiting directing instructor, Mary Olden, who would be with us for week two. I had overslept and was late to class. She turned out to be a woman in her fifties who had a body like a baby elephant. She talked about the tension between what you see and what you hear on stage, about how it's more interesting to see someone look at their watch as they say I love you than to see someone blowing a kiss while saying I love you. She asked us to provide a creative visual analogy for the class, for what we were doing at that moment. I raised my hand.

"Yes?" she said.

"We're cannibalizing," I said. "It's like we're standing over the operating table, dissecting your parts, trying to figure out whether what's in your liver is useful, you know, poking around for knowledge, inspiration, ideas, maybe whole organs to consume."

She laughed abruptly, almost angrily. Her eyes were cold and heavy-lidded, like the eyes of a reptile.

At the end of class I asked her what I'd missed.

"Get the assignment from someone else," she said, and walked on, lumbering up the stairs.

What I'd missed was an assignment to create a composition over the coming week using at least two of the elements—fire, water, earth, air—and specific chunks of text from Gertrude Stein's *Four Saints in Three Acts*, which I found incomprehensible.

"But that's what's liberating about it," Doug said in our small group when we sat around on the floor trying to figure out what to do.

"Yeah, *liberating*," drawled Shisha Pope, who was tall and black and beautiful, with astonishingly well-muscled legs that went up almost to my shoulders. She was commanding on stage, although she didn't always know what to do with her hands, which, like her feet, were large. She could be very silly and had a fabulous deep giggle, but she was serious when she was working and she scared the shit out of Doug.

"Don't you think so?" he asked, turning to me. He had flushed a deep, determined red.

I murmured something indistinct. Doug, the overeager mouth-breathing Edmund from the first day, had taken an unfortunate shine to me.

Nicky Pickler, a skinny blonde dancer with a dancer's tics and grace, said, "I think we should just figure out who's saying what. Just assign the text."

Nicky liked to look bored and above everything, but she was always checking everyone else out. She had beady little eyes that roved up and down everyone, constantly. Sarah had told me on the day we went out for coffee that she had privately nicknamed Nicky *the bean counter*, and I was so grateful for this confidence that I found myself regarding Nicky the bean counter with great warmth, which undoubtedly confused her.

"I don't think there's an easy or obvious division though," Ann said.

"I think we should do something in the ocean. You know, to embrace the elements!" Emily volunteered. A spasm of pain crossed Shisha's forehead, which happened almost every time Emily spoke.

Early on, maybe already on the third day, Emily had asked if I wanted to get lunch and I said sure, okay. The instant we were walking out into the sunshine, I knew it was a mistake. She smelled powerfully of patchouli and neediness. While we ordered from Mac's window, I remembered the previous day's class in Improvisation with Jorge Meringue, a high-energy teacher of the kind that makes me most apprehensive. He had us throw out a word to the person standing up in front, who would have to riff on that word, doing a kind of physicalized monologue made up on the spot, with certain verbal and physical constraints, like not using the word "and" or hopping on your left foot. (Sometimes I think acting teachers create these exercises for their own sadistic entertainment. For instance, I know that's true whenever they want you to be an animal. I hate a lot of things, but that is way, way up there on the list. If you saw what it was like in a room with students bouncing about as rabbits or pretending to prowl like cats or wriggling over carpets like snakes, you would understand *exactly* what I am talking about. I bet people—perfectly talented people—have left the acting profession altogether because they were asked to be an animal one too many times. I am not kidding.) In the improvisation exercise yesterday, when Emily stood up for her turn, buoyant like a sturdy balloon, someone yelled out the word, *euthanasia*. She started talking, bouncing her hips from side to side and it took a moment before I heard snickering and realized that she was chattering earnestly about the hardships of children in Asia. *YouthInAsia*.

My French fries were cold almost on arrival and I pushed the plastic basket away.

"Are you going to throw that out?" she asked me, in an edgy way.

I watched her eat them two at a time. I was thinking about friendship, about how unlikely it is and how much I don't really like people. Emily jiggled nonstop, and had a habit of making a small noise in her throat, a small grunting sound. She could not go more than a minute or two without making it, although she seemed to be totally unconscious of what she was doing. I got so I couldn't hear what she was saying when she was speaking because I was anticipating that sound so much. All I could hear was the pulsating erratic muted bass line of *grunt . . . grunt* and each time, I tensed with irritation and dread. At least when she ate there was less of this noise. During the reprieve I looked over at her carefully.

She was one of those white people who are almost translucent, the veins on the backs of her hands prominent, the skin dry. She was thickly built, somehow middle-aged looking, as though she wouldn't really find her calling until she could be cast as a beleaguered television mom trying to get stains out of someone's soccer jersey. Something about her on the bench eating congealed French fries with her spidery hands seemed so sad that I didn't want to know anything more about her, or be let in on any intimacies, not the shampoo she used or her parents' divorce or what pajamas she wore or her last boyfriend or whatever she was talking about at the moment. I closed my eyes to block her out. Then I had to have a vision of her bedroom with a ballet barre and giant posters of the Thompson Twins and Tom Cruise in his *Risky Business* sunglasses. This was incredibly depressing for some reason. It kind of made me want to hang myself.

"Using the ocean might be a little impractical," Geoffrey with a G said to Emily then, not unkindly. "Right? I mean, we don't even know what time of day we're performing."

Emily nodded vigorously, although her mouth was a little wobbly. Everyone else looked at Geoffrey with gratitude. He was maybe the only one in the group who you could always count on to listen—to really listen—when you were in a scene with him. He told us on the first day that his mother was Mexican and his father was Swedish and he was a sophomore at Brown. These facts had instantly merged in my head till they seemed inseparable. I couldn't manage to think one without thinking the other two at the same time. He was usually calm, and he looked both slick and muscular, like a very assured mob guy, but somehow gentle at the same time. He smoked constantly and could make the most intricate piece of Shakespeare make sense. No matter what he was playing, he was always telling a story that you could hear. I think you could have understood him even if he were speaking Urdu.

It was good that we had Geoffrey, because creating a theatre piece in a group in the early stages means there are no leaders yet and there's a lot of straining and trying, hanging back and uneasy jockeying. No one wants to be held responsible for getting it wrong and everyone is worried that they aren't as good as the next person. Geoffrey operated as our diplomat, our maître d', our air traffic controller. He was reliable and he had skills, but he wasn't showy about it.

Some of the group had already surprised me. Lanky Chris, for instance—who looked like he wished he were Douglas Fairbanks, as though he could be ready at a moment's notice to swashbuckle, or lounge against a doorframe with a cigarette draped from his fingers—he was at his best in stage combat class and in our brief exposure to historical dancing, when all his affectations seemed to fall away, or maybe they suddenly had the right outlet. Suddenly, strangely, with the minuet he was completely at home. (Do not ask me why we had a historical dancing class because I don't know, except that the program had managed to recruit a woman named Janice, tall and nervous like a disturbed crane, who was some kind of historical dancing expert. She came in one week and was gone the next, taking her ancient record player with her. Actually, I found I loved the minuet, the precision, the arched feet, the up and down of it.)

The Gertrude Stein assignment was hard for all of us because it was so determinedly open-ended. We were responsible for most of the text of Act III, not that it mattered since there was no more or less coherence in that bunch of text than in any other.

"Are we supposed to make sense of this?" Ann asked. "'Pigeons on the grass alas? Pigeons on the grass alas? It was a magpie in the sky?'"

She seemed to be frowning, but Ann had dark eyebrows that grew together in the middle so it was hard to tell when she wasn't frowning. I asked her one day on break why she was here. She was sitting on the window ledge of the main room in the art gallery, reading the *New York Times*, which she did every day. She would roll the paper up carefully and return it to her blue and white Yale canvas bag. She had a complicated system for unfolding and folding the newspaper so that all the time she was reading, it remained the size of a large book.

"I'm a math major," she said, pushing her glasses up her nose. "I thought it would be good for me."

"That's amazing," I said. "You wanted to spend your summer in an acting workshop because you thought it would be good for you?"

"Yes," she said, and returned to her paper. She seemed to be the person Titch would refer to as the LCD, or the lowest common denominator, which maybe Ann might have appreciated at least in theory, although not in application: the LCD is the person you know is likely to be the weak link, so you don't have to be.

But then Ann turned out to be a great fit for Stein. She had the idea to create a grid on the floor that we all moved on, she came up with the water gun, and she suggested we make hard and fast rules for movement—Shisha pitched in with this too, and Geoffrey, we all did. But with the imposition of a spatial structure and the specific movements, the text started to fall into place. We divvied up the lines, such as they were, and we began making our own sense of them. Relationships sprang up. Suddenly it was sinister and it was funny, speaking this gibberish, one day more film-noir-ish, the next the story of Christ on the cross.

All the groups were rehearsing at the same time, in the same building where we had gathered on the first day. We met there for the first four hours of the day every day for the second week. At the start there was a strange territorial, secretive feeling, people looking out of the corners of their eyes to see who else was doing what. Bursts of laughter from other groups derailed our efforts in the beginning, but we had begun to gain our momentum already by the second morning.

I wasn't looking so much at other groups as I was constantly looking for Sarah. I couldn't help it. I was always conscious of her.

When you want a flock of sheep to go somewhere—into the barn to administer worming boluses, let's say—you position yourself almost casually in opposition to them. You have to stand your ground enough not to have a wave of panic sweep the flock and cause the ewes to surge over you. You have to be calm and steady and purposeful, slow moving and nonchalant, and not look anyone in the eye. Look a sheep in the eye and she will generally assume she is up against the firing squad. I countered Sarah in the room as best I could, keeping soft eyes, knowing where she was without looking directly at her much, or at all. Once though, in the middle of the second week, I was watching her as she was looking out the window. She was pulling at the neck of her T-shirt, frowning, distracted, a piece of hair stuck to her cheek. She looked over quickly as if to catch me, and my face flamed because we both saw it exposed—my stupid naked desire. But then she came over to me after and looped her arm through mine. I stopped breathing. *Can't wait for the weekend* she said and it seemed for a moment magically like something about the two of us, that we were woven through the word *weekend*. This wasn't the case. She said she was going to New York; she had plans. After the party Friday night, she would be away for all that free time.

The party on Friday night was at someone's house in Provincetown. It was to celebrate the first round of performances—the performances of everyone's chunk of *Four Saints in Three Acts*, all strung together in a row—at the end of our first two weeks together. *Are you going?* she'd asked. Was she kidding? It was a chance to be near her in after-hours rooms, in anything-can-happen rooms. Was I going? Are the pigeons on the grass? Yes, in case you were wondering. Yes, they freaking well are.

I'd never been to Provincetown on a Friday night before, and it was the Fourth of July weekend, so it was even more than usually flooded with people and color, explosions of light and noise. It was a little like being at the World's Fair in Tunbridge, Vermont, at night when the party really gets going. Totally different crowd of course, but I had to resist the same urge to stare at everyone in my path, people with their mouths too large and slippery from drinking, a kind of garishness everywhere. It was a little scary and I almost wished I'd talked Titch into coming with me.

But then.

I slipped my hand into Sarah's at that crowded party. What I thought was, *I'll just get her attention to say goodnight.*

We did not look at each other.

The world was between our palms.

When I drove home that night, I went fast around the corners, reckless, impervious, chosen, untouchable. The windows were down, the smells of salt water and stagnant marsh came gusting in on a cool breeze, the tires rasped over the sand on the asphalt. It was quiet at home. In the driveway in Truro, I stood on the floor of pine needles and leaned against the car door, breathing in the night air. Everything was hushed, with only the wind causing a gentle stir, before settling down again. It felt like the night, all but asleep, had gently readjusted her covers. Then it was very still, cavernously black. Time passed.

I climbed the stairs two at a time. I was carrying a new country in my chest.

Titch was up that night. She wanted to know about the party. Usually she's quiet, unobtrusive, like a really talented robber, using her skills to get information, in and out, no fuss, no theatrics, nothing direct, nothing at gunpoint. But she circled me in the kitchen that night, while I fished for leftovers in the fridge, cold wet bedraggled salad, chilly clumps of spaghetti. I hadn't eaten anything at the party. I had had no awareness of food, no ability or memory of how to chew. Now I was ravenous. My body was humming. I perched on the counter to eat. Titch leaned against the counter opposite me.

"So was it fun?"

"Mmm," I said, or something equally noncommittal.

"Who was there?" she asked, casually.

"Just about everyone from the program."

"Was Sarah there?"

"Mmm."

She didn't ask me what she might have wanted to ask me and I didn't volunteer anything about Sarah, about my heart, anything. The hair on one side of Titch's head was completely flattened down, as if she'd fallen asleep on it. I thought she had probably been waiting up to talk to me. But I kept my spaghetti bowl between us, inhaling long strands with pointed concentration and thinking, *There's nothing to tell*, which was true and not true.

How do you know? Titch would ask eventually, shyly but determined, her upper lip working slightly. She meant, *How do you know how you feel?* About Sarah. About girls. *How do you know?* she would ask, almost fiercely. But not for a while yet. Now she narrowed her eyes at me and held her thoughts to herself, while I pretended to be innocent, unconcerned, ignorant, hungry.

When did you know? Titch would also ask eventually. *When did you really know?* And I would say, *Never. There was no one moment that I knew.*

But I think I knew right then when I didn't tell Titch. That's when I knew.

CHAPTER 12

The phone rang well before 7 the next morning. Titch called *it's for you* in sleepy displeasure and my heart sprang up like a dumb dog. Sarah said *hey do you want to go to New York today, can you call in sick or something* and I said *yes give me ten minutes* and then I tore around the house scattering clothes and hair products and cat food in my wake. Titch emerged from her bedroom in her off-pink pajamas from when the reds ran. She watched me silently as I spun around, as I left my semi-fluent lie on the voice machine at work, as I banged cupboards, and clattered down the stairs out the door to Sarah's truck, jumping in, flushed, triumphant, instantly utterly shy. Titch was still standing at the top of the stairs as I pulled the truck door closed with a bang. I waved. She did not wave back. I forgot her immediately.

Sarah looked over at me under her lashes and said, "You look like a Catholic schoolgirl."

"Do I?" I said, giddy. I had on a knee-length skirt, a white V-neck T-shirt.

"Mary Margaret."

"Mary Rose."

"Mary Gallagher."

"Mary Patrick."

"Mary Malone."

We beamed at one another, enchanted. I thought the sight of her hands on the wheel—her thumbs barely touching, the delicate gold-linked chain bracelet slipping down her wrist—

might actually make me faint. She put the gearshift in reverse, turning her head crisply around, and the sharp definition of the long bones in her neck leapt toward me, the hollow in her throat, her decisive chin, the swell of her bottom lip, the confident, easy way she handled the truck—we were not out of the driveway and a light sweat had broken out on my forehead. I gripped the door handle on my side and tried to breathe in deeply, feeling drunk from the cool morning air pouring in the window and blowing my hair all around.

The light was coming up pink on the horizon and the asphalt was glistening from the rain the night before. We stopped at the Hot Chocolate Sparrow in Orleans and bought carrot muffins and large cups of coffee with cream and sugar.

By the time we hit the city, we were both famished and ate an enormous breakfast at a French place on 9th and 21st, with giant bowls of café au lait served by skinny, sullen, glamorously disheveled waitresses, who either were French or gave a great French impression. We had found a parking place right off of 9th Avenue and Sarah pulled into it with a flourish. She said I didn't understand what a miracle it was. Stepping out of the safe containment of the truck was jarring at first, the pavement bone-jostling. When I nearly tripped on the sidewalk, Sarah caught my elbow for an instant to steady me and then when I looked up all the faces we passed looked luminous to me. Even the angry, hurried, and sick people on the street had halos, like the light distortion that happens when you have a migraine, but glittering with happiness instead of pain.

Sarah had an appointment to get her hair cut at a place on the corner of Bank and West 4th Street. It was not like any hair salon I had ever seen. It was like visiting someone's oversized elegant foyer, with giant urns of flowers and floor-length windows, with heavy drapes of amber-colored raw silk pulled back with oversized sashes. Two ornate retro barber chairs sat before marble counters and long mirrors with tarnished silver frames. The basins for washing hair were discreetly tucked away in the rear. A regal pug dog named Honey came to greet us and then returned to her place of honor on a large red velvet floor cushion, with a bowl of water. I sat and watched while Sarah chatted to her hairdresser, a man with a big, hard stomach and white hair, an expressive, rubbery face, and glasses with owlish, pink plastic frames.

He asked me questions about my home and told Sarah where she should take me to eat and what we needed to see in the city over the weekend. I basked in his friendliness, sitting cross-legged surrounded by old copies of *Vogue* on the sunny velvet window settee.

Outside on the street again, Sarah was shy and kept fingering her hair.

"Hold on," I said to her and she stopped obediently while I pressed a thumb to her temple and removed two small golden scissored hairs from where they glinted against her skin.

Just then a red-haired man passing by us said, "Look at you pretty girls," and there was no harm in it, only blessing, an admiring acknowledgment of our shininess, the way her light bounced off of me and the way we gleamed, like new pennies. Anyone who could have seen us would have said the same. There's no denying that kind of radiance. I thought I might crack from happiness. I thought—giving in, entirely breaking my seams with glee—I have met my match: *I am matched.*

Sarah took me to Kiehl's on Third Avenue then, with its white-coated, bristly salespeople, the clean lines of the bottles with their tidy black graphics. The potions, the samples, the impossible numbers of products you could spread on yourself; it was intoxicating. Everything looked or sounded delicious, from the swimming pool blue of the astringent to the pineapple facial scrub. Sarah was serious and intent in this setting.

She fit right in. She picked up various items—shampoo, conditioner, lip balm—with the stern efficiency of a seasoned shopper. She rubbed heather-scented lotion on her hands and held them up for me to smell. When I wandered aimlessly in different parts of the store, no matter where she was I could feel an unbroken yellow ribbon of happiness and complicity stretching between us, which would unspool in a leisurely way and then just like that quickly wind us together again. I was more content than I could remember being in that lazy, dog-paddling day, not needing to be anywhere, unconnected to my previous life, miraculously transported, everything right with the world.

We walked all the way back across town, and stopped at a bodega on the corner of 9th Avenue and 23rd Street, close to Sarah's apartment. The bodega was empty except for a tall slender woman with a lush brown ponytail who was browsing the magazine rack. She looked over at us twice sharply and then called out, "Sarah?"

Sarah turned away from me to greet her.

I heard ponytail girl ask her, "How's Bess?" and Sarah say, "She's fine."

Her shoulders were hunched up protectively. The woman tilted her head to one side, looking around Sarah over at me, slightly bemused. She gave me a careless once-over, which made me feel sweaty and ungainly. Then she said, "Well," gracefully flapping her hand at us, "enjoy the day."

When the woman had gone, Sarah turned back and smiled at me, an odd, tight, apologetic smile.

"I don't like her much," she said.

"Who is she?"

"Well, she rooms with some friends of mine from NYU and she models. She thinks she's a very big deal because she has the same agent as some of the hotshots."

We paid for our Diet Coke, and left.

"Was Bess your girlfriend?" I said, trying not to leave the conversation behind in the store, trying casually, nonchalantly, to pick up the threads. I had met Bess once at the house she and Ruby shared on the first weekend we'd arrived on the Cape, but I couldn't picture anything about her in this moment except that she was tall and had red hair. The mention of her name seemed to make Sarah grow stiller. I felt like I was approaching a distrustful animal.

"Yeah. We broke up in the spring and it's been a little sticky since then. I don't know. You know she's an artist?" Sarah asked. She was frowning, looking down, fiddling with the handle on her bag.

I shook my head.

"When we broke up, she made a whole set of children's furniture, tiny tables and chairs, and she painted the word LEARN on them in bright primary colors and then stacked them up in a heap." Sarah said this seriously enough, but her mouth twitched and I couldn't help it. I laughed. She grinned back at me then, only slightly ruefully.

"That's the silliest thing I've ever heard," I said, boldly, feeling giddily superior, daring.

"It is, isn't it?" she said, and laughed suddenly, happily.

I didn't want to let on how heady I found this conversation.

"Come on I'll buy you a soft ice-cream cone," she said, catching my hand.

"But it's going to rain," I said, thrilled, hanging on like a child. The sky had gone a deep greenish color and there was an ominous rumbling. Flinty New Yorkers were walking at their regular speeds, not acknowledging the sky, while a few—tourists, Sarah said, laughing—were looking around worriedly and ducking under awnings, searching their oversized bags for umbrellas.

"You don't mind a little water, do you?"

I told her how, when I was little, my grandmother used to

hand me a bar of soap and send me outside naked in the rain to wash.

"And what was that like?"

"Oh so cold," I said, "I mean you wouldn't believe how cold. And I don't know how clean I got because I used to slide on the grass. But I loved it."

Sarah looked at me then with such tenderness, her face very close to mine, that my heart jumped. But all she did was tug my hand and pull me across the street to the Mister Softee van.

"Come *on*," she said.

Just as I had eaten the top of my ice cream, the first big fat raindrop splashed down. I saw it hit Sarah on the forehead and watched her turn her face upward, blissful, as the rain started pelting down harder and harder.

"My ice cream!" I yelled in protest, covering it, gobbling it as the rain sluiced down my cone and the whole thing fell apart in my hands. She stood and laughed at me, rain pouring down her front, and seized with happiness, I threw the remainder of my cone at her. It caught the bottom edge of her shirt and she just laughed harder, holding the shirttail up in the rain to wash it out. We were drenched in minutes, looking out at one another from behind our scraggly and dripping hair. A giant crack of thunder opened up around us and she turned in circles, jumping in puddles. She was yelling something at me and I couldn't hear her over the noise.

Eventually, we squelched home to the apartment, which she shared with a friendly guy named Dan, a plump waiter waiting for his acting break. Inside, she stripped down easily while I stood frozen for a moment looking anywhere and nowhere at the same time.

She held out a long-sleeve T-shirt to me. It was a soft washed cotton in purplish-blue. It smelled of fabric softener and Sarah.

"It's your color," she said with authority and I took it, mute, damp, shivering, blessed.

Walking to the restaurant I told Sarah about the last time I had been in New York, which had been on a college visit the previous spring with Titch and Amy Klein. Amy's parents had driven us to the city and we all stayed with Amy's aunt, who had a large apartment in the Apthorp building on the Upper West Side. The place seemed very romantic and nineteenth-century, the way I wanted New York to be.

But then after the Columbia University tour ended, before Amy's parents met up with us, Titch and I had gone off to a grubby café just down the street from St. John the Divine. We were feeling very worldly with our herbal tea and our unfamiliar pastries—*hamentashen*, the girl behind the counter said, her voice thick and foreign and bored—two girls, out and about, loose in the big city. Then a man came in to the café, took out a gun, and threatened the girl behind the counter, who didn't speak much English. He was yelling. She was hysterical. I don't remember feeling anything but wonder when the gun swung around the room, dipping toward us, jerking away. Somebody to my left was crying quietly. A man behind me said, *Oh Lord Jesus, Oh Lord Jesus, Oh Lord Jesus* and groaned. Someone else said, *Shut up*, viciously, like a wet slap.

I remember noticing that the edge of Titch's mug—that heavy indestructible white crockery so many restaurants use—had a lipstick smear on it. She was breathing hard. She grabbed my hand under the table, crushing the bones of my fingers together. It was over so fast—there was a plainclothes cop in the room, it turned out—that we barely had time to register what had happened. We didn't tell Amy or her parents because her father panicked easily and we thought he might not let us finish the trip. I think he would have been thrilled to have an excuse to get out of New York. All the way on the drive down from New Hampshire, he talked about the crack epidemic, the homeless epidemic, the AIDS epidemic, which, to hear him tell it, began in the West Village of New York City, not in San Francisco or Africa at all.

I asked Titch and Amy the first night we were there, when we were getting ready for bed in the guest room, if they thought there were always so many epidemics, or if it was true that there were really more epidemics now than ever before. If we were living in the time of epidemics. They didn't know. Also Amy wasn't really interested in that kind of conversation. She wanted to know whether she'd be able to take classes at Columbia if she went to Barnard. Whether there'd be boys.

Anyway, the danger was over so Titch and I didn't say anything. We didn't talk about it until we were home and alone together again and even then, not much.

But for the rest of the time we were in New York and even after we went home—for about two weeks altogether—I discovered that whatever comfortable protective shield I must have usually had up in front of me was down. I was a magnet for deranged and desperate people, for sick animals, for beggars, for anyone raw and unprotected. Outside of NYU Admissions, a homeless woman hit me over the head with her large shopping bag, which felt like it was filled with rocks. A man with only one working eye followed me down 8th Street, yelling about getting rid of the demons. Another younger man put his head on my shoulder, crying, on the subway train. It wasn't just New York, either. The first day back home, in the parking lot outside of the mall in West Lebanon, a rabid raccoon staggered toward me across the pavement out of nowhere. I mean this raccoon got me in his sights and tracked me down. It was completely unnerving. But I must have been approachable. After the holdup I must have dropped some guard I didn't even know I had.

Sarah didn't say anything when I told her about this. I had meant it to be kind of a funny story, a worldly story, but she just glanced over at me from time to time, seriously, intently, while

I was talking. Then she paused on the street, reached out, took hold of my necklace, and slid the clasp, which had migrated around to the front of my neck, around to the back. I felt her fingertips lightly on the nape of my neck. "I'm so glad you were okay," she said.

At dinner, we were quiet. I was playing with the red candle on the restaurant table, tilting it one way and then another, watching the wax pool up and re-form, picking at it with my fingernail, concentrating, self-conscious. She took the candle from me and poured hot candle wax into her mouth. It made me wince and she laughed, delighted, and peeled a red wax rose from her tongue. If she had pulled a rabbit from beneath the table it would not have surprised me. She was magical. She had tricks up her sleeve.

When we left the sanctuary of the restaurant, I was aware again of the strangeness of the city, its looming darkness pressing in, an unexpected piercing scent of wisteria. By the time we were walking up the flights of stairs to her apartment, I could hear my breathing, feel the pulsing in my neck. The entryway smelled like old cat urine.

I was a little light-headed. For the first time, nervousness pricked my chest. I focused on Sarah, moving purposefully ahead of me, in her jeans with a green tank top and Blundstones on her feet. She was all bare brown arms and humid neck, her hair pinned up at the back of her head somehow, straggling bits sticking to her skin.

Her roommate Dan was already asleep. His small mop-like dog came to visit us, toenails clicking across the linoleum, and then sighed and collapsed, legs shooting straight out to the four corners of the room so he looked like a miniature bear rug, belly to cool floor. The air was gluey from the city smells. The shapes of furniture in the dark living room seemed ghostly now, blockish, unknown.

I want you to hear this song, she said. Okay. We were sitting kitty-corner in chairs at the kitchen table with a tape player and glasses of water. She pressed play. She leaned in toward me and brushed her cheek against mine so lightly it was more like warm air than skin. She dipped in again and we rested there for a moment barely cheek to cheek, barely breathing. *This is what they mean*, I thought confusedly, *about cheek to cheek*. The softness the warmth the nearness was dizzying. We did not kiss. We put our heads together and touched noses and cheeks instead, as inquiring and velvety as horses who visit by lowering their satiny muzzles together. In the background, Nina Simone sang "Lilac Wine," crooning gently. (*I lost myself on a cool damp night/Gave myself in that misty light/Was hypnotized by a strange delight/Under a lilac tree*.) We breathed on one another. (*I made wine from the lilac tree/Put my heart in its recipe/It makes me see what I want to see/And be what I want to be*.) I tried to hang onto the words of the song to steady the happy jumble of my mind, the huge pounding in my chest. (*Lilac wine, I feel unsteady. Lilac wine is sweet and heady, like my love*.) I tried to listen to what Nina was singing as a way to hold on, but I wasn't capable of holding on. I was already beyond, over the edge of delight. The words slipped away from me in the wash of joy, of breath, of the revelatory softness and the mild lush sweet scent of her skin. It was the smell of happiness. My whole body rolled over in warmth, like a dog in deep grass in the summertime sun.

When Sarah did speak, it didn't make any sense to me at first. She said, *Hello beach plum*. Then she said, *Oh, Nina*. Her eyes were unfocused. Her voice did not sound like anything I had ever heard before.

CHAPTER 13

One of the first things I noticed this summer about living in a new place is how I map that place, how I carve it up and use it. On the Cape, I learned the routes to places that I went regularly for practical reasons—the produce store in Orleans for example, the cheap gas in Eastham—as well as the way to a few places I had adopted as my own—Bound Brook Beach, the quietest pond tucked away in Truro—and once I'd hit a certain number of each kind of place—places I needed and places I liked—I trucked back and forth to those spots, digging my trail, rarely getting off course. I did this on foot and by car. There were whole unexplored areas of the Cape, probably hundreds of overgrown scrubby sandy roads that I never even considered going down. That way I had a gradual feeling of mastery over my own tiny map. For a landscape, a place, to be familiar, I need the doing and the doing of it, the same step by step across it, a repeated physical habit to learn the terrain.

But with Sarah what was known, what was familiar between the two of us, was immediate. I'm not talking about feeling smug because we'd both really read our Edith Wharton like those insufferable couples everyone knows. I'm not talking about shared interests or those seemingly amazing discoveries when you're first crushed out on someone and you learn that they hate Elmo too or when you admit that you both grew up listening to Dolly Parton and you adore her. Those moments might make you feel destined to be with the other person, but really they only serve as confirmation of your own ego and tastes (every right-thinking *Sesame-Street*-watching self-respecting person hates that wannabe-Muppet and *of course* you loved Dolly and you were right to do so). I'm not talking about this kind of mutual self-congratulatory pleasure.

What happened was that we were skin of the same skin.

I had felt something similar to this sensation once, long ago when I was little, with a slender boy, slippery and loose-limbed, double-jointed and lithe like a circus performer. He could have curled himself into a small box such as might hold a bakery layer cake or a tall hat, and he was graceful in a way that very few boys are. His name was Nico. He said that when he grew up he wanted to be a circle. He said this as though it were about the same thing as wanting to be an astronaut or a fireman. It made perfect sense to me. He made sense to me, in his being. We met and regarded one another for less than ten minutes before we pounced and leaped and rolled. It was the summer after I had moved home to Vermont to live with my grandparents. We were both six years old, our birthdays only one day apart.

Nico's father was working a job, digging out the pond at my grandparents' home, and Nico came along to ride on the giant machinery. He could have been my twin. The first morning we stretched out lengthwise at the top of the long hill behind the house, arms stiff by our sides, and rolled down faster and faster in the meadow grass, which was blousy, spiky, smelling of sun with whirling pockets of damp ripe earth, crisp prickly sweetness. When we landed in a heap at the bottom my nose was tucked in the hollow of his collarbone, which smelled like the peepers sound, which is to say, like home. I licked his neck, which didn't startle him at all. He rested his face in my hair. His heartbeat was too close to the skin in his skinny boy chest. It was a strange sensation to be near him because his oversized heartbeat made him seem at once fragile and all encompassing.

It gave me the same amazed feeling as cupping my hands around a songbird, the way the heart pounds all through the body, that wide terrifying embrace. He was all heartbeat, all heart. In the one picture someone took of us, we are both in denim overalls, hand in hand, dirty and victorious, not girl or boy but shining eyes in grubby faces. He has a high, worryingly vulnerable forehead, enormous impish glee, a mop of dark hair, large dark eyes, and a beautiful mouth.

For two months, we played together seriously, with abandon, every day but Sunday. He was my brother and my true love returned to me. We were our own litter of puppies. We were joyful and unashamed.

This did not mean that we agreed on most things or much of anything. Once we found a dead cat in the road behind the barn, its eyeball lying apart in the dust like an iridescent blueberry, or that shiny dark reddish blue skin of a wild grape, pulpy and battered. I wanted to investigate it, but he cried and wouldn't look at me. I thought we should move what remained, the matted fur, the flattened forelegs, off the road. He didn't want to touch it or have anything to do with it so I hunted up sticks to pry up the body. He looked at me all streaked with tears and snot, like I was a traitor. He would not touch me on the walk home.

When his dad was done with the job, he was gone from one day to the next and I never saw him again. But I believe I would know him anywhere, at any time. I believe that all my bones would rise up and clatter together like noisemakers to greet him, in jubilant recognition, just as they did the very first time I saw him.

Sarah and I didn't always see eye to eye either, but we too are from the same litter. When she curled over me in sleep, in love, from the first night on, we would find ourselves later in the most remarkable, unlikely positions without strain, with our earliest limberness, our baby bonelessness, allowing for an intertwining, a merging I never knew possible. The ease was astonishing, unknown to me. This was not sidling up for comfort—although it was comforting—this was not passionate gymnastics—although it was passionate—this was being drawn, drawing to your own skin, inevitable, magnetic, necessary.

It would be better not to remember this.

But if I do, when I do, what I remember is waking up in the morning, that first morning and many, many others, deep in soft folds of bedding, naked as a jaybird, heavy with ease, limbs entangled, basted top to toe with happiness, just drenched in it, smeared with it. Her face on the pillow smiling her lazy smile at me, her hair mussed, her slow heavy-lidded familiar blink, smiling her smile, completely undefended, as assured and content as the cat that has drunk the cream. The first time I saw her unguarded smile, I was undone. I was done in. I was done for. Her whole face opened and unfurled when she looked at me, as uncomplicated and joyful as a sheet shaken out and billowing in the sunshine. The first time I saw that look on her face, I knew she loved me.

She believed in good bedding, in a feather bed, a mattress piled high with a downy comforter, soft, soft sheets, a decadent pillowed place to burrow in and bed down. In it, we made our own rules. In it, we were a fort that could not be taken; we were sheltered from all the elements. In it, we belonged to each other and nothing in the world could touch us.

After the weekend in New York, without any discussion, we were together for as much time as could be squeezed from the day, which seemed expansive, like an opening accordion, for us. Between classes, whenever possible we would lag behind walking from one location to another, backing each other into corners, crushing the morning glories on a dilapidated trellis, pressing up against the back of a building, curving into the cool musty stone stairway to the basement of the church, locking the door in the girls' bathroom at the library. At the end of the day, I liked to wait for her on the landing outside her place in town and when she was finally done with the workshop and I heard her footsteps crunching on the driveway, I would bolt down to meet her and leap off the fourth step from the bottom, the way the lambs race up the manure pile and sail off the other side into the open air, knees bent, ears out, for no other reason than because they can.

We were on an unnamed mission, ferocious and tender, giddy and determined. She tucked love notes and flowers, pears and secondhand books in my bag. She could look at me across the room and I would be flooded, my heart beating foolishly at the thought of the sourness inside her elbow or the soft baby hairs at the nape of her neck, the focused concentration of her gaze, the unexpected softening of her face. She could be watching a scene in class with attention and I would be able to see only her face swimming toward mine through a heated haze, to meet up at the pillow.

Out of class, sometimes all night long, we talked a blue streak. I can't tell you what we talked about because mostly it was random stuff—careening between the fantastical, the totally specific, and the crazily big picture—like whether there was a limbo and what it would look like; which names of the Greek mythic figures would make good names for cars (the Ford Medea); whether Meryl Streep really was as great an actress as all that (I said yes, in *Silkwood*, Sarah, yes, in *Out of Africa*); our family dramas; what names we would give our children (she was partial to Ben and Lily); what rules applied to dreams; how jeans should fit; the relative merits of Chrissie Hynde, Simple Minds, Tom Waits, David Bowie, the Smiths, Stevie Wonder—maybe Sarah's hands-down favorite—and Nick Drake ("Just no," was all Sarah had to say about Nick, and when pressed: "Too sad"); absolutely anything we'd read, or heard, or seen; where we would travel and live and how we would spend our lives. Nothing and everything, all-over-the-map talking.

I can tell you what she was like when we talked. She was like a big cat cub. When she spoke, she snapped off her words, pouncing on her tail, biting it soundly, and then looking up, pleased, not admitting to pleasure. Sometimes we would scrap conspiratorially in conversation, biting one another's tails until we were caught in a tailspin, round and round in dizzy, batting, contradictory joy.

She could be very severe. This thrilled me. I wanted to be her target; I wanted her to take me for dinner, to wrestle me down so that I could surrender, neck presented, belly up, her occupied territory, her plaything. I wanted to carry my love for her in my teeth and drop it at her feet a hundred times a day.

I attempted this in class but only cautiously, only as much as was seemly, by unobtrusively leaving the occasional cup of coffee at her elbow, or a shared sweater at whatever spot she had chosen on the floor. She did not acknowledge any of these gestures directly. She was always focused on the work in the room, serious, attentive, and professional. I had a new ease in classes, brought on by having survived the first round of performances without too much to be ashamed of, but mostly because I was chosen. And more than that, I had a whole new life, a secret splendid explosive life.

I thought it was a funny thing, our kissing, because as far as I could tell most people didn't seem to think that's what we were doing or could be doing. It didn't *occur* to people. At the same time I was thinking *I can do this* and if I could, anybody could. I actually wanted to march up to people sometimes and let them know, no kidding. It made me want to take girls and kiss them on the mouth, because I had discovered that I could and I thought it was very likely it simply hadn't occurred to them that they could too. *Doing this will break your world open*, I wanted to say, looking over during class at Emily's woe-begone, overeager face, or Ann's furrowed, pinched one. *You have no idea. There will be a before and an after like no other.*

It's strange to do something you have never seen done. I didn't know if it was peculiar to wish this, but I wished there were pictures of Sarah and me kissing. Or a short film with a handheld camera, like the black-and-white ones Titch has of herself running around the yard as a toddler in her striped playsuit, or naked jumping in and out of the wading pool, hamming it up. Not a long film, just to see what it looks like from the outside. I'd never seen two girls kissing, not really. Not in any real sustained way. It felt different from kissing a boy and I knew it must look different too. I do know it was pretty and I wish we could have stepped outside it once in a while to admire, or just to know. I didn't know I could be so hungry to *see* something or to have something *seen*.

CHAPTER 14

One person and only one person in the workshop knew almost immediately.

Three days after Sarah and I came back from the first weekend in New York, all the members of Group 6 were eating lunch companionably outside at the picnic tables, with seagulls screaming occasionally in the background. Sarah was with us, casually, at the far end of the table. I was wearing my hair up at the back of my head, which had prompted a mindless conversation about haircuts.

"You should cut your hair," Emily cried, with her usual suffocating enthusiasm. "You would look so sweet with bangs. My friend Paul cuts hair and he'll be up this weekend. You should totally have him cut your hair."

"She's not going to cut her hair, she's not getting *bangs*," Sarah said abruptly, as though goosed, but reluctantly, into this conversation. "Don't do that," she added to me.

"I've got to get back," she said then, standing gracefully and sweeping up her paper trash in one hand. The others began following suit, chattering.

Shisha was seated next to me when this happened. She watched Sarah's departing back with her head tilted to one side, and then turned to me.

"How long has that been going on?" she asked. She seemed amused.

Startled but deeply gratified, I said, attempting nonchalance, "Oh, a while."

She kept looking at me steadily, a look with compassion, verging, I thought, on something almost like pity, which made me confused and uncomfortable. I felt my face getting hot. I thought maybe I was supposed to say something, but I didn't know what.

"What?" I said finally, with more irritation than I meant to. She just shook her head gently.

I didn't know Shisha very well, but I knew in a roundabout way that she had a girlfriend. Judith. I'd seen Judith because she sometimes came to collect Shisha at the end of the day. And one day there had been something about the way Judith had her hand on the car door as Shisha got in that smacked of possession, and not of the car. Judith lived in Boston, but she came out most weekends to their rental place in Orleans. She was a slightly terrifying white woman in her forties, skinny and erratic, with a hard, lived-in face, and a throaty laugh. And then there was the day, in the first week of classes, when Shisha had had a long stretch of bruises on her ribs and I asked her how she got them.

"Oh, Judith loves me," she said as though that was what I had asked about. She was pulling her T-shirt over her head and spoke through the cloth. "But she's jealous and she's got a temper. You know. She can get mean."

I did not know, and I shied away entirely from the conversation like a skittish horse. It spooked me. It was actually inconceivable to me at the time that one woman could hurt another this way, so the fact of what she said—what it meant—fell right out of my head the minute she said it. Or maybe it was Shisha herself who made it seem inconceivable, with her happy, deep laugh and those legs that could kick you into next week.

"Be careful," she said that day at the picnic tables, with such kindness that I couldn't take it amiss, although I balled up my napkin in my fist, feeling baffled and cross. I stared down at my feet through the slats in the table. My toes looked blunt and stupid in their sandals.

"Your first is a big deal," she said, "that's all. She looks like a lot of work."

"Well, who isn't?" I said defensively, exhaling heavily through my nose, in a small tizzy. My first? How did she know these things?

Shisha stood up. "That's not what I meant," she said. She sighed. She was very tall, standing there. "Look, I like you," she said. "That's all."

"By the way," she called back over her shoulder, when she was about a dozen steps down the road, "she's right. Never bangs for you, no bangs. Much better without."

The only other people who had to know right away lived right next to Sarah. When we got back from New York, whenever we weren't at the workshop Sarah and I spent most of the time at her place in Wellfleet. It was handy for the program, because all we had to do was roll out of bed and dash into town. Since I could borrow Sarah's truck for longer trips, I told Titch I wouldn't need the car. I went back to the Davidsons' to pick up clothes and to feed the cats, but spent almost every night at Sarah's. And because Sarah's life was crowded with people and places to be, my dance card was immediately full as well.

She lived in a small apartment in the top of a house that had been converted as a result of a Massachusetts program to reclaim old, falling-down houses and transform them into low-income housing. The collection of apartments had year-round tenants paying low rent. Sarah and Eddy were in the top two apartments, and Dennis was on the ground floor. Eddy was the boss at my weekend job at the catering outfit in town, and Dennis was a finish carpenter. The decade that the low-rent order had been in place for the apartments had passed, but no one had moved on or showed any signs of ever moving on, and

Luke, technically owner and landlord, showed no signs of asking for more money from the group that was essentially his family. Luke lived in the small house he had built adjacent to the apartments. The three men had all moved permanently to Cape Cod sometime in the previous two decades and they were settled into their ways with and alongside each other. They groused a lot about one another, but in a friendly, grubbing sort of way, the way your favorite uncles talk who drink too much and have grand, failed schemes. A fair number of conversations revolved around winning the lottery.

The three of them had unofficially adopted Sarah two years before when she first came to the Cape, and now they folded me into the mix by extension and apparently without hesitation. All of them—and everyone else I met who lived year-round on the Cape—worked multiple jobs to stay afloat. At least one of those jobs was guaranteed to be catering to the rich people, the summer people. The people whose houses sat like giant empty insults, dark all winter, huge vacant windows eye-balling the town. Everyone who really lived here turned some kind of trick in the tourist circus, throwing pizza, or tiling floors, feats of carpentry, roofing, bartending, and waitressing. And as far as I could tell everyone had at least one other true vocation: painting, sculpting, translating, writing, making movies, breeding dogs, working a boat.

Luke was the hub. It was impossible to tell how old he was. He had a thickening middle and a face that had lived outdoors, that had been turned up to the sun, worked out in the sun. There was a picture of him on his strange-fangled Scandinavian refrigerator with its freezer on the bottom. In the photograph he has longish shaggy dark hair, blue bell-bottomed cords, and is squinting happily with his head tilted back in the sunshine. He might be in high school. There's a crease in the photo that runs across his heart. He looks as though he were stumbling around arms extended feeling the soft air the way girls in elementary school used to pretend to be Helen Keller when they weren't busy drawing horses in their notebooks.

The first Sunday after I met Luke he had a big plan, which did not, it would turn out, distinguish that day from any other. The big plan was to build a chicken house. Never mind that he had no chickens. (Details.) He would buy chickens. He would use the chickens to heat the downstairs/greenhouse/basement of his little house and to create a fabulous source of compost. He had been researching how to make this happen and had found a woman on Martha's Vineyard who had created an ecological system based on a chicken house. He had spoken with her, but had then promptly decided that he could improve on what she did. His construction would be bigger, better, smarter, and more effective, something he was now calling the chicken cathedral. (*Chicken house is thinking too small*, he had confided to me that morning in the radish row).

Sarah and I went into town to buy a Sunday newspaper and by the time we came back Luke was stretched out on his back on the lawn fast asleep with one arm thrown up over his face, exhausted by his own ideas. I learned, gradually, that this was the way: the chicken cathedral embraced in a rush might get returned to off and on but would have to share the table with an infinite number of ambitious plans, vying for Luke's attention like so many mistresses.

To say that Luke was a guy who knew his own mind is like saying Hitler had some notions. I'd never met someone so set in their ways, so convinced of their rightness, so easily rattled by variation or adjustment. The use of the wrong brush to scrub the dishes brought on palpitations. This didn't strike me as a sign of age though. He seemed like a person who as a child would have had fixed opinions on everything from how to tie shoelaces, to which was the right glass for juice, to what kind of balls bounced best. He would absolutely have had his own system for winning foursquare. He had shown up an authority. He had reasons, rooted in a science of efficiency and rightness all his own, but at the same time, he was one of the slowest, dreamiest people I had ever met. If his entrenched sense of correctness hadn't been coupled with enormous pleasure and curiosity about the world, it might have been insufferable. As it was, he did irritate plenty of people. Shoulders stiffened when he helpfully pointed out the better way to nail in a board, or to park a car. Plenty of people—including Eddy and Dennis—couldn't resist baiting him from time to time, although I always thought this was like shooting fish in a barrel: you could misuse "hopefully" in a sentence, and watch him shudder in his agitation to set you straight. The ease of provoking him made it seem like poor sport. If you listened instead, even marveled at the apparently limitless reach of his idiosyncratic knowledge, you could appreciate the sweetness, the energy with which he responded to the world. Besides, he was inclined to like me, so he often gave me a heads-up so I could defer without being confronted or challenged or corrected. He might say, jovially, "You're not one of those people who . . . " (doesn't know how to clean out a cast-iron skillet; would put any old thing down the toilet and not respect the plumbing; would use a butter substitute). I had a distinct, unexpected advantage with Luke because of my grandmother, who taught me to clean with vinegar and baking soda and to take care of old things, who made a practice of recycling her teabag at least three times and never used the drying machine but hung everything on the line. The information I could bandy about that my grandmother had imparted to me—like how to nibble on red bee balm, or what to do about Japanese beetles—was received with great interest. I would know I was secure in Luke's affections when he declared one day, *She's not one of those people who doesn't know how to bank a fire!* I was so happy to be *not one of those people*, to be *one of these people*, happy neither to agree nor disagree with his dictums but remain mute and contented, buoyed along by his faith that I shared his worldview. I wanted him to love me as he loved Sarah. Loving her had made me love him instantly, emphatically, almost painfully.

CHAPTER 15

When we entered the third week of class an array of new teachers joined us for shorter increments, usually for two or three mornings to hold forth on specific topics. On these occasions, the groups were all mixed up together. It was fun to be in the same room as students we had seen only on the night of the Gertrude Stein performances. Two different people came to talk to us about auditioning in the first full week of July, the first a casting director from a New York agency named Marg Hawthorne.

As we were arriving for the first session on auditions—leaving our bags lined up against the wall, along with jumbled piles of sweatshirts and notebooks, shoes and scripts, water bottles and coffee cups—Nicky Pickler the bean counter sidled over to me.

She said with characteristic shrewdness, "This woman is a really big deal. She casts Woody Allen's films and a lot of series. It's a big deal if she likes you. She's very well connected."

I looked at the woman who was a big deal. Although she wasn't fat at all, she reminded me of our elementary school librarian, Jean Keen, whose chin capsized into her neck. This woman was small, round-cheeked, with the same combination of dryness and softness. Dryness in the skin, but softness in the cheek. She looked like she would know how to train dogs.

Those students who had headshots had set them out on a long table by the window. Everyone else eyed them with private judgment and curiosity.

Sarah's headshot, which she'd told me was an old one, made her look like a young Jane Fonda, not in an idiotic pinup way, but because she had that breathtaking stark naked gaze that Jane used to have, something a little stripped down. Not workout Jane, not *9 to 5* Jane. Jane with the seventies shag haircut that's so ugly that her face looking out through the hair is even more plainly beautiful. Marg paused in front of the headshot and then looked over at Sarah assessingly.

"It's a good picture," she said, "But it won't get you any comedy work."

Sarah turned pink around the ears, but bent over the picture and asked Marg a question I couldn't hear, the back of her neck serious and intent.

In the sleepy slog of that afternoon we had scene work together with Group 4. I was assigned a scene from a Wendy Wasserstein play. Marg Hawthorne presided over us. She sat patiently through various versions of the same scene, in which one character approaches another at the end of their college friendship to say goodbye. The scenes droned on.

"Why the faces?" Marg asked when we had sat through three versions, everyone lolling on the floor of the library's spare room and picking at the hairy carpet thread.

"Sometimes you get stuck with material you don't respond to, but it's your choice how you handle it, what you bring to the table. You can make me attend to the phone book if you have to. And you might have to."

She looked around at us, and then pointed to me and my scene partner, a tall willowy girl named Alicia with a long nose, long dark glossy hair, and a high opinion of herself. "You two," she said, "again."

Before we began, Marg walked over to me, gripped my elbow, and whispered, *You're in love with her*, in my ear. I stared at her, startled, and then we played the scene again. Alicia bobbed along in her own self-absorbed world and I was more and more crushed and furious that I couldn't reach her, although I tried in every way I could. When we finished, the class murmured a little ripple of appreciation.

"Alright then," said Marg restrained, but approving. "It's the strength of the choice going into the scene that makes it play or not. It's how high the stakes are. Nice."

I sat down on a cloud of self-congratulation, feeling understood.

"What did I suggest to make that happen?" Marg asked at large.

Ann, in her unpredictable rabbity way, piped up, "That they are in love?" and I looked over at Marg's pouchy cheek nodding in profile and thought, *What did she see in me to ask me to do this.* I thought, *She sees me,* and, overcome with shyness and pleasure in equal parts, I stared so hard at the floor that I saw black spots.

"Raise the stakes," Marg was saying to the room. "Always raise the stakes."

"Does that mean she can tell?" I asked Sarah afterwards, outside in the parking lot. "How can she tell?"

Across the street from the library, a delirious chorus of frogs was singing their raucous social hearts out.

Sarah said, "Well, she's been around. She's good at her job. And she's gay."

This didn't help me. What I meant was, if it was something Marg Hawthorne could see, who else could see it, and what were they seeing? What did it look like?

Sarah looked across at me. "You've never been asked if you want the lesbian discount at any store in Provincetown, have you?"

I said no.

"Well, then," she said, dismissively, opening the truck door and slinging her knapsack behind her seat. "I wouldn't worry about it if I were you."

"Have you?" I asked her through the window as I came around to the passenger's side, but she was looking straight ahead and didn't answer.

"I wasn't worried," I said, when I got in, which was not entirely true.

I knew that if Sarah didn't answer a question immediately, I was never going to get an answer. This didn't trouble me in the slightest. I felt we were in complete accord at bottom and her occasional refusals to speak didn't touch my certainty. Certainty was in her mouth, the slope of her silky bent head, the downy small of her back, the spaces between her ribs, her heartbeat. As long as I had access to these, I had all the information I needed.

Also it wasn't only that I couldn't necessarily get clear answers out of Sarah. I was unfathomable to myself a lot of the time now. For instance: I said I was a biter when I was a child. Well, from the beginning I bit Sarah without even knowing I was biting. I didn't know why I did it; I hardly knew when I did it. I bit in an unfocused, determined haze, in lovely snatches of ferocity and desire, marking cheeks, sometimes shoulders, arms, calves with purply blue crescents. We would gaze with wonder at these developments in the early light like they were new moons around Jupiter, suddenly two shy amazed girls.

The same night we worked on audition scenes, we ran right into Marg Hawthorne on the street in Provincetown.

"You did a nice job today," she said to me with unexpected warmth. "You could have a future."

I squashed the urge to say I sincerely hoped so. Her cheeks looked very pink.

"Thanks," I said, instead.

"Where are you going to school?" she asked, ignoring Sarah.

"I'm not. I mean I'm still in high school. In New Hampshire." She nodded at me and then her eyes slid over to Sarah.

"Sarah, right?" she said and Sarah nodded. Marg started talking to her about a workshop in the city in August—the development of a new television pilot filming in NY—that Sarah should audition for. She said Sarah should call her about it.

"Are you going to do that?" I asked, when Marg had said goodbye.

Sarah shrugged.

"It won't come to anything," she said.

I was watching Marg Hawthorne's departing back. It seemed to me there was a walk, an identifiable walk. The robust, no-nonsense march of Jodie Foster, Mary Poppins, Sally Ride, and the thousands of girls whose hips drive straight ahead and not side-to-side. Because in addition to trying to comprehend Sarah-and-me, which was kind of a full-time job, not to mention reciting my Shakespeare and memorizing lines and negotiating the other students and workshop demands and remembering to show up at my weekend job and absorbing the new landscape, I was studying a whole new people. I watched everyone, asking roundabout questions when I thought I stood a chance of gleaning any useful information without looking too stupid.

Provincetown, with its bare-chested men in leather pants and dog collars, the orange tans, the muscles and chains, the rainbow flags and stickers in shop windows, the drag queens with monstrous high pink wigs and teetering heels and aggressive eyeliner, was terrifying, astonishing, and educational all at once. But it was overwhelmingly about men and their efforts either to see or to pretend not to see one another. It was much harder for me to track and understand what happened between women.

"Who's that woman?" I asked, about, for instance, a small wiry brunette sitting with Sarah's friend Jean, who worked as a bartender. We were out late in a small smoky hole in the wall on a Wednesday night when I should have been home in Truro, curled up with a script and a cat.

"Her name's Peggy. She's not gay," Sarah said, in her brusque indifferent way. "She's just trying it on for size. I think she's married to some poor slob actually."

I pressed for more but Sarah insisted there wasn't much to it.

"She comes out here and she's with Jean," she said, shrugging it off. "But Jean's deluding herself. She gets a little worked up about this stuff. And she's always falling for straight girls."

This kind of exchange left me in a muddle. I had an insatiable appetite to know more, but Sarah would only ever say as much as interested her. She was full of unexpected, inflexible judgments, often witty, usually caustic. She did half-jokingly subscribe to the idea that a gay woman's ring finger was likely to be longer than her index finger. I had never heard of such a thing. She took my hand like a fortune-teller, straightened my fingers out toward her, and said, "What have we here," teasingly before kissing my knuckles. She also claimed there were telltale signs of gayness, like the line of the jaw. But she disliked anything overt, mullet haircuts, pink triangles, rainbow bumper stickers. She passionately hated the use of the word "partner"—"What are they, cops? Lawyers?" she would say derisively, of anyone who referred to a girlfriend or boyfriend this way—although she didn't offer any alternatives.

I didn't tell her I was kind of mesmerized by obvious announcements, all the physical signposts and actions that said this world of women was a world of its own. That included appraising looks from women, or the way some women's breasts, heavy and unrestrained, pulled at white T-shirts under leather jackets, or the leather jackets themselves, with those incomprehensible mesmerizing silver clips and zippers and buckles hanging off them everywhere. *What were they for?* I was kind of drawn to the looking, to being on the receiving end of that frank, curious, often amused assessment. I wouldn't have thought it would be different to be checked out by a woman as opposed to being checked out by a man, but it was and I found it exhilarating. It made me want to skip a little, it put a hiccup of flirtation and pleasure in my day, warmed me slyly from a safe distance. I had never had this experience of being with a woman in the company of other women with women and I found it heady, intoxicating.

When did you know? Titch would ask squinting past my left ear. And later still, *But how did you know? Are you gay?* (This very quietly, so self-conscious but determined that her face was almost entirely scrunched up, like a ball of crumpled tissue.) *I mean is that it? Do you know? When did you know?*
Never. There was no moment that I knew.
The truth is I never thought of myself as one thing or another, as straight or gay or as anything other than Sarah's person, as she was mine. That was the only category that made sense to me.

Sarah didn't identify herself in any way either; she didn't like to be aligned with any group as far as I could tell. The question seemed beside the point of us. It's true that in classes I continued to be careful about how I behaved with and toward her because clearly she did not want to be in a couple while being our section leader and all. She never said she didn't want to say anything about the two of us, but she didn't have to. We never touched one another in class, or even put our heads together to whisper. She treated me very much the way she treated everyone else.

Out of class, away from the other students, we were immediately, emphatically, happily joined at the hip. Also at the hand, the shoulder, the forehead, the cheek, the mouth, the belly, the leg; whatever was handy. I never had any doubt about what I could make Sarah feel when we were alone, if I wanted to (and I wanted to). Publicly, we were entirely in one world or the other depending on the context: with her friends in Wellfleet or in Provincetown, we were physically merged, inseparable, a known commodity, an established pair, as we were in private; in class or anywhere near it, we were physically apart, removed, at a marked, strategic distance from one another.

Of course these apparently tidy distinctions tripped into uncharted territory before long. One evening after class, when we had nothing in the house for dinner we drove to Orleans to go shopping. On the way, I said I wanted to make cookies and Sarah said she didn't want cookies around in the house because she didn't want to eat a lot of them, so I said I would bake them and we would give them away to Luke and Eddy and Dennis. Then the house would smell like cookies—which is my favorite part of baking—and we would make the guys happy. She thought this was very funny for some reason.

Inside the store, I was in the baking aisle and Sarah had headed in the direction of produce, when I heard someone call my name. I turned around, holding a bag of chocolate chips in one hand. Titch's stepsister Ruby was standing immediately in front of me, looking tan in jean shorts and carrying a shopping basket over one arm.

"Hey you!" she said.

"Hey!" I answered, more enthusiastically than I meant to. I hadn't seen Ruby except from a distance since the first week after we'd gotten to the Cape.

"I haven't seen you in a while."

"Yeah, it's been really busy," I said. "The workshop and working and everything."

"Where's Titch?" Ruby asked looking behind me, and at

that moment Sarah reappeared around the end of the aisle, brandishing a watermelon.

"Look what I found!" she called out, and then slowed down when she caught sight of Ruby beside me.

"Hi Ruby," she said, pleasantly, holding the watermelon in front of her abdomen lightly, with her fingertips, like a basket-ball.

"Hi," said Ruby, cocking her head on one side, inquisitively. They were smiling at one another like it was a game of chicken and we were waiting to see who would blink first.

I blinked.

"We're just picking up some groceries," I said, weakly.

"I see that," said Ruby, and her smile spread into a smirk, unattractively.

"You're not at the restaurant? I mean obviously you're not at the restaurant, but I thought you worked evening shifts, I thought you would be at work now," I said, hearing myself digging a deeper hole and starting to blush because of it.

"No," she said slowly, thoughtfully. "No, I'm not at work now.

"How is Titch?" she asked me then. "See much of her, do you?"

"More than you do," I said, cross now. I took the watermelon from Sarah and dumped it into our shopping cart.

"Ruby's harmless," Sarah said, as we were carrying our shopping bags out to the truck. It was still twilight, and the mosquitoes were out. The parking lot smelled of heated asphalt and gasoline. "I mean, sure, she can be gossipy and mean-spirited and petty—"

"But harmless," I said, waiting for her to open my door.

"Right. Anyway, so she thinks she knows something. Big deal. It's not like this is news to Titch, right?"

"No," I said slowly, although of course I still hadn't actually said anything directly to Titch about Sarah. I wasn't thinking about Titch, though. I was wondering if Ruby's news—about Sarah and me—would be news to Bess, Sarah's ex-girlfriend and Ruby's housemate. Either Sarah wasn't thinking about this, or it didn't matter to her. I didn't know which and I didn't ask.

CHAPTER 16

When I moved out of the Davidsons' I didn't call it that. I didn't say anything at all. Although some of my stuff stayed in Truro, I had pretty much moved into Sarah's the week after we returned from New York. In the beginning, Sarah came over to the Truro house a couple of times, but I always felt shy and divided, unsure of who or what to protect, or how to be. Titch seemed dark and unforthcoming, suspicious and snarky; Sarah seemed imperious and flip. I didn't want to be shared ground so I ducked the whole problem. For a while, I'd call the house when I knew Titch wasn't going to be there and leave a message saying, "Hey I'm staying in Wellfleet tonight," but before long I stopped even bothering to do that. Titch called me too off and on for the first two weeks after I got home from New York and moved into Sarah's, but she didn't like to leave messages—she has a phobia about answering machines—and even when we were there we didn't always answer the phone.

I got back to the Davidsons' in order to feed the cats and tried a handful of times to overlap with the time I knew Titch was home in the late afternoon, but after two weeks she stopped being home then anyway. I didn't ask if her work schedule had changed or what was up. Mostly I was glad not to have to make the effort.

For a while she stopped by sometimes at the end of the workshop day, as she had since the beginning of classes. That was easy because Sarah was always occupied with her job at that point, after the rest of us students were released for the day. Sometimes Titch would show up and we might meander into town to eat ice cream with a few of the other actors, or go to the pier and sit by the water. And sometimes she would come with me back to Sarah's apartment and hang out on the lawn in front of the house. We'd put our feet up on the iron-work café tables that Dennis had soldered, surrounded by strange, slightly menacing metal sculptures, and we'd drink iced tea with Luke after his daily bike ride, or with Dennis, if he wasn't napping, or with whomever happened to be around.

After one of these occasions, I had the happy thought that maybe Titch had a crush on Luke. If I was harboring a small hope that her interest in Luke might draw her into the Wellfleet crew and make her part of that world, she nixed that idea right away. She scowled deeply when I raised Luke's name, although the tops of her ears flushed a light pink and the color spread across her cheeks. She appeared to be sweating slightly.

"We are not going to talk about it," she said, perfectly calmly.

I had stopped by the house in Truro after having not been there for two days, to do a load of laundry and, guiltily, to clean litter boxes and play with the neglected cats, Chester and Jack. Titch joined me in the living room where I was sorting socks. When I made the mistake of mentioning Luke though, she got up almost immediately afterwards and went into the kitchen.

"Titch?" I called, "hey, I'm sorry. Come back."

"I just have to finish something," she said, distantly. "I'm boiling rags."

"Oh, okay," I said, helplessly, rolling my eyes at the cats. "If you're boiling rags."

Where she had been hesitant about actually stopping by Sarah's apartment to look for me before we had this exchange, now she was much worse. She would walk by the house, eyes averted, staring blindly ahead or twisting her whole body away from the house as though intent on the neighbor's lilac bushes as she walked down to the pier. If she stopped to see if I wanted to go by Mac's and eat a fish burrito she would stand at the bottom of the outdoor stairs leading up to the deck and call up quickly. If I didn't appear immediately she would have darted off again, her sandals crunching over the broken pieces of oyster shells in the driveway. I would see the back of her head, ponytail swinging, disappearing down the drive.

Once she had come up the steps to the apartment and Sarah had answered the door in boy's white briefs and a tank top with no bra. She was eating a piece of watermelon and the juice had run down her arms. We were laughing. Titch had blinked into the cool dark apartment and looked panicky when her eyes focused. Then she fled. That was the last time she came up like that.

We still saw each other, but more and more only by accident. One Saturday night, after I had been staying at the apartment for the better part of three weeks, Sarah talked me into going to the drive-in movie theatre in Wellfleet. We both should have been working on lines for scenes we were in, but it was still and hot inside the apartment and we were restless.

Full-blown summer had arrived finally, at the start of July. I had gotten used to the cool nights and intermittent sunshine, the short bursts of rain. But then without any warning, everything erupted in green heat, lazy and pulsing. The marsh, which for so long had looked like the back of a sick or preoccupied lioness—tawny but with unwashed tufts sticking up along the spine—transformed. It melted into lush, corn silk loveliness, looking magnificently inviting against the razor blue sky.

It happened when I wasn't paying attention, during the stretch of weekdays when I was inside, cantering to trochees, rehearsing lines, breathing into my soft belly, or on Saturdays, cutting baguette rounds, washing endless dishes, staying up very late at night. Sometimes I liked the mindless rhythm of cutting and chopping at work, the washing and drying, the squawking radio perched above the giant double sinks, the soapy water underfoot, the clatter and bang and smell of frying. Increasingly, with the arrival of summer, there would be a whiff of the outside, especially in late afternoon, of the lazy sunshine and, just out of reach, the sea coming in through the screen. That made work a little harder.

Then one day I stepped out the back door of Jake's Edibles to join Eddy in the gravel by the dumpster where he was smoking. The screen door whined and banged, and the world broke open over my head.

I said, "It's summer," blinking, dazzled. Eddy just squinted at me, not unfriendly, and sucked in hard like his cigarette was an asthma inhaler or the very dregs of a joint. Eddy was a good enough guy, not talkative, with a slight hangdog look. He never had much positive to say about the Cape, although he had spent his whole life here and had lived in the apartment next door to Sarah's for the last ten years. If you didn't know he was a co-owner in the catering business, you'd never have guessed because he was kind of diffident and hollowed out, like maybe he didn't get USDA pyramid nutrition in his formative years. His skin was slightly yellowed and he sucked on his teeth when he worked, but in the kitchen his hands flew. He was very, very fast. He was not exactly a fan of Sarah's, although he wasn't mean about her. They seemed to have a mild, joking antagonism. When he saw me watching the screen door for her he said once, *A lot of trouble.* I ignored this because it was my trouble and if it was trouble, if she was trouble, it was trouble I wanted. Besides, although he seemed unprepossessing to me, he was rumored to have had a long string of random girlfriends and he didn't seem like a particularly reliable guy to be dispensing romantic advice. We stood outside basking, in amicable silence.

All my life I have felt like spring is a relentless gauntlet of budding and blooming, growing and chirping; it assaults you. That busy, feverish cheer gives me a hectic, fractured lonely feeling, a sick sadness, a real spring fever. Even when there are moments of exhilaration, spring is still a hard, bright green, indigestible lump in the chest, the whole rabbit that the python swallows.

Summer is different. If you pitch forward into spring, you fall backward into summer. It's a wide expansive hammock, an endless space, a cavity opening under your feet. When I was little it was terrifying because there was no end to summer, no clear definition or way to navigate that wide open green madness, nothing but dreams and heat and loneliness yawning in front of you from the end of one school year (the screen doors in, the lilacs blooming) until the start of the next (a dark narrow promise, a shutting down in the fall). The space in between school was the distance to the moon, measured in broken book spines. But this year, this summer, for the first time in my life I wanted to drag my heels in the dust, to make hard grooves, to slow the time down.

What this meant is that whenever Sarah said, "Let's—" I would say *yes*. There was all the time in the world and still not enough time in the day, the summer, the universe for her. So that hot Saturday night when she said, *Let's go to the drive-in*, I said, *Yes. Let's*.

We got there after the first feature had started, and the air outside had begun to move a little, the promise of coolness coming in through the truck's rolled-down windows. Between the two movies, I went over to the concession booth and waited in line on the trampled grass. Almost immediately I saw Titch walking toward me with Camille, the first person I had spoken to—or rather who had spoken to me—on the very first day of the drama workshop, and a few times since in passing. I said, "Hey!" And Camille nodded her head at me gloomily. Titch stopped behind me in line and Camille continued on in the general direction of the restrooms without pausing. When she'd gone by, I tried to smile at Titch, but she didn't smile back at me.

I said, "I didn't know you guys were hanging out. She's gone to smoke, right? She smokes like a chimney. Camille."

Titch just stared in the direction of the lighted counter in front of us, at the backs of people's waiting heads, as though I had not spoken.

I said, "You know she listens to Twisted Sister too. It's not ironic either."

When she still didn't turn her head, or speak, or crack a smile, I said, "What is this, the silent treatment?" And her eyes finally swung toward me.

"Oh, I'm sorry," she said, "are you talking to me? Are you trying to be funny? Because you're not funny, Nina."

"Okay," I said, startled, raising both hands in mock surrender.

Titch was looking hard at me now.

"What?"

"Did you get my message?"

"No," I said, but for some reason it didn't sound at all believable as I said it. I was thinking guiltily that the light had been blinking on the machine when I had gotten back to the apartment that afternoon, and I had ignored it.

"Okay." She looked away from me. The big screen behind her had begun to flicker to life again with the opening credits of the second movie.

"What did you call to say? Is everything all right? Titch?" And when she didn't answer, "What's the matter with you?" I asked, irritated.

She snorted. "You're such a jerk, you know that?"

"I don't know what you're talking about. What did I do?"

"It's not so much what you do," Titch said, "as what you don't do."

"Yeah?" I said, exasperated. "Like what don't I do?"

"Well, you don't call. You don't come home. You don't listen to your messages. You don't talk to me. You disappear. You know, little things."

"I've been really busy, Titch," I said, and my voice sounded self-righteous and unconvincing.

Her face was lined with contempt. I wanted to smack her.

"Anyway, you're here having a good time, right? Maybe you should just do that."

"Yeah," she said evenly, sarcastically, "why don't I do that?" And she turned and stomped away from me.

I stood there with my arms dangling, like a fool, watching her leave.

Titch abandoned me in the second half of eighth grade, after we'd been best friends for four years. It was the worst, really the worst pain I'd felt at school until that point. I would roll over in the morning, my legs leaden with despair, and lie there in a tangled, cobwebby haze for a few minutes before I'd remember what was wrong.

She had taken up with a cluster of popular girls who all wore L.L. Bean boots and men's tweed overcoats from vintage stores. They weren't staggeringly pretty individually. Once I was lab partners in Chemistry with one of them, Nicole Peske, and close up I was surprised to find she was not particularly shiny or remarkable. She had kind of a squashed nose, thin lips, and one of her eyes was smaller than the other. But collectively all their shortcomings were more than equalized. Any flaws only added miraculously to their combined sheen. The sheer devastating power of all of them bunched together— with their long gleaming hair, their laughter, their linked arms, their eyes all turning toward you at once—it could flatten you like a truck. Just thinking about it would make you want to shrivel up and die. When they walked down the hall headed out of the school it was like a flock of barn swallows turning tail, all their matching coats flaring out behind them.

I had fantasies of becoming a knife thrower and felling them one by one with a knife lodged smoothly, and hard, between their tweedy shoulder blades. I would round the bend in the hallway by the senior lockers, dressed like I was in a western. (Like the cowboy on the cover of my grandmother's paperback copy of Owen Wister's *The Virginian*, which I was reading at the time. Right down to the boots and spurs and the shadowed face. I imagined it like that.) My knives would split the air, brilliant indecipherable flashes, whizzing by the principal's office. I could see how one after another each girl's mouth would be caught in a wide open *O*, her arms flailing out in slow motion, her body plunging forward facedown, one after another, all of them, downed like so many bowling pins. I even practiced knife throwing in the garage with an old rusty Swiss Army blade that I found in the toolshed, until once I scratched the side of the jeep enough to warrant notice. I had so much hatred and violence in my belly for them that sometimes I thought I would throw up. I thought I might even enjoy throwing up.

All I ever did in retaliation really was to steal stuff from Titch's locker once or twice. Her locker combination was my birthday, and mine was hers. When I discovered she hadn't changed the combination my throat seized up. I took her calculator, which I disemboweled in the driveway before burying the evidence, and one of her mittens, which I cut into small pieces and then flushed down the toilet for good measure. Also I prank called her home in desperation over and over. Once her mom answered and said kindly, *Is that you dear*, into the phone, which left me silently gasping with anguish like a hooked fish. Anyway Titch came back to me the next fall, which now that I thought about it probably gave me a false sense of my own power. In this moment, as I watched her narrow back disappear into the milling people at the Wellfleet drive-in, I didn't want her to go but I didn't want to go after her.

"I just saw Titch," I said to Sarah, when I got back to the truck.

"Are those Junior Mints?" she said. "Really? Well, where is she? Oh, peanut M&M's. That's more like it. You take those. Does she want to join us?"

"No," I said, "no, she doesn't. She came with Camille. And anyway, she's mad at me."

Sarah raised an eyebrow. "About what?"

But at that moment a building exploded on the screen and her attention jumped forward. "Noooooo!" she cried, happily. I looked at her profile in the movie light, and laughed. I couldn't help it.

When we got back to the apartment that night and Sarah was brushing her teeth in the bathroom, I pressed play on the answering machine. Titch's voice rose hopefully, uncharacteristically breathlessly from the black box. She sounded about six years old.

"Hi, um, it's Titch calling for Nina. Nina, I just wanted to see if you wanted to go to the movies, I was thinking maybe it would be fun to go to the drive-in? I haven't been since we went to that one in Fairlee, whenever that was. I could pick you up, say around 8? I don't think it starts till late, um, until it gets dark. I don't know what's playing, but I don't really care. It would be really nice to see you. Anyway, let me know."

I called her right then to say I was sorry, but she wasn't home or she wasn't picking up the phone. I left a message. She did not call me back. I felt guilty, and relieved.

CHAPTER 17

W e were already nearly at the fourth week of the program, in the middle of July, with five weeks left of the summer. At this momentous juncture we in Group 6 finally arrived in front of the head of the program, the director Bill McNeil, for the first time. He didn't look any friendlier or more awake than he had on the first day, but he was all ours for five full days and a kind of thrill of possession rippled through the group. He doled out harsh criticisms and we flocked to him for more.

"What are you doing?" he asked sarcastically of Doug one day, when poor Doug was struggling through a Chekhov scene. "You are acting like a crazy person. You are like Frankenstein. Solyony is all heart. He might be *the* heart of *Three Sisters*. You are strangling the life out of this part. You are turning him into a robot, a soulless, useless, pathetic robot. Don't take what's on the page and stop there, like a moron. Don't you know anything? You can't play what's on the page. What's underneath? I am telling you—I am telling all of you, LISTEN UP PEOPLE—Anton Chekhov is a *genius*. You should be so lucky to be cast in any of his plays. You are unlikely to find better material in your entire miserable careers than what this playwright delivers. So *don't fuck it up*."

Doug was his favorite target. I thought Doug might actually make Bill McNeil pull his own hair out. The angles of Doug's head were so unattractively blunt—like someone had put him together from unfinished slabs of clay—and his breathing was so labored with effort that I frequently felt sorry for him. To his credit, although he huffed and puffed and blundered through his scenes, he never stopped trying.

Shisha was the only one who could reliably make Bill McNeil laugh sometimes, although he didn't think she took acting seriously enough—"It's not enough to half-ass it! I can tell when you haven't done the work!" he would yell at her—but he left her alone more often than not. Geoffrey too he usually treated more as someone who had already passed a test. The rest of us, though, were on the receiving end of varying degrees of nonstop antagonism and criticism.

To Emily: "You are going to have to gain a lot more weight, or lose it. You have to be really fat or not at all. Otherwise you'll never work in this business."

To Ann: "You are always like a mouse. A crazy, scurrying mouse. Stop it. Straighten up and stop squeaking. I mean it. I can't bear it. Your voice is hurting my ears."

To Chris: "Jesus Christ, stop trying so hard and being so drippy. It's painful to watch you. You make me want to kick you. You are like a wet noodle. Stop emoting so damn much. Grow a fucking spine."

To Nicky: "I have no idea what you are doing up there. Just none. Are you related to these people? I have no idea. Is this person your husband? Do you like him? Do you wish he wasn't your husband? Does this seem like important information to you? Did you make any of these choices in this scene? Because I'll be damned if I can tell what you're doing. For the love of *God*. Make. Some. Choices."

And I got: "Don't be so bloodless. Make a fucking mess for Chrissakes. What are you afraid of? There's no room for fear here. There's no room for caution. Don't be so careful. It's all technique and brain with you. Take some *chances*. Show me *something*!"

And to all of us, almost every day: "What was that? That

was abysmal. That was such crap. Oh, *God* that was bad. There was not one redeeming moment in that entire scene. Haven't you learned anything, any of you? Go away. Don't talk to me. Do it again."

It was the way I imagined boot camp to be, although to be fair my entire understanding of boot camp comes from the movie *An Officer and a Gentleman*, specifically the scene in which Richard Gere gets fantastically covered in mud and hosed in the face by his drill sergeant. With Bill McNeil nobody escaped the abuse. But spurred by the criticism, most of us tried to up our game. We also began to feel like we were in the trenches together, in a new way. The best any of us could hope to get from our sadistic sergeant was a kind of grudging noise of acceptance, a "that'll do" kind of grunting acknowledgment, and if you heard that you'd be high as a kite all day afterward, everyone else shooting you envious glances. Much more often he would launch a full-on attack. We didn't care; we were converts to the school of Bill McNeil.

For five days, it was all Chekhov all the time. It was new to me, and I loved it. Somehow what looked so dolefully, beautifully Russian on the page made everyone wildly cheerful in the room.

Occasionally, Sarah would fling her arms wide—coming down the steps from the apartment for example, on the way to class—and cry out some Chekhovian line, like *How are we going to live our lives?* She was kidding, and she was not. One time she issued this battle call, and I cried, to match her, "*Bravely and hand in hand!*" Which she loved, and then that became the answer. Call and response, a game we liked to play.

How are we going to live our lives? one of us would say.

Bravely and hand in hand! the other would reply.

Out of nowhere, the less context the better, with the confidence of angels.

How are we going to live our lives? Bravely and hand in hand.

When we had to bid Bill McNeil a reluctant farewell the next week—he did not give us a backward glance—we settled in to work on contemporary drama scenes and monologues. This was much less dramatic than our full immersion into Chekhov, but still we were all digging in deeper because of our time with the Russian. Just about everyone was making braver leaps, and we were cheering each other on in the leaping.

On the second day we were assigned a number of two-person scenes by our visiting acting teacher. I was opposite Shisha in a scene from Caryl Churchill's *Cloud Nine*. We had to play the scene as though one character was absolutely in charge and then play it again, with the power dynamic reversed. It seemed like an elementary and uninteresting demonstration of the importance of choices, the need for clarity, whether you're acting or directing, and the ways in which the best writing isn't set but allows the balance of power to shift from moment to moment or to upend altogether. It depends on who's calling the shots, who's seeing the story, and who's telling it. It turned out to be surprisingly fun, especially to watch how different people interpreted the question of being in charge. I liked working with Shisha, who would almost always do something unexpected and who was always game. We wound up laughing a lot.

"That's such a good exercise," I said to Sarah, who had been deep in the much more discouraging world of Harold Pinter all afternoon, trying to help Ann and Chris, who were struggling with a scene from Pinter's *Betrayal*. I was exuberant, bouncing from the class.

"What do you want for lunch?" I asked, pulling my shoes on.

"I don't know," she said, distracted, looking around the empty room. "I should really finish clearing up in here."

"I say we get sandwiches and make it to the beach. We can get to Newcomb. Come on, there's time."

She shook her head, her hair swinging, but there was a

helpless look on her face that I was familiar with, and I smiled, chin out, Cheshire-like, jubilant.

On the beach, standing high up on the dunes, she said, "It's so beautiful. How can anyone stand it?"

The wind was picking up, and the waves were sparkling. It was so bright out that my head hurt. I bounded down ahead of her towards the water, my knees buckling, pitching forward, nearly somersaulting in the sand, calling back over my shoulder.

"How are we going to live our lives?"

"Bravely and hand in hand."

"Well, get on down here and kiss me." And she did.

Bravely and hand in hand.

I believed this.

CHAPTER 18

O ne night I came home to the apartment later than Sarah, which was unusual because she always had to organize various spaces, and ferry about and cater to the visiting teachers once the day's classes had ended. But today I had gone out with Chris and Doug to rehearse a scene after classes were over, and then they had decided to order dinner and while they waited for it we had wandered over to Mayo Beach and then we stayed there, longer than we meant to, wanting to watch the sun finish setting.

"Where've you been?" Sarah called from the shower, over the running water, when she heard me come in the door. "Have you eaten? There's not much in the fridge. I had to eat the old cottage cheese. Who runs this joint anyway? Oh, hey, there's a letter on the table for you. I found it there when I came in. I think Titch must have dropped it off."

I picked it up and the MP's handwriting lurched up at me. It wasn't the first letter, more like the fifth that he'd sent. I tried to read the first one, but then I felt ill when I looked at the envelopes and I didn't want to read any more. I would look over the pages, my eyes completely glazed, unable and unwilling to focus.

Sarah hated the MP. That crazy sonofabitch, she said when I told her about him and the entire spring, that's fucked up, he should never have gone near you. *I'll kill him if he ever goes near you again.* And she would be very serious when she said this, lean and mean and tough, like she was going to protect my maiden honor in the woods, or like she should be wearing a shirt with cutoff sleeves and the collar turned up, like what the boys from *The Outsiders* dressed in, clothes she didn't own and would never have worn. I loved that she hated him. I didn't bother to straighten out what was certainly an unfair perception of the situation—that he was a monster of exploitation and I was his vulnerable victim. Somehow I was exempt from any judgment in her version, which was fine by me. I basked in her protective rage. He seemed so far away from me when I told her about him that he might have been a grotesque character in a fairy tale I invented.

"Is that from him?" Sarah asked, gesturing toward the letter with her elbow. She had come into the kitchen and was resting one hip against the counter while she toweled her hair dry.

"From the MP? Yes."

"Are you going to read it?"

I looked down at it. "I don't really want to."

She wrapped her hair up in the towel expertly, and swung open the door of the woodstove with a flourish, which I countered by shoving the letter in on top of a pile of cold ash.

"Do you want to do the honors?" she asked, offering me the matchbook.

I hesitated, and she put her head on one side, looking at me more closely.

"What's up, buttercup?"

"I don't know," I said. There was a prickle of guilt or remorse in my throat. I didn't owe him anything, and it made me feel cross to be harassed by his handwriting, but it felt slightly bad anyway, like a betrayal, to burn his letter, not even to pretend to read it.

Before I had left for the Cape, by May anyway, things had gotten completely out of hand with the MP. I was flummoxed because it seemed like he should have been able to handle the situation better, or at *all* for that matter. He was the bona fide fully certified right-there-on-his-driver's-license adult. It seemed like his extra twenty-eight years should have given him a head start on matters of the heart, like he might have lapped the course a bunch of times and just been able to take things in stride as he loped towards home, but apparently not. Instead he began to cry a lot. He kept breaking the rules that he had originally instituted about contact between the two of us. He was unraveling right before my eyes and it was deeply unnerving.

For instance, once I was walking uptown with Lynn Nichols for ice cream after school and I saw the MP's battered blue Honda circling the Dartmouth green and creeping up and down Main Street and I knew he had spotted me and was trailing me. I made Lynn sit with me in the Village Green until I was sure he would have had to move on and even then I detoured through the Hopkins Center and tagged after Lynne to the Howe Library in case he was parked somewhere waiting for me to surface. Where I had once gone looking for him in school, I had begun hiding everywhere and anywhere from him, in school and out. And he had started hunting me down.

Ever since I had finally told him that I was heading out of town for the summer, he began unraveling over the phone regularly. I had told him he couldn't call me at home, but he did anyway, sometimes pretending to be other people. It was appalling, but sad too. It made me feel desolate in my bones. When he talked to me, he morphed into some hunchbacked animal, some caved-in beast—he actually whimpered, a sound I'd only heard from him in entirely different circumstances. Here that cry had turned into its unforeseen evil twin noise.

I couldn't bear it, but I'd replay that sound in my head the way I was resigned to replay in my head various ugly things I'd seen and heard. I had distilled a loop of ugliness that ran in my head like a short film, kicking off with excerpts from an actual short film, an educational gem about avoiding rape that Mr. Hingham, the school counselor, made all the girls watch when we were twelve. (Because the girls are the only ones who need to be educated about rape. Because it's going to be our job to get away.) That's minute #1 on my horror loop—a woman desperately scrambling away in the underbrush from a would-be rapist she had picked up while driving. (Because I was about to pick up hitchhikers when I was twelve and four years away from even getting my license.) That visual stayed with me for a very, very long time. Even much scarier incidents in my own life could not dislodge it. It might crop up when I walked home after dark, or all of sudden when a car slowed down beside me in the middle of a bright and sunny afternoon. Cue tape: that woman's ragged, panicky, futile breathing, her victim breathing, would thrum in my ears, along with the crashing, flailing, hunted animal sounds of underbrush snapping. That clip would hang around for years, along with soundtrack noises like the tiny gasping sobs of the MP and a whole limping pack of sad, bad, and ugly dog-eared, well-fondled fodder that can make me unsure in the belly.

Titch, whose bible and constant point of reference is William Goldman's *The Princess Bride*, both the book and then the movie, would refer to these kinds of mental intrusions as ROUS's, Rodents of Unusual Size, the mythical but finally conquerable nasty beasts that waylay the story's hero and heroine in the Fire Swamp. Titch was fanatical about *The Princess Bride* from the moment she encountered it, the way most boys are about *Star Wars* or *Star Trek* or apparently *Star* anything. Not that Titch was immune to Harrison Ford, either, but then in *Star Wars* (or in *Raiders of the Lost Ark*, or my favorite, *Witness*) he has the same attitude as the whole of *Princess Bride*—the perfect ironic lip curl of the anti-romantic die-hard romantic. I tried to follow Titch's philosophy on scary unbidden thoughts—ROUS's—mostly I said fuck it to them and tromped on their heads when they jumped up wanting attention. Something about what was going on with the MP made that harder. I was battling some ominous knowledge I didn't want to let in, that I was flailing to keep at bay, about as effectively as beating off a cloud of gnats in a bog.

Two days before Titch and I drove to the Cape that bit of knowledge broke open over my head when I was standing in line at the Main Street drugstore to pick up my grandmother's glaucoma medication. Marianne Franks, the tetchy dry woman who had lived behind the drugstore counter for my whole life turned to me and said, *Now what can I do for you*, and right then I fully grasped this much: the MP couldn't do anything for me, couldn't help me, because he couldn't even help himself and so was not *grown up* as I had understood that state of being. And he was not alone in this. Any of the grown people waiting behind me at the pharmacy could be fakers. Any number of people masquerading as adults might look to *me* for help, they might be needier than babies, soft in the middle, weak sacks of want. It had nothing to do with age. There was no essential line between adults and me anymore, if there ever had been. More: if I had thought that being with the MP meant that I was grown up, I saw in an Alice-in-Wonderland topsy-turvy flash that actually it meant more about him than about me, that what it really meant was that he was a child. This thought was so dizzying that I clung to the edge of the drugstore counter. Amazing, deeply distressing, not to be believed. But there absolutely, irrefutable in the MP's tiny cascading moan, that pathetic pleading baby cry, *don't leave me, I need you*, as fixed, as certain, as naked as an ugly prehistoric bug suspended in a fossil. Marianne Franks, who was waiting on me, not patiently, held out her hand and asked again. I saw her mouth moving, but the only thing I heard was that shriveled shameful bedroom sound.

In the kitchen, I turned away from the sound in my head and from Sarah, lit the match, and set the MP's fat envelope on fire. I watched it burn, my eyes searching for words as the flame licked and curled and smoldered the paper.

"Hey, sweet girl," Sarah said, from behind me then, lightly touching between my shoulder blades. "Are you okay?"

And in the moment when I turned around to her, I was. I was more than okay. Because I knew it wasn't that I had been running away from the MP—although obviously I had done that too—it was that I had been running to her. It had all been so that I could be with her. I twined my arms up around her and locked my wrists behind her neck at the same instant that she caught and pulled me to her. I slid against her as easily as a fish slips through the warm waters of the Indian Ocean. I could feel my heart pound through her chest, our clavicles and hip bones joined, our pulse points clicked together like magnets. We kissed and I was home. She could do that.

CHAPTER 19

That was the week we arrived in the room with director Patty Trout, a woman appropriately enough with damp eyes the size of platters, magnified by enormous red-rimmed glasses. Bill McNeil was in the room when we were gathering, half sitting on the windowsill, smoking and looking around the space without much interest. But when Patty appeared, dragging what appeared to be an enormous ragged carpetbag and a yoga mat, Bill McNeil jumped up and gave her a big hug. They talked together in low, warm voices. He introduced her, and seemed to take it for granted that he would stay and watch her class, although he had never done this before.

"You're in for a treat with Patty," he promised us, smiling maybe the first real smile I had ever seen from him.

All the groups were present at once this day, and it was sticky in the room, humid with nervous sweat. Everyone was having another run at a Shakespeare monologue, for the whole day. The whole week we had been revisiting the same piece of Shakespeare, for most of us our chosen text from the very first day, in a wide range of classes. We were supposed to say the words over and over and over again until they became our own, stopped making sense, and (we hoped, I guess) started making sense again. I was heartily sick of it.

Emily from our group went first. She stood in front of the whole crowd, radiating anxiety in a huge smile, before embarking on her text, which, she informed us, was a monologue of Cleopatra's from *Antony and Cleopatra*. She looked very much the way a cat does after being set down on the metal table at the vet's, when it can't get a purchase on the slippery surface and it begins to purr frantically in a desperate bid for humanity. Emily's smile was like that purr. I found I couldn't watch her, because her dread was so palpable and it was feeding my own. Anticipatory fear was blossoming on my palms.

The thing about theatre is, you never know moment to moment what is going to crack anyone open, what will get someone to go the distance, to let everyone else in, to make the leap or the connection—however you wanted to think about it—to be an actor. At least, I never seemed to know, which is maybe part of why I am not as much of an actor as I wish that I were.

My first acting teacher was a voice teacher, but she was also an actor herself, or had been. I was nine years old then, and it was before I had ever thought seriously about being an actor, even before Titch and I were reciting poems in assembly and staging scenes in the backyard together. Back then what I thought about doing was politics, about which I had a very dim understanding. All I knew was that politics was what my parents concerned themselves with, what they seemed to take seriously, and what they claimed took them away. By the time I was nine, I had privately boiled down this vague interest in politics into a focused, if crazed, desire to take over the world, which I knew I couldn't really say to grown-ups—*I want to take over the world*—nobody was going to find that anything other than alarming. Maybe it's permissible in a toddler, but not in a preadolescent. So I would say only that I wanted to go into politics. Given an opening, I would spin off on how my role models were people like Gandhi and Frances Perkins. This would make grown-ups fall all over themselves with enthusiasm. Ben Kingsley hadn't yet played Gandhi, although when he did, it would mark the only occasion in the history of our school that students made a trip to the Nugget, the town cinema, right in the middle of the day. I felt pretty good about that choice. But Frances Perkins was even better. You could always see right away which grown-ups actually knew her and which ones would narrow their eyes and nod knowingly instead. (I only knew about her because of Female Leaders Day in Social Studies. Not even a *Unit*, just a Day. I guess we were lucky it wasn't Female Leaders *Hour*. Also, Maggie Thatcher made that list, and don't get me started on Margaret Thatcher with her mean little eyes. It was a crap day at school, like so many others.) Frances P. was at least Secretary of Labor under FDR. The first woman in the Cabinet. She was the best part of Female Leaders. Even grown-ups with no idea who she was ate it up when I casually dropped her name.

A woman overheard this I-want-to-be-a-politician rigma-role at some work dinner party of my mother's when she was in town. I was spinning like mad and praying to be excused so I could go back to my room, climb out of my dress, and brood on my plans to dominate the universe. But this woman at the party, tall, with too many splotched freckles, like a mutant Dalmatian, kept pushing her hair back and concentrating on me. She had to double over in the middle to see me, her spotty pale moon face hanging at the end of a long tunnel of hair. She was a dancer or something, modern dance, and she said I should go to a voice teacher if I wanted to make big speeches! And she knew just the person!

This turned out to be a fat dusty Englishwoman named Gwendolyn Murdy who claimed to have coached Vanessa Redgrave, although not, she insisted, to stand up at the Academy Awards and talk about the Palestinian Liberation movement with a fanatical gleam in her eye. I was a little disappointed by that, but figured there was no harm in her. For a voice teacher, she talked a lot more than I did, but one of the things she said in our first meeting and nearly every subsequent one was that I had an "*s* problem," which other less

well trained people might call a slight lisp. It was hard for me
to see how this was a problem for world domination and I
pointed to a number of people—Barbara Walters an obvious
contender—who seemed like excellent reasons to hang tough
with the *s* problem and maybe even increase it to a *t, u, v*
problem. Gwendolyn Murdy didn't get this at all. When she
didn't get something I said, which was often, she would leave
her mouth hanging open for a minute, then snap her jaw shut
hard and shake her head from side to side violently, wattles
flying, like there was water in her inner ear.

But I liked her and I made half-hearted, dutiful, largely
unsuccessful efforts to improve under her tutelage. We ate a lot
of strange German cookies—Lebkuchen, I think she called
them—that tasted like gingery paper and reminded me of puff-
ball mushrooms that explode so satisfyingly when you jump on
them in the woods. The cookies let loose a similar small *poof* of
air when you bit into them. We sat around, showering pow-
dered sugar on top of the dust in her apartment, which was
filled to the brim, just knotted up with fake cloth and plastic
flowers, new to me except in graveyards. With Gwendolyn
Murdy, I developed a new appreciation for the intricacies of
teeth. This was partly because I'd been forced to keep the tip
of my tongue touching my lower teeth as I enunciated
monopthongs and dipthongs, but also because Gwendolyn
Murdy had a big mouthful of English teeth—manic like tall
brownstones after an earthquake, just tilting every imaginable
which way. It's the small funkiness in teeth, the gaps, the over-
laps, the snaggles that I find compelling; the snowflake teeth,
the true originals, that produce their own bite patterns and
noises like nothing else, whistles and clicks, brilliant sibilant
plosives all their own. Gwendolyn Murdy had singular teeth,
but when she spoke a piece of text, she would be transformed,
she would be unrecognizable, because what she was saying, the
very language, the heart of it, the meat of it, the gist of it, would

overtake her funny, dumpy, strange self. When our lessons were finished, my s problem was intact but I had a new and deep curiosity about acting.

What I observed with Gwendolyn Murdy and ever since then is that a lot of acting is alchemy. And you need alchemists to make it happen, people who genuinely believe in the transmutation of base metals into gold. If you don't believe that this is possible it will never happen.

Patty Trout was an alchemist. She wasn't messing around. In no time she had her first victim, our tightly wound Emily, on her back on the floor with her eyes closed, her arms supporting her lower back, her legs over her head, knees slightly bent, toes turned in toward each other, and vibrating slightly. This might have been a funny sight, the way her bottom and her thighs were jiggling, but nobody giggled. Our restraint wasn't out of any kind of respect or politeness or even fear about our own upcoming humiliation. It was because the sound that came out of her in that unlikely position, the unexpected clarity, the looseness of her breath, and the lushness of Cleopatra's language, was marvelous. Only Patty Trout looked unsurprised. It was like she had taken Emily—needy, unhappy Emily—turned her upside down, given her a good shake, and caused a kind of sensuality and a kind of truth to fall out of her. Suddenly Emily's hunger had teeth.

Patty Trout manhandled everyone, thumped people between the shoulders, put them into strange positions, shook their arms to loosen them, nudged the backs of their knees, confronted and coaxed them, asked all kinds of questions, out loud and murmured, and startlingly, occasionally yelled students' text, by way of example. It was terrifying and electrifying all at once.

When I stood up, finally, to face her, she looked at me for a minute and then began stroking my jaw down gently with her crooked index finger.

"Let that go," she said, and again, "let that go." I grimaced.

I stumbled through the text once. Then she moved in on me.

Was this a face/To be oppos'd against the warring winds/To stand against the deep dread-bolted thunder? I said, and she pressed in for the kill.

"Who left you in the wilderness?" Patty Trout asked.

I didn't answer the question. It didn't make any sense to me.

"Who have you left in the wilderness?" Patty Trout prodded.

"No one," I said, resisting, forging on.

"Who have you left?" she asked, placing a hand on the back of my neck.

"Why are you asking me this?" I said, stiffening. I didn't mean to sound huffy, but I did. I was digging my heels in.

Patty Trout smiled at me, faintly. "It's sometimes a fine line between leaving and being left," she said. "And it's affected you. Just say the lines in response when I ask you something."

I started to speak again.

"Stop." She said. "Repeat the line." She moved her hand onto my belly, firmly but kindly, and placed the other on my shoulder. She said, "Breathe into my hand." I did. Up close she smelled like all the spices you need for pumpkin pie, which was deceptively reassuring.

"Look at them," she said, indicating the rest of the students. "Take them in. Talk to them."

That seemed like a spectacularly bad idea. I looked at the lot of them with deep animosity.

This time she actually leaned in so close that she touched the side of her forehead to the side of mine, lightly, and as she did she asked me, with both quiet determination and compassion, "Nina, who have you abandoned?"

I made a fast rude face at her without meaning to, and just

as immediately remembered being eight years old waiting in the jeep in the parking lot of the P&C in White River Junction. (This was the supermarket called the Price Chopper. Although why then the "and" in between the P *and* C? I chewed on this kind of thing—misplaced conjunctions—like someone the English teacher gods had reached down and touched in utero. *You will strengthen our numbers.*) Sometime earlier, my grandfather had shambled off like an upright bear into the supermarket. I could tell time but had no clock. I started counting cars in the lot and then black or blue cars that drove by and finally the seconds between blue and black cars, *one Mississippi two Mississippi.* Once I reached a hundred before a green Subaru wrecked my streak. He didn't come out. It started to get dark and the lights from the store glowed invitingly like a spaceship. Every time I thought *he'll come out if I count to 100 or 500,* I'd count, but he wouldn't materialize and I'd just start all over again. I watched people come out hugging large paper bags, a quarreling teenage couple with matching gelled and spiky hairdos and a middle-aged woman with no waist. I was worried by the dark and felt pinned down by it like I couldn't leave the jeep now that it was dark, but also like I might wind up sitting there all night. Who would know? Who would know to come out to me and how would I know if they could be trusted?

Inside the jeep was the smell of the sun-warmed plastic window flaps, a smell being released now into the cool cover of night, a smell like rubber sheets on a baby's bed, intimate, vaguely disgusting. Also, more happily, the rich familiar smells of machine oil and hay dust, bits of which were embedded in the seats. I picked at them with my fingernail until I got a hay splinter.

I don't know why I didn't go into the store with him to do the grocery shopping. I usually did because there was always a treat in it for me—a stale gumball from the big pink machine, or better still, SweeTarts, which I liked to pretend were pills for some devastating illness I had. I doled the candy out, self-medicating, seriously and sorrowfully all the way on the drive up the hill, staving off my final collapse and privately practicing my last words, guilt-inducing but bighearted pardons for all the wrongs done to me. I had a number of popular scenarios, but my favorite involved my being propped up on pillows with my inexplicable gently wasting Beth March kind of disease, while the weeping, distraught face of my father hovered at my bedside, begging for reconciliation, and suffering much more than I was. *I will never forgive myself*, he would say.

Eventually, the assistant manager brought my grandfather out to the jeep. I saw his face surface in the plastic window sheet like a mammoth fish coming suddenly into view at the Boston aquarium, a big white blur. He said, "That's my daughter," with assurance, and the assistant manager (Scott Something on his tag) looked at me for confirmation, help-lessly. A skinny, leggy kid, Scott, with enraged acne. He had no idea what to do. I was confused, but I nodded because I couldn't see what else to do either and I was glad not to be alone anymore. My grandfather climbed into the driver's seat, a little shaky on his hind legs. He looked mad and turned inward, unlike himself. It should have been reassuring to have him back, but it wasn't quite. He didn't seem to know where he was. His wool barn jacket at least was familiar, comfortingly steeped in wood smoke. We sat for several minutes before he reached to turn the key.

I should have gone after him, my grandmother said. She was uncharacteristically short with me afterwards. I never found out what happened in the store. It was some unnamable shame, like whatever strange spell had him in its grip when he came back to the jeep, like the wave that sometimes rose up in front of his eyes. *Why didn't you go in with him?* she said, but I didn't know. I didn't know what was wrong with him or even for sure that something might be. Nobody told me. I didn't know he needed me. Why didn't anyone tell me that he needed me? Why didn't I know? I would never have left him alone, not for an instant. But I thought I was the one who had been left behind. Then he went into the woods, opposed the warring winds, and froze to death.

In class I was crying, but hadn't noticed.

"Say it again," Patty said insistently, gripping my arm.

Was this a face/To be oppos'd against the warring winds/To stand against the deep dread-bolted thunder?

"And."

Mine enemy's dog, though he had bit me, should have stood that night against my fire.

"Against what?"

Against. My. Fire.

"And."

Alack, alack. Tis wonder that thy life and wits at once had not concluded all.

But they had. They had concluded all. *Alack.* A lack. *A lack.*

"From the beginning," Patty Trout said, and I did, with a drive from some internal place. She said, "Nice work," and released me.

I was exhausted, depleted, sodden. I tottered over to Group 6 and slid down the wall to sit with my people. Shisha leaned over to me, pressing the length of her upper body against mine, and said, quietly, "That was the shit," and I smiled at her. The coolness of the skin on her arm made me realize how flushed I was. Geoffrey was smiling his slow beatific smile at me and even Emily stopped her constant jiggling long enough to stretch out her foot and nudge my thigh gently in appreciation. I looked around for Sarah and saw her looking straight at me from across the room, a troubled inscrutable hard-edged look; I had no idea what it meant. There might have been tears in her eyes, or there might not. I could not tell.

During our lunch break that day, Bill McNeil passed our table and rapped me lightly on the head with his knuckles. "That was passable work today," he said, and then the glimmer of a smile—like the shadow of a beautiful exotic butterfly—fluttered lightly over his face. He said, "What are we eating here?" and sat down between Chris and Nicky, immediately appropriating and rifling through Chris's bag of potato chips. Even his benevolent presence put something of a damper on the conversation, although we all felt the unconscious honor. Nicky dug in her bag and produced a cigarette for him, which he promptly took without thanks. "I'll see you lot later," he said, and headed over to where Patty Trout was stretched out on her back on the grass on her yoga mat, a big floppy hat pulled down over her face, apparently passed out.

That night there was a party at a house that a group of eight students were sharing, including Chris and Doug. It was a recently built soulless grey rental house, out on Chequesset Neck. When I went upstairs to find a bathroom, the first open door revealed a bedroom that looked like the inside of a suitcase had exploded. There were clothes everywhere. The bathroom was cold—someone had left the window open—and it smelled like old bong water. Someone had scrawled a smiley face in coral lipstick on the corner of the mirror. I saw my own face in the mirror, surprisingly round and pink and buoyant.

Downstairs someone had cleared the main living room and pushed back the sofa and chairs so that people could dance. Someone had hooked up speakers and the music—the good, the bad, and the ugly—was all equally loud.

When she saw me come downstairs, Emily ran over and pulled me onto the dance floor, spinning me around clumsily, bobbing and weaving and laughing. Only yesterday, this would have felt oppressively like an unnecessary, grabby, heavy-footed cheer, something to escape. But now I was equally effervescent, glad to join her and grateful that she did not know how I had misjudged her, or if she did, that she forgave me. The bounty, the beneficence. We were in the middle of a clump of red-faced people jumping up and down, and Katrina and the Waves were singing *Ohh-ohh. I'm walking on sunshine, ohh-ohh*, which is exactly the kind of music I find irresistible and Sarah condemns out of hand. I don't know how anyone can object to that kind of contagious peppy ridiculousness. I was happy to give in to it, to give in to Emily, and to all the beaming, sweaty people bumping into me.

Toward the end of the song, I caught sight of Sarah hovering near the edge of the room, not dancing. We had gone there separately—she had to go to a meeting with the other section leaders at the end of the day and I had gone out with the rest of the group for pizza—and she looked alone there somehow, disconnected, contained. I headed over to her and gestured with my head to the dance floor. I didn't know if she'd join me, but it seemed harmless enough to ask. At least two thirds of the people were mingling on the floor. Then I threw open my arms, but she just looked at me steadily and took a sip of her drink. I dropped my arms, foolishly, but I couldn't release my good mood, the fizzing in my chest and head from the day's praise and beer and dancing.

Feeling bold, I came up right next to her, closer than I would usually in any group and leaned in close to speak to her.

"Is my kiss on your list?" I asked, repeating the song lyrics that were playing now, speaking into her ear.

She pulled back from me, looking at me very seriously, and I thought for a minute that she was going to shut me down or ask me how much I had had to drink, but then she leaned over and said into my ear, her face expressionless, "I can't believe you did that. I can't believe you Hall and Oatesed us."

"You're such a snob!" I yelled over the music, happily.

"About Hall and Oates?" she said. "Are you kidding me? Absolutely."

"It's not such a bad song," I said loudly, overemphatically. "It's catchy."

She looked at me, shook her head in mild disgust, and looked away again.

"It's not like I'm confessing to owning REO Speedwagon, or *Journey*, or *Phil Collins*," I shouted, on a noisy and happy roll.

Sarah grinned at me then, broadly, briefly. Looking away from me, out across the room, she leaned over and spoke directly into my ear again, her breath warm.

"Oh, go ahead, honey," she said. "Embrace the cheese. I'm not stopping you. I might have to shame you, but I'm not going to stop you."

The teasing tone, the word *honey*, the word *shame*, her breath in my ear and down my neck made my shoulder blades fly together sharply and my whole body stand at attention. She knew she was doing this, but her face stayed removed, faintly amused. She lifted the bottle in her right hand easily to take a sip of a beer. I wanted to grab her by the wrist and crush all the bones in her hand.

At that moment the music changed and Sarah put her bottle down on the windowsill, still without looking at me, and began to move toward the center of the room.

"Oh, now you're dancing?" I called after her. "Now you are?"

"Prince is the real deal," she said, over her shoulder. "It's not even worth discussing."

"I wasn't trying to *discuss*," I shouted. "I was trying to dance!"

"Emphasis on trying," cracked Geoffrey, who slid suddenly into view on my right.

"Oh shut up," I said, relieved and entertained. "I can kick your ass in the minuet and you know it."

"Too bad there's not much call for that," he said, dancing away again.

"If I had a list of the best things in life, you would be on it," I called to Sarah, loudly, recklessly, over and above the other people in the room. She was turned away from me, dancing, and she threw me a glance, but whether it was warning or warm, I couldn't entirely tell.

CHAPTER 20

T he next day we were headed out to breakfast, which was what we usually did on Saturdays before I went to work at noon. Sarah liked to eat mostly in Province-town despite the drive, which meant an early rise before the road was too clogged with beachgoers funneling back and forth. We almost never ran into anyone from the program there, and when I was getting dressed that morning I wondered for the first time if that was part of the reason we went so far. Sarah came out of the shower after me and was hunting through a pile of clean T-shirts lying over the back of the chair in the bedroom. I dove toward her and we fell backward on the bed.

"There's no time for this," she said sternly, and then she burst out laughing at the mock consternation on my face.

"Oh, goodness. Come here, greedy girl," she said, and scooped me toward her. I rested my head on her chest for a moment, luxuriating. I could hear her deafening heartbeat in my ear and feel her still damp skin on my cheek. She smelled citrusy from the shower soap, and underneath that like her own naked slightly astringent self. She was the most gorgeous tawny color all over, even her breasts, which were a revelation. I had never had much truck with my own, which I found inconvenient most of the time, heavy to carry around and hard to dress, intent on straining my shirtfronts and popping open buttons. Their only virtue had been their appeal to boys, and that was at best a mixed, unsatisfactory advantage. I never could understand what boys were responding to; in fact the interest boys had in breasts always seemed to me like a clear marker of how inane most of them were. They were so easily contented with seeing or touching a breast, but they never seemed to know what on earth to do with one, once it was revealed. It's not that I was any help with this; I hadn't had any idea what to do with breasts either. What was the point? What was being craved? What possible purpose was being served here? But I had to reconsider this position when I met Sarah because I was entranced by her breasts, which were in every way different from my own. She did not need to wear a bra, although she almost always did, but whereas my breasts are like heavy soft cushions, mild-mannered flotation devices in the water that require constant corralling and support on land, hers stood up of their own accord like gravity had nothing to do with them. Her breasts were all at once so pretty and so single-minded, so businesslike and so pleasing. Like all of her body, they were straightforward, beloved, desired, merged to me and mine. They did not lie.

That Saturday we eventually made it to Café Heaven in Provincetown. We were waiting for our food, when a woman at the table next to ours decided to move toward the window, saying to her friend in tow, "There's more light up here and I like to go toward the light."

"Does that seem like a good idea?" I asked Sarah, *sotto voce*, and she laughed, her bursting pealing laugh, bumping her coffee mug and spilling a little on the newspaper, just as our food appeared.

"Can I have your French fries?" I asked immediately, reaching over toward them.

"Don't be so impatient," she said. "You're so impatient." But she shoveled a pile onto my plate.

"Look what you give me," I said happily.

"Not as the world gives do I give to you," she said, scooping sugar into her coffee and clanking the spoon twice, emphatically, on the edge of her mug.

"That is so true," I said, reaching for her ketchup.

Right then the café door opened and Bill McNeil came in. I started to wave and then I saw that immediately behind him, smug and twitchy at the same time, was Group 6's very own Nicky Pickler, wearing a purple windbreaker. She waved at us, and I waved back brightly. Bill looked around grumpily and sat in the far corner by the window, his antennae up, not acknowledging us at all.

Sarah looked at me and said quietly, "Your mouth's open." Then she said, "Well. Tricky Nicky."

We didn't say much else over our eggs and we didn't eat off each other's plates as much as usual. Sarah read the Arts and Leisure section from front to back. I snuck looks at their table. They didn't appear to be speaking much.

"Do you think he's sleeping with her?" I asked as soon as we were out the door.

"Looks that way," Sarah said, unperturbed, head down, rooting around in her slouchy patchwork velvet bag.

"It's just that she's kind of a dumb bunny," I said.

"Well, I doubt he's in it for the conversation."

"Okay, but she's an idiot if she thinks that's going to lead to anything. It's not like he's going to cast her in something because he's sleeping with her."

"You don't know that," Sarah said, then conceded, "okay, probably not."

"Anyway," she added a minute later, "everyone's in a relationship for a reason, everyone's getting something from someone else." She sounded dark and irritable.

We were walking by the drugstore on Main Street where a grizzled old man in the window gazed out unseeingly over his newspaper. He looked filmed over somehow, or maybe it was just that the window was dirty.

"Really? What are you getting with me?" I said jauntily, turning away from his vacant look.

"A soul mate," she said breezily.

And just like that she could switch from an incomprehensible, aloof, moody person filled with judgment and misgiving to someone who made me weak in the knees. There was no pausing, she just shot around the game board and landed on love.

What would I be impatient for, if not for this?

CHAPTER 21

D id you know about Nicky and Bill McNeil?" I asked
Shisha the following Monday, on a break, at the picnic table outside the church. The two of them were
standing in the distance, smoking together. Nicky had one
hand jammed in the back pocket of her jeans, and she was
turned away from the rest of us, pretending indifference.

"Oh yeah. It's hard to miss. She's practically wearing his letter jacket."

The thought of Bill McNeil owning a letter jacket seemed
so hilariously heretical that it made me snort like I was in grade
school and slosh juice in Shisha's general direction.

"Take it easy there, sport," she grinned, moving my bottle
to a safer distance.

"What are we talking about?" Ann asked, scootching cautiously closer to us on the bench.

"Bill McNeil, and Nicky wearing his letter jacket."

"What?" Ann was completely scandalized, her eyebrows
flying up and out like bat wings. "NO. Really? He's old enough
to be her father."

She looked over at them, anxiously, and then back at us, her
head waggling from side to side as though she could not control it.

"That's a real draw for some people," Shisha said.

"Maybe it's about power, getting access to it, or you know,
feeling powerful," I said vaguely, screwing the lid on my bottle.

"Oh yeah? Power? Whose?"

"Both parties," I said, picking at the label on the bottle, affecting unconcern, and then to escape the conversation, "what do you think he lettered in?"

"Bill? Pussy."

Ann's face came completely undone and she let out a horrified yelp. I wanted to be unflappable, but I blushed instantly, unstoppably. Shisha laughed her big honking laugh. Ann snatched up her blue and white canvas bag and headed back inside, while Nicky exhaled smoke and shot a squinty look in our direction.

"You scared her," I said, looking after Ann's agitated back, feigning composure. "That's not kind."

Shisha shrugged. "What about you?"

"What about me?"

"Are you and Sarah going public or is this undercover shit going to last all summer?"

"We're not undercover," I said defensively. "Anyone who's paying attention would know now."

"Sure," she said affably. "Because people pay such close attention."

"They do here," I said. "Could anyone be more in anyone else's business than this crowd?"

"Okay. I was just asking."

"I think she feels awkward," I said, after a pause. "I mean because she's the group leader. Like it might make the group dynamic strange. And she's a very private person."

Shisha looked at me like she was trying to decide whether to let this pass, and then she smirked and stood as Nicky came up alongside us.

"Time to go in?" she asked, cheerfully.

But then. We were still doing scenes of Shakespeare usually once a week in the afternoon with Bertie. We would take the text all apart and dissect the language and put it back together like technicians. The table work was tiring, but then we'd get up on our feet and play and it was great fun. One hot, lazy afternoon, Bertie asked Sarah to play Rosalind in Act I, scene 3 of *As You Like It* and then looking around the room, he landed on me and said, *Nina, you take Celia. Doug, Duke Frederick.*

We hadn't done any scene work yet together all summer, and I felt my eyes start to go helter-skelter when I got up and walked toward her. I felt unsteady and exposed. I had done this scene before, three years ago in another lifetime with Titch, but this was different and new.

The scene was the one in which Celia's tyrannical father, Duke Frederick, banishes his niece Rosalind from court on penalty of death, and Celia (me) comes passionately to her defense.

I was too young that time to value her;
But now I know her: if she be traitor,
Why so am I; we still have slept together
Rose at an instant, learned, played, eat together
And wheresoe'er we went, like Juno's swans,
Still we went coupled and inseparable.

I heard my voice wobbling a little and I tried to slow down and breathe. Then when I looked directly into Sarah's open face, I felt a great swell of courage, and she met my shaky eyes head on and they steadied and the lines were simply true:

Pronounce that sentence then on me, my liege:
I cannot live out of her company.

When we paused, Doug was standing stock-still looking at us. I realized Sarah and I were holding hands, and I felt a change in the room, a change in the breathing, maybe just my own, or maybe more than my own.

"I think that's a good place to stop," said Bertie, with his giant goofy smile. "Very nice."

We didn't say anything to one another in class. But I waited for her that day after classes were over, on the stretch of grass outside the church, and no one questioned it, no one asked me what I was doing, or why I didn't join them as I usually did. Ann offered me the sections of the *New York Times* that she had finished before she went off with the others for dinner and I thanked her and took them, although I didn't read anything. I lay on my stomach and watched people walking toward Commercial Street in the warm light of the end of the day. When Sarah finally came out, she waved goodbye to her fellow assistants and came loping toward me seamlessly, smiling, like we did this every day.

"I thought you'd still be here," she said. "I was hoping you would be."

She told me on the way home that the next day's visiting instructor was going to lead a singing class and I crossed my eyes and stuck out my tongue at nothing in particular. I am deathly afraid of singing in public. It makes me panicky.

She laughed. "It won't be so bad," she said. "You just focus your mind on the person you are singing to—imagine you are singing to a child if you want, or anyone you know and care about, imagine you are putting someone to sleep if you want—and don't forget to breathe."

The only time I sing is with my grandmother, who sings and hums all the time, whether she is washing dishes or feeding the cat or pulling up burdocks at the sides of the road. She sings Elizabethan rounds and popular songs, nursery rhymes and made-up songs. My grandfather sang as well. Walking home with Sarah that day I was thinking of something catchy like "I'm Forever Blowing Bubbles," and how their singing it could make me feel as lightly suspended as swinging in a hammock on a summer day. I was used to piping alongside my grandmother, but it was easy because my voice could chime underneath and be enveloped by hers. I never want to sing by myself in front of other people.

It turned out that I was not alone in my fear of singing and in the end Sarah had to stand up to sing first. Part of her job as group assistant was always to go first if nobody else was leaping into the breach. She sang that sad song "10,000 Miles," and when she got to the end she sang it directly to me. I couldn't believe it was happening, in front of everyone, so openly, not in the course of a scene or in any kind of veiled way. She had a lovely singing voice, clear and sweet. I had never heard it before. The bit of the song that I remember was, *Oh come ye back my own true love/And stay a while with me/If I had a friend all on this earth/You've been that friend to me.* I know it wasn't your usual love song or anything—she could have picked something much more obvious. But it was so beautiful when she sang it that I was struggling not to cry. When she was done she walked over, sat down right next to me, like it was the most natural thing in the world, and took my hand between hers. I didn't know where to look, so I looked at the floorboards and wept a little and tried to pull it together. I didn't want to cry, really I didn't, but I couldn't seem to help it. (Of course, there's more to that song. *Farewell, my own true love. I'm going away.* And: *Don't you see that lonesome dove, sitting on the ivy tree/She's weeping for her own true love, as I shall weep for mine.* For example.)

After classes were finished that day, Bill McNeil asked everyone to gather in the big room of the art gallery in order to discuss what we should do with the final weeks of the workshop. Sarah was sitting near Bill, with her back against a wall. She had her red notebook open and was taking occasional notes on the conversation. I weaved in between all the students, who were strewn across the room, sitting, lying down, inconveniently lumped together, until I got to her, and then I squeezed in beside her. She smiled at me. A heated debate was going on around us about whether to attempt a full-length show—probably a *Three Sisters* cobbled together in a way that would enlist everyone in some capacity—or to present scenes, or not to do any final performances at all. The logistics were making my head swim. Bored, I reached for Sarah's pen and scribbled, *3 Sisters are you for it or agin it* in her notebook. Sarah looked down, paused, closed her eyes for a long moment, opened them, and penned quickly, *Whatever I'm for, I'm for you.* She bent her head and her hair fell forward so I couldn't see her face, and she wrote underneath that, *Whatever's for us, for us.* Then: *I will hold you always no matter where no matter when no matter what. You're my person.* She underlined again, *Whatever I'm for, I'm for you.* She paused, looked away. My hands were thick and stupid, my heart flopping. *You're my person.* She lifted the pen again and wrote. *I think this is passion I think this is true.*

Do you? she wrote. I started to look over at her, but then, unexpectedly, she touched my hand, tracing lightly between my fingers. Her hand jumped a little. Without looking at me, she underlined what she'd just written again, in a single, shaky dark line, *Do you?*

Yes. I do. Of course I do. *You know I did. You know I do.*

(This is how the broken heart squeals: between tenses. The sticky clutch, the grinding gears, the sound of a ten-car pile-up.)

This might seem like nothing, the whim of two girls too young to drink legally, but the worst of it is that this connection doesn't come often, sometimes doesn't come at all. And once had, it colors everything. If you don't know what I am talking about, I don't know whether to say, *I hope you never do*, or to say, *Whatever you do, never settle for anything less.*

You know how there were those things you didn't know about until you did? Like what a semicolon is used for or what it would feel like to be really kissed. When I turned ten some grown-up said to me, "You've entered the double digits,"

gloomily or cheerfully I can't remember, but it didn't matter
because the suggestion seemed so alarming—a life sentence,
since you were likely never getting out of the double digits.
Suddenly a corner had been turned and I didn't even know I
was turning it. Around that time I started keeping a mental list
of things you didn't know about until you *knew*, like the arrival
of the ATM to our town because once that happened no one
ever said, *Did you get to the bank?* on Fridays anymore because
it didn't matter if you did. Then there was the matter of high
school terminology when I was little. I knew you were a senior
in the last year but I didn't know which year was sophomore
year and by the time I was ten it seemed like I had passed the
moment when it would be okay to ask.

I tried to glean meaning from context, which is what my
grandparents always told me to do, *Listen to the word in the
sentence.* I looked things up a lot in the encyclopedia and
learned to be extremely serious about words and about never,
ever writing in books, or breaking their spines, or dog-earing
their pages. Words were sacrosanct. But my mother was fond
of teasing. Once when I was eight, while spending the summer
plowing through P.G. Wodehouse, I asked my mother what
aspic was and she said serenely, "What does it sound like?"
Which left me a little worried. Or once she made me believe
that a family friend's last name was Wasserperson (it was
Wasserman), which entertained her and infuriated me. My
grandparents did not do this. I don't like being tricked, but
more than that I think being in the state of unknowing, the
state of unknowing and asking, deserves honesty and respect.
It's not precisely the same as innocence or ignorance even, it's
another state of being, which can be hard to say goodbye to
mostly because you never know when you are going to shapeshift
into a new state of being until you do. It's dizzying to think
about really, the constant rollover.

For example: I used to babysit for this little boy I adored, named Matthew. He had just turned six years old, and we'd been practicing his letters for a while and then suddenly one afternoon he'd begun to read. Very soon after that we were in the car on the way to his swim lesson, and he burst into tears because, he said, no one had ever told him that once he *could* read, he would never be able *not* to read again. He had understood reading to be a consensual, voluntary process, which would mean that he could read whenever he chose, but he didn't have to read if he didn't want to. But now and forever when he saw a stop sign, he would have to read *Stop*. He would have to read *Yield* and *Construction Ahead* and *Two for One at Wendy's!* and *Are You On the Right Road?* And that was just the beginning. He had no idea the full scope of what he was going to have to read or the full extent to which he was going to be a prisoner to literacy. But he had an inkling. And he felt furious and betrayed. Which I completely understand.

Sometimes you can be crafty with change, outmaneuver it a little. Like when I finally got glasses in ninth grade. I was walking on Hovey Lane and I looked up into a circus tent of maple tree leaves with my new glasses on and I was amazed because the leaves had edges. I had needed glasses for at least six years but wasn't having any of it. Instead I had gotten so I could distinguish the walks and general outlines of people from way far away down the hall in school, and I was an excellent note taker because I could never see the board. But all that time, I had had no real idea that leaves over my head, the leaves I walked under almost every day, spring, summer, and fall, had edges. The definition was extraordinary, heartbreaking. Then I took off my glasses and saw the familiar comforting blur of gold and green, the dappled light, the big, peaceful movement. I love having bad eyesight because I can see either with soft focus—shut the world out, push it to the gently fuzzy periphery, and see only what's right in front of me—

or I can see with cold sharp brisk vision, the way most other people do. But I get to choose.

It wasn't like that with touch and Sarah, she opened me up and revealed me and there was no choice and no going back. *Whatever I'm for, I'm for you.*

In fairy tales when the princess signs away her firstborn and then whinges about it later, I always thought, listen you dumb cluck you don't mess with the spirit world you don't mess with the fairies or the gods, if you sign on the dotted line or your word's as good as a signature then you better believe you will pay the price and that oath is irrevocable. But when the time came, I signed, I promised, I was all in and I didn't even know it had happened. It's hard when you don't know something's irrevocable until it is.

PART 3
THE END OF THE FAMILIAR,
THE BEGINNING OF THE END

CHAPTER 22

The first Sunday morning in August, I went along with Sarah and Eddy and Luke to the Swap Shop, the community exchange on Cole's Neck Road, which was also the Transfer Station and Recycling Center, or the dump. They were on a mission to find whatever the summer people had started to leave behind. I'd only ever been there to leave garbage before, never stopped in to the Swap Shop to look around. It turned out to be full to the brim with dishes, glassware, pots, pans, games, puzzles, toys, lamps, speakers, sporting goods, LPs, umbrellas, chairs, and books.

"It's funny to go trash picking like this," I said.

"Well, it's a far cry from dumpster diving," said Luke robustly. "There's great stuff here. It's remarkable what people will throw away or leave behind."

"Look at this!" said Sarah. She was balancing on a pile of old cushions and she had hold of the arm of a blue and green upholstered armchair from a recently deposited collection. "I could get this back to New York in the truck easily. It's beautiful. Nina, come and help me."

"Why do you want that?" Eddy asked. "You have furniture."

"Why not? And anyway it's beautiful. It's only got one chip on its foot. It's completely sturdy." She kicked the pillows away, dragged the chair a little way away from its pile, and sat on it. When I walked over, she grabbed me around the waist and pulled me in as well.

"Okay, ladies," Luke said, fake harrumphing, "this is a serious mission we're on. This is no time to fool around."

"What exactly are we looking for?" I asked, not getting up.

"Anything that appeals. One person's trash is another person's treasure."

Sarah had spotted a set of blue glasses and nudged me off her lap.

"Look at those," she said. "They're gorgeous."

"You have glasses," Eddy said.

"Not as nice as these."

"That's the thing about you, Sarah," he said. "You're never satisfied with what you have, you always want something else."

At that moment, Luke dived into a box and emerged with a triumphant cry holding something yellow I couldn't identify right away.

"What is that?"

"What is that? That," he said lovingly, "is a marigold-colored espresso machine. Oh, now this is a find."

"Does it work?"

"It will," he said, turning it upside down and investigating its nether regions. "It will work for me. Once we've had a chat."

I laughed and Eddy laughed when I did. He began digging through a pile of records. For a moment, all three of them were quiet, absorbed in their discoveries, and I stood there, unable to stop smiling, not needing or wanting anything but that company, that dusty sunny moment in time.

When we got home from visiting the Swap Shop, I was struck with a cheerful urge to see Titch, and I ran over to visit her at work.

It's true that we weren't speaking much or at all at this point. We hadn't really crossed paths since our run-in at the movies. I didn't care. But that day Sarah had work to do for the program at the apartment, and it seemed suddenly like the perfect time to go find Titch, so I went down the road and crossed over West Main Street to Briar Lane. Then, just when I walked into the sandwich shop, I saw a tall redheaded woman gather her bags and exit out the back. Sarah's ex-girlfriend. Bess.

"What's the matter with her," I asked Titch, rolling my eyes, trying to make a joke of it. Titch was working behind the counter, wearing a green apron and a cap with the store's logo, looking hot and grumpy. When I said this, she shot me a look of infuriated disbelief.

"I just thought I'd say hi," I said, and when she didn't answer me, "I can wait."

I went over near the register while she assembled a sandwich.

"I said no mayo," said the bearded man with a threadbare backpack at the counter. Titch dropped the bread in the trash can with disdain and started over in a concentrated fury.

"Do you have spelt or some non-wheat bread?" a pinched-looking woman inquired. Her nostrils appeared to be glued together. She was wearing flip-flops and had a beach towel draped around her leathery neck.

"All the breads are on the board," Titch said with elaborate politeness, spearing pickles.

"Come on, I mean she didn't have to leave," I said to Titch, when she had rung up Scruffy Backpack Man. "What's her problem?"

"I see the bread," Pinched Woman said, "but all the breads have wheat, they're all wheat breads. I don't do gluten."

Wordlessly, Titch took change from Scruffy Backpack Man and stared hard at the woman.

"I guess I could have the special salad," the woman said weakly.

Titch began shoveling greens in a bowl.

"Your mom called again last night," she said, finally, not looking at me. "Also the MP has left four messages."

Out of the window, I could see Bess. She had come around to the front of the store, and was squatting down beside a spindly old bike, fishing for something in her bag, her skirt dragging a little bit in the dust.

"I don't know what you want me to say to him, Nina, but it doesn't seem like he knows the two of you are done. Why is he calling? I thought you said it was over."

"We are, it is," I said, frowning. Now Bess was knotting the end of her skirt in front of her. She swung her leg over the bike and balanced precariously.

"Yeah? Did you forget to tell him, is that it? You just don't talk to anyone anymore?"

"Just don't answer the phone," I said, annoyed. "What do you care? It's not your problem."

"Actually, it is, because I live there and, news flash, I know him too."

"Fine." I said. "What am I supposed to do about it?"

"Don't make me take care of your crap. That's all. Also, I'm not going to cover for you when your mom calls," Titch said, still under her breath to me, head down, snatching at the red onions violently with her plastic tongs.

"Nobody asked you," I said.

"No radishes," the woman customer wailed, but softly, like a child who's been put down for a nap and still wants you to know it's under protest. When she had paid and sat down at the table by the window, I turned back to Titch, who was now resolutely wiping surfaces with a cloth. I flicked the glass of the display counter with my fingernail, hard, exasperated.

Bess was still visible. She was stopped at the corner of Holbrook, resting on one foot, adjusting the strap of her grey messenger bag across her chest.

"She's your sister's friend," I said, "I don't even know her."

"What are you talking about?" Titch said. "Everyone knows about them. Didn't she ever tell you—didn't Sarah ever talk to you about it? You met Bess, didn't you? I mean what did you think was going on? Why would you think it wouldn't matter to her?"

"Well what does it matter to me?" I asked hotly. "They broke up before I even got here. So what if Sarah never talks about it. Obviously, it's not important enough to mention. And what do you care? Why are you taking her side?"

"I'm not taking her side. This isn't junior high. There aren't *sides*. I'm saying they were together for almost two years. You don't think that counts for something?"

"Well, obviously. But it's over."

"Okay," (slapping the dish towel down on the counter, turning her back, noisily pushing dishes under the tap, refusing to look at me), "whatever you say."

I looked at the back of her sunburned neck murderously and then slammed the screen door on the way out as hard as I could, making Pinched Woman cough up a cherry tomato.

The reason Titch and I became friends was because she marched up to me on the playground at the beginning of fourth grade and asked if I wanted to be friends—which, who does that? I was talking to Molly Hartman and I just looked at Titch like she was crazy. I can still see her coming over and standing for a minute with her hands shoved deep in the pockets of her blue CB jacket. She was chewing on the inside of her cheek. When Molly and I paused to look at her, she said, "Nina? Do you want to be friends?" She said it firmly, too, without any kind of hesitation. I think I said *yeah, sure*, in an unconvincing disbelieving way, in a way that was meant to be totally discouraging. It startled me that she said my name like that, that she seemed to have so completely and decisively chosen me. She nodded once, crisply, and turned away and I probably even rolled my eyes when her back was turned. I said yes because she looked kind of intense and she scared me a little, with her directness, her determined chin, and the way she stood there, all pointy and hopeful like a newly sharpened pencil. Back then, white girls in Vermont and New Hampshire—and there weren't many other kinds where we lived—all wore turtlenecks with patterns on them, like tiny red hearts or blue whales, under big, baggy sweaters that often went down to the mid-thigh, very preppy ugly and all about hiding breasts and butts, whether you had them or not. That day she had tiny green alligators sticking up on the neck of her turtleneck. She was skinny and angular, flat front and back, with a long neck and thick, slightly frizzy shoulder-length dirty-blonde hair held back with two green and white beribboned barrettes on each side of her head. (It was also the time of beribboned barrettes, colored ribbons braided through plain silver, gold, or brown metal barrettes and left to dangle at the ends. Listen, we didn't know. We were just in it, and when we were together in it we were happy too.)

But the truth is I found it impossible to talk to Titch about Sarah. Sarah and I were in our own world and I didn't want anyone crashing about in it asking questions, making me feel common when we were so clearly not like anyone or anything else. The arrogance of it, the staggering, joy-filled superiority. More than anything I didn't want Titch's slyness, her sharpness—all things I loved about her—needling my happiness. She had no place in it.

Also Titch was right that the sight of Bess troubled me. Mostly I skated right over her existence. If you grow up in a small town, having routine blind spots for people is second nature. But I would still see her out of the corner of my eye with some regularity, going to work at the restaurant, or at the liquor store, or once at Hatch's buying cherries, or coasting down the street on her shabby, ancient bike, her red hair flying out behind her in a show-offy way. The blotch of her red hair was like an irritating floater in my eye, skimming around the edges.

Her old bike tapped at my chest though. It was like a bike you might come across in the recesses of a dusty secondhand store or upstairs in a barn, it was a bike with a history, a cracked seat, a bell.

Sarah had startlingly little to say about Bess. This was the sum total of what I had learned: Bess was an excellent baker and made great fruit pies. She taught yoga. She knew about wine. She was thirty-two, impossibly old. She spent a lot of time in her studio, making sculptures. She was saving up for a new lathe. The dust from the studio had bothered Sarah. They didn't have much in common. Once they had taken a vacation to North Carolina and Sarah had been horribly sick, vomiting all night, and Bess had not held Sarah's hair back for her while she was throwing up. It was like a small pile of mismatched laundry, this information, unusable but impossible to throw out.

CHAPTER 23

I had sent my mother and grandmother four or five chatty, uninformative letters and an arty postcard, as well as calling a handful of times, but now that Titch had given me the heads up that I was missing my mother's calls, I preemptively phoned home that same day. I said that with my schedule it was best to call on Sunday afternoons, and after that I hustled over to Truro for my mother's weekly call. I wasn't happy about making the trek, but it was better than drawing attention to the fact that I didn't live there. If Titch was around and got to the phone first she would make an elaborate show of calling my name and delivering the phone to me, which I tried to ignore.

In these conversations, I mainly listened to my mother and didn't speak. She had a lot to say and didn't ask much. She seemed really distracted. She told me a little bit about what was happening on the farm, about how much hay the neighbors had brought in from our field, about how much we still needed, but mostly she was fretting about my grandmother. She said my grandmother wasn't talking to her much at all, although I pointed out that she hadn't said much of anything for a couple of years. It didn't seem alarming because it was such a gradual creeping kind of silence. Also she was very communicative, for a silent person.

"It's as though she's given up," my mother said, one Sunday. "I mean some days it feels like she's not even really here anymore. Like this is not my mother anymore, but more like a remnant of my mother."

All I could think about was how when my grandmother read to me when I was a child, I used to hold up my thumb and index finger to my eye to make her manageably tiny, blurring the light of the lamp with her head. I could hear her clearing her throat, I could hear the knitting needles, that soft clicking and rubbing together, the pages turning.

"I don't know what to feed her," my mother went on. "She's not eating very much. I keep thinking about whether I should get some help, except you know that she's not going to tolerate strangers in the house. Also I can't get her to wash without a fight. But it's more like civil disobedience than a struggle. She goes sort of limp."

I wasn't accustomed to this kind of conversation with my mother. She sounded tired and forlorn, with only a small familiar undercurrent of crankiness. Also my heart clutched a little when she talked about my grandmother this way. Was it true? Was she slipping?

"Maybe she doesn't need to wash," I offered. But my mother wasn't listening.

She sighed. "I think she misses him. I didn't know it was this bad. I'm so afraid that she's going to lose her mind too. Oh, you know, not the way he did. Jesus, I hope not like that. But still."

When she said this, I was sorting Sarah's laundry in the bedroom in Truro and I had two sudden, vivid memories one right after the other:

First: on a hot green summer day four years after my grandfather's death, my mother and I are at the Lippitt Morgan Horse Show in Tunbridge, Vermont. In the show ring, holding a fidgety brown filly and her slightly sway-backed dam, is an old man, a stranger with a ridiculous hat, a floppy green sun hat secured under his chin with white elastic that cuts into the wattles on his neck. His face looks out with a clouded stubbornness, a veiled fury, not sour but deep, upsetting. A familiar look. A look of dementia, a demented look. My mother's face contracts and she grabs my arm, hard.

Immediately this memory jumped, like a slide projector clicking back, to the sight of the back of my grandfather's hand. The skin, loose and brown-spotted like crackled roast chicken skin. The dog has bitten him right after dinner, and blood is running freely out of the gash in his hand onto his pants. He can't see it. My grandmother approaches with white gauze bandages, but he waves her away with his bleeding hand, shaking his head no, his twice-broken twice-healed wrist trembling. He can't feel the bite. He continues to shake his head, agitated, lost, while she wraps the wound, accidentally smearing his blood on her cheek with the back of her hand.

He watches her, shaking his head, defeated but apprehensive. He is like a sheep in the flatbed of a moving truck: no thought beyond the moment, the disoriented struggle to stand, but still a vague, larger sense of loss of control. A sheep will lean against you heavily for support if the truck turns a corner, always breathing distrustful milky breath, eyes wet, unknowing. The docility of my grandfather's heavy hard stomach is hard to bear. He would walk into the woods that very week and he would never come back.

On the day of the dog bite he nibbled at the bandage surreptitiously, shredding the gauze like a sneaky teething child, while my grandmother gazed out the window at the unoccupied bird feeder.

And then, unexpectedly, he put his head down on the table and she cleared her throat, laying a hand on the back of his neck. Her stomach gurgled. I put my cheek down too on the cool wood surface and looked over at my grandfather at eye level, like we were looking at one another in the crack underneath a door. His eye knew me, for an instant in that narrow sliver of space, and I knew it back. *Was this a face to be oppos'd against the warring winds?*

"She likes Jello," I said to my mother, fully expecting to be reminded of the disgustingness of Jello, its nasty unacceptable ingredients.

"Jello," she repeated. "Jello."

CHAPTER 24

Things started to go wrong. In the final stretch of the workshop, something was shifting underground. Sarah's dark moods seemed a little darker, a little more frequent, although she could still be nuzzled out of them most of the time. It made me vigilant and a little uneasy. I knew she worried about money, she worried about working, but the dense grey mushroom cloud that settled over her from time to time didn't seem connected to anything specific. It made her burrow deep in the covers and struggle to come out. I went in after her. I thought it was my job. I understood it to be my job.

There was almost never a trigger that I could see or predict though. Also the off moments were tiny at first, causing me only pinpricks of bewilderment, a sensation like when you are coming down stairs and think you've reached the bottom step only to discover abruptly that there's six inches of empty air still to go before your foot hits solid ground. A momentary lurch, a lost heartbeat.

We had received our assignments for the final collective show of *Three Sisters*, which we were supposed to muscle together into a coherent production in the remaining two and a half weeks. I was acting in most of Act 1 and then directing two more scenes in Acts 2 and 3. It was hard to hold all the pieces in my head, so I didn't try. Instead I focused only on what I was doing when I walked into my assigned rehearsal room each day. Sarah, along with the other assistants, was responsible for the big picture, for paying attention to the lines of continuity throughout, as well as for scheduling, stage managing, organizing props and costumes, and corralling the actors, as much as that was possible.

The day we started rehearsals, Sarah was away. She'd driven into New York very early that morning to audition for a television pilot workshop. I didn't wake up when she left, but I was up early and at rehearsal before anyone else, looking forward to it. I was pleased because I was playing Masha—my favorite, the middle sister—alongside Shisha as the oldest sister, Olga, in the opening of the play. Another girl, Jeanette, a little blonde elfin presence, more like a wafer than a person, was playing the youngest sister, Irina. Doug was directing us, and he showed up with a sheaf of notes, bristling with self-importance. He looked like in his mind he was wearing a monocle. We sat around with our chairs in a circle while he lectured us.

"This opening moment is when we establish the relationship between the sisters, so it's terribly important that we get it right."

"Is it?" asked Shisha. "Is it *terribly* important?"

He shot her a look. He was so used to her wise-assing by now that it barely broke his stride. But when we got to work it was great fun, and even Doug relaxed and let us play.

Once we were finished, I had the afternoon off, and instead of hanging out with the others or learning my lines as I was supposed to be doing, I decided to make dinner for Sarah. I was in the middle of cutting onions for spaghetti sauce when I heard her pull in to the driveway. I could see the top of her head as she stepped out of the truck, but I couldn't tell much from the way she was moving. She looked tired, maybe a little hesitant.

"How did it go?" I called to her from the top steps.

"I don't know," she said, her back to me, yanking her bag out of the truck. "Okay, I think? Maybe. I don't know. I guess I'll find out."

I ducked back inside the kitchen, rinsed my hands off in the sink, and kicked the open oven door closed with my foot. It was hot, and I was sweaty from the stove. Sarah came into the apartment and stood in the doorway, her bag dangling from her hand, looking at the table, which I had set, and at the flowers in the middle, black-eyed Susans, purple butterfly bush, two sturdy blue hydrangea stems, and some pink salt spray roses, which I had gathered on my walk home.

"I made a peach pie," I said, pleased, unable to sit on the news.

She just stood there, no color in her face. She bit her lip.

"Where did you come from?" she asked.

"What are you talking about?" I said. She looked suddenly, astonishingly, like she was about to dissolve in tears.

"I didn't think this would happen," she said, very low, looking down at the floor, sounding almost stricken. "This wasn't supposed to happen."

"What wasn't supposed to happen? Sarah?"

She gestured weakly, taking in me and the room.

"What are you talking about?" I said again, confused, and when she didn't respond, "You know everything that's going to happen, do you?" to tease her, to lift the cloud.

Her face rearranged and began to return to itself. She looked up.

"I used to," she said. "You were a surprise."

And then, recovered, "And peach pie. I would not have predicted peach pie."

Another time: at a party in early August at the beachside home of Marilyn, the introductory woman with the dandelion fluff hair from the first day of the workshop. All the actors were stumbling around, playing Frisbee, drinking beer, grilling hamburgers, and shucking corn. Marilyn was drinking too much, wearing a giant brown and purple caftan. Bill McNeil was skulking around the kitchen, faithful Nicky the bean counter by his side and a cluster of other students hanging on him worshipfully. But Sarah was nowhere. I looked for the better part of an hour until I finally found her outside, all alone looking at the water. I slid my arms around her ribs and pressed my nose into her cheek, that safe harbor. But she didn't turn. She didn't turn in toward me as usual. Her cigarette-flavored mouth was cold.

"You've been smoking?" I said. She scowled, shoved her hands in her pockets, and almost turned her back on me, not speaking.

"Sarah?"

No response.

Nothing too serious. A momentary lurch, a lost heartbeat. But it got rapidly stranger, and worse.

One night toward the end of the first week of August we were coming out of a restaurant in Provincetown, gaily, laughing. A face floated up in front of us, a pale face hovering like a balloon at the end of a long stick thin body. I thought for a moment that it was a mask only it wasn't Halloween, or a carnival, or a parade. A cadaverous face, gaunt, barely human, marked.

"What was wrong with him?" I asked Sarah as soon as we were out of earshot.

"KS," she said.

"What?" I asked.

"Kaposi's sarcoma," she said repressively, as if that was the end of it, and I was chastened, couldn't ask again. I looked back over my shoulder at the man's long narrow back, and saw a shorter, bald man walked beside him holding his hand, as though he were keeping the sick man's scary balloon head from floating away into the night sky.

Sarah was silent in the dark all the way to the truck. When

we got inside, she reached over and turned on the radio. Patsy Cline was singing, but I didn't want to leave the conversation behind the way I usually did when she set up a roadblock. My voice sounded weak to me, though, and I had to ask my question twice before she even heard that I was speaking, so I switched off the radio and her head snapped sharply toward me.

"I said, that man who was sick, why does it upset you so much?"

"Why doesn't it upset you more? You think it can't happen to you? You think it doesn't happen to anyone like you?" She sounded clipped, bitter.

I was silent. I did think that, pretty much. Despite the various warnings we'd had at school, or the murmurings I had heard on the radio, the only people I knew for sure who had been affected by AIDS were gay men and drug users and maybe some unfortunate people who got contaminated blood from transfusions. And even that much had been hard for me to believe; the whole thing just seemed so implausible and foreign and unreal.

"People are *dying*," Sarah said, and she sounded really angry. I looked out the window. It was a warm night and the air was sticky with salt. I could hear a man calling drunkenly, mournfully, to someone else, over the noisy sounds of the bar behind him.

"Okay, but why are you angry with me?"

"I'm not angry with *you*," she said, sounding angrier still. "I'd like to go home now though, is that okay?"

I bit my lip. She started the truck and we drove to Wellfleet in silence. When we got there though, she took out the key and held it for a minute, twisting the chain in her hands. I waited, unsure of what, if anything, was coming.

"Eddy's sick," she said, after a long pause. "He tested positive."

"He is? I mean, he did?" I was really shocked. Eddy with his lanky frame and his cigarettes, his clowning around, his unexpected friendliness, his efficient way of moving about at work, what I'd heard—from whom I couldn't remember—about his many girlfriends; I couldn't put it all together. I thought about how he had said of Sarah, *a lot of trouble.* Why did he say that? I looked over at his apartment, which was dark. I had only been in there once and we almost never saw him there, only sometimes pulling on a jacket over his bony shoulders, his long arms, his hands jerking out of the cuffs, as he hurried down the steps from his side to work or wherever he was going. He was almost always in a hurry, unless he was smoking, in which case his whole world seemed to come to a short, meditative halt until the cigarette was done.

Sarah was looking out of the window in the direction of the bay, where the water was slightly darker than the night sky.

"How did he get it?" I asked tentatively.

"Who knows?" she said, only marginally less impatiently. "And who cares? He's twenty-nine and he's going to die." But when she turned to look at me, her face was pale, wiped clean of anger. "He slept with the wrong person, I guess."

I was confused, and silent. I wanted to say, But isn't Eddy straight? How do you know he has AIDS? Did he tell you? Why did he tell you? How long have you known? How long has he known? Do the other guys know? Does he know who made him sick? Do they know? And how come he doesn't look sick? Is he definitely going to die? And, underneath this, the unaskable, the unthinkably selfish, what does this have to do with you and me? The questions were still coming along one after another in my mind as Sarah was getting out of the truck and walking away, they were still coming one right after the other as her intractable back marched up the stairs without me.

When I saw Eddy next, which was at work, I tried to

behave normally, although I couldn't help watching him out of the corner of my eye. "Hey, kid," he said, with warmth when I arrived and was standing by the door, struggling to pull my apron over my ponytail. "Hey," I answered, and he stopped to knot the apron tie behind my back for me. He didn't seem any different from the way he always had. He didn't look marked. But then nobody does, until they do.

I had an odd, sinking sensation under my ribs about all of these people I thought I was coming to know, these people who had started to feel like family. I thought, *I don't know them at all*. I was an interloper, a stranger, a tourist. *Who were they?* Instead of being closer to everyone, I could suddenly, jarringly, be farther away. Even—although I didn't think this, I couldn't think this, I refused to think this—farther away from Sarah, maybe especially from Sarah. From one minute to the next, with a new disconcerting regularity, Sarah could all of sudden be standing behind a plate of glass, unreachable, unknowable.

CHAPTER 25

A round this time Sarah told me her mother was coming to town to see her. We were finishing up dinner in Luke's kitchen when she told me. I asked her if her father was coming too. She said something noncommittal about his work and about his needing to stay home in Indiana with the family dog, an ancient ailing Siberian Husky. When she was saying this, Luke was drying dishes at the sink with his back to us. He didn't look over, but it was as if he had. Several bars of jaunty jazz music played into the silence that descended on the three of us. Sarah sighed.

"He's not a bad guy, but he can't do *this*," she said then, unexpectedly (gesturing almost inadvertently to herself, a repeated small stirring movement with her right hand in front of her chest). "He doesn't believe in it. It would be much worse if I were his son, but as it is, it's. Bad enough. Not his thing. He's not a bad guy," she said again, her voice trailing off, "he just doesn't know what to say or do with me really. So, you know, he doesn't. Do anything."

Luke turned around then, wiping his hands on the dishtowel. "Coffee?"

I knew very little about Sarah's parents beyond the most basic information, but the timing of Sarah's mother's coming filled me with relief and focus. I thought it meant that Sarah and I would be reunited on the same team, we would be co-conspirators together again. Having her mother visit would be a distraction from whatever dark corners we had accidentally stumbled into. I would almost certainly learn more about Sarah—about the place she was from and about her people—more than I could ever learn only from her account. Better yet, I would be connected to her family; her mother at least would know who I was and connect me to Sarah. And Sarah would see anew what an asset I could be. Because I'm terrific with parents. Fathers love me. Mothers love me. Other people's families love me. All week before her mom arrived, I was looking forward to it.

But from the moment Lenore, Sarah's mom, took my hand limply, reluctantly, I knew how wrong I was. She was a wiry querulous person with an anxious, kind, deeply weathered face. I couldn't see Sarah in her, except possibly in the refined bones of her jawline and the high forehead. She had trouble looking at me directly, although she did seem shy with almost everyone except the waitress, with whom she was chatty and warm. She looked constantly apprehensive, even panicky, as though she was prepared to be shocked by the customs in this strange place, or as though she was afraid all the time about what might spring out at her around the next corner.

We had dinner at the Waltzing Lobster in Truro with Luke, to whom Lenore seemed to cling. He took good care of her, pulling out her chair and exuding his avuncular charm. I was grateful to him, but unable to stop being worried and unhappy that I couldn't win her over. No matter what I said, she behaved as though I were speaking a foreign language, joking in a foreign language, and she was struggling to keep up, to get the punch line. She was never rude. But although she answered my overtures and queries, she did so with circumspection, remoteness, refusal. She did not ask me anything. She did not want to know anything.

It had never occurred to me that I could be an undesirable girlfriend, that anyone's parent would not only be disappointed by me, but would wish fervently that I did not exist. But suddenly it seemed as though I was a problem. I was a liability. Even more dumbfounding it seemed as though I might be *the* problem, as far as Lenore was concerned. This idea was so unfamiliar and so unfair that it could not register; for well over half the night I simply could not find any place inside me for the idea to take up residence. But by dessert, it was a fact that had wedged itself in my chest, like a sharp stone, a flinty arrowhead I had swallowed.

Unbidden, my own mother sat with me during this meal and I thought of how she would have behaved if she had been there, if she knew about Sarah, which of course she did not. But I had to conclude that she would have done better than this. She hadn't much cared for Titch when I became friends with her, but she had changed her mind, eventually. I liked to think that she had finally trusted that there was something there that she couldn't see, something that made me happy. I was surprised that my mother surfaced here, surprised that I recruited her to be in my corner. But she materialized in this moment because I knew absolutely, knew grudgingly and with an unwanted upwelling of gratitude, that while my mother might have been wary and judgmental, she would have talked to Sarah. She would have made the effort.

It would have been hard if Lenore had just disliked me, but what happened was much worse. Sarah had been a little discouraging about the visit, but she had not warned me in any way about how her mother would regard me. As a result, not only did I feel like I had plunged into another reality with Sarah's mother, but I also felt like Sarah had dropped me there, whether unwittingly or not I couldn't tell. Sarah was quiet at dinner, attentive to her mother and once in a while checking in with me, but she made no effort to draw a connection, to open any kind of avenue between us, to relay any kind of warmth. She already knew what I was learning: that this was a lost cause.

After dinner, Sarah drove me home. Her mother was staying with her in Wellfleet. My stomach was uneasy because my distress was curdling the cream sauce from dinner. I thought maybe Sarah would attempt to reassure me and tell me it hadn't gone as poorly as I thought. I thought maybe she would be able to explain some of what had gone wrong. I thought maybe I should say something comforting to her. Neither one of us spoke, or even so much as acknowledged that anything had gone wrong, which felt a little disastrous.

I thought with her mother in town that Sarah wouldn't want to come in, that she would have to go right home. But we were kissing in the car and she slid out of the truck and followed me up the stairs. She had hold of the waist of my jeans, her fingertips slipped in and holding lightly where my jeans gaped at the small of my back. We moved totally silently, wholly in sync, like seasoned and yoked pack animals. We went right past Titch's room with her light still showing under the door. We didn't turn my light on. She closed the door softly behind us. Before I had finished pushing piles of clean laundry off the bed onto the floor, she had her shirt over her head. When I turned around, she was already standing stripped down and focused at the end of the bed. She meant business. She was on task.

But before she left, she rested her cheek in the pocket of my hip bone and sighed. I could see a silvery strip of moonlight running down her bare back. Her spine looked like a necklace of beads laid out in a line. Her hair was spilled across my stomach, rising and falling lightly when I breathed. After a long minute she rolled over on her back. I reached over her for the cotton blanket to cover us and she gripped my hip bone in her hand fiercely for a moment. We sat up, clung together, wound around each other like seaweed. After a moment she gracefully and silently rose. I watched her dress. We did not speak. Fully clothed, she paused by the side of the bed and traced the side of my face and my mouth with her thumb. Then she slipped out the door and down the stairs, holding her shoes in one hand. I had my arms wrapped around my knees in the midst of the rumpled bed, listening to the motor start up as she backed out of the driveway with the lights off. The sound seemed acutely, unaccountably sad.

The next morning, I was nursing a cup of coffee in the kitchen, holding it in both hands up to my cheek when Titch came in and stood at the end of the counter. She regarded me for a moment, weight on one hip, so still and silent that I began to feel awkward. I wondered whether she had heard us the night before. I couldn't tell if she looked accusatory or what, because I had to hide my face in my mug.

"This came for you," she said finally, crossing behind me to the fridge and dropping an envelope in front of me. It was yet another letter from the MP, always the same handwriting, slanted to the right, legible but ugly, careful cursive, every round "a" with its tail. When I had opened the first envelope pulverized dried flowers coated the paper and my hands in a fine dust, making me sneeze. I looked at the latest squat little cream-colored envelope on the counter. I did not need to burn it; I did not even have the energy to throw it out. I carried it into the bedroom, and shoved it in the drawer by my bed, unopened, with the others. I could feel Titch's eyes on my back as I left the room.

I didn't see Sarah the rest of that Saturday, while her mother was in town. I was in the house in Truro and I didn't have to go to work. Titch didn't have to work either, as far as I knew, but after puttering about for an hour in the glassed-in patio, which she had turned into a kind of painting studio, she took the car and went out without speaking to me. I heard the car reversing in the driveway from my bedroom. It was a damp, grey day and my joints hurt. I curled up on the sofa with the cats, who were all over me, Jack springing on my feet and biting, Chester lying heavily by my side. I read *Three Sisters* and tried not to wait for the phone to ring.

CHAPTER 26

S arah did call, but not until the next day. At first she sounded like herself again on the phone. I was as relieved that her mother was gone as I had previously been that she was coming. I was prepared to forget all about it, if that was possible. Sarah had to go up island to Hyannis to find a list of props and costume pieces for the final show. I said I was happy to go along, but by the time we left, it was late and Sarah was stressed and absorbed by the task. She couldn't be teased out of this mood, even though in a better moment she would have granted me at least a smile. When I couldn't get more than a half-hearted response from her, I gave up and just listened to Stevie Wonder, who was singing in his unfailingly upbeat and sweet way.

Then when we were walking down the street to the vintage clothing store, I reached for her hand, and Sarah instantly slid her hand out of mine. *Not here*, she said, frowning, not looking at me.

I looked around but I couldn't see anything. A distracted mother with one child in a stroller and another tugging at her pant leg. Two older men in conversation in front of a hardware store. Why not? I asked. Because, she said, just because.

After we had crossed off most of the list, she turned to me with a half apologetic smile. "I'm hungry," she said, "and cranky. I'm sorry."

"That's okay," I said. "I'm hungry too. We should eat."

As we were sitting eating our sandwiches, I asked her

tentatively about her mother's visit and she shrugged me off, her face closing. "I don't want to talk about it," she said.

I was tired and without meaning to, I began sniffing into my sandwich.

"Oh, Jesus," Sarah said then. "Nina. Really. It's *okay*." She reached out for my hand and brought it lightly to her cheek for an instant.

"No, I know," I said. And we did manage to smile for real at one another then, for the first time that day, mine a little wobbly. I was so focused on Sarah that I didn't notice a dark-haired woman who had come up beside our table. She was smiling at both of us, gently and warmly, so I smiled back but I couldn't make sense of what she was saying.

"It's a sin," she said again. "I'm sorry?" I said, but Sarah's left hand gripped the table hard and her right hand crushed the bones in mine. Her face was chalky.

"Go away," she said.

"I just want you to know the Lord loves you."

"What?" I said. "What are you talking about?"

"Go away," Sarah said again and this time her voice was thick. She was furious, but she also looked on the verge of tears.

"I know that it's easy to be confused," the woman said kindly, "but you can turn away from each other. You can be saved."

"Oh, you don't understand," I said. "We love each other." My nose was still running and there were leftover tears on my cheeks that I wiped with the back of my sleeve.

"I know you think you feel that way, but it's a sin. I want you to know that if you listen to God's word, you can be saved."

She set a leaflet on the table between our plastic cups, and turned to go. As she did, she touched my shoulder lightly and said, "I'll pray for you."

I felt exposed, defiled, ashamed. Everything seemed dirtier and uglier after she left, the café's concrete wall and its peeling mermaid mural, the plastic spoons and paper napkins, the salt and pepper shakers in the shapes of anchors, the top of the metal lattice table. People around us were pretending not to have heard, were turned toward one another, their eyes slipping toward us and away again. My face was very hot.

Sarah said, "Bitch," fiercely but too late, and without complete conviction. Her chin was trembling, and she did not reach out for me. She had pulled her hands under her side of the table.

But the woman hadn't been a bitch. I felt caught by the net of her gentleness, which trapped us in some cloying, ugly, confounding haze, like it had made it impossible for us to see each other clearly. The pamphlet between us read *Christ is Coming*. Well, let him come. We weren't stopping him. I couldn't grasp how someone could have looked at us and responded the way that she did. I thought again, she just doesn't understand, and I said this, but Sarah snapped back at me, "Oh, she understands. And it's not like she's the exception. She's the norm."

For what felt like the umpteenth time that week, I said, getting teary, "Why are you mad at me?"

"I'm not," she said exasperated. "But you don't have any idea about this, you don't understand."

"What do you mean I don't understand?" I was hissing at her now, furious too. "What are you talking about? Why are you talking to me this way? What's wrong with you? You think I don't know we can't hold hands everywhere? I'm not stupid, Sarah."

She looked at me, from a million miles away.

"I think you haven't had a lot of experience with the kind of ugliness people have against people like you and me," she said, finally, evenly. "That's all." But even though she had put us back together syntactically, I didn't feel better. I didn't feel united. I didn't know how to get back to that place.

We drove all the way back to Wellfleet in silence, and she left again immediately to drop off the props she'd found at the gallery. But when she came back to the apartment, she walked directly up to me, put her hands on the sides of my face, and kissed me as hard and long as she ever had, with her eyes closed. Then she cupped the back of my head and looked into my face with so much naked love and remorse that there wasn't anything to do but kiss her back.

CHAPTER 27

The MP called again," Titch said when I saw her a few days later. She was frowning at a collection of paintbrushes spread out in the breakfast area, some drying on towels on the floor. It smelled of turpentine, even though the sliding doors were pushed back so that she was surrounded on two sides by screens. She didn't sound as unfriendly as she had recently; she was totally immersed in the art project in front of her, speaking to me as though from a great distance.

"Did you tell him I was eaten by a great white shark?" I said, lightly, my stomach dropping. I had come to Truro for the afternoon, skipping the workshop, nursing a sunburn, and feeling very tired. I was hoping to be alone. Sarah's apartment had no bathtub and I had an idea about having a nice cool bath, maybe with baking soda in it—a recipe of my grandmother's for soothing just about any ailment in the summertime (hot milk with honey was her wintertime remedy). Sarah and I had napped on the beach at Duck Harbor the day before and I had a swath of itchy hot pink skin down my left side, where my shirt had slipped off while I slept.

"Don't be ridiculous," Titch said, not looking up, but still with no outright hostility. "That was Martha's Vineyard, not Cape Cod. Ripmip is no fool. I think you better call him back this time though. He sounded funny."

"*Technically*, cinematically speaking, it was Amity Island, and I don't know what he is, but he's something worse than a fool," I said.

"Yeah," she said. "You should call him though." She looked over, distracted, and then seemed to register me for a minute.

"You look terrible," she said bluntly.

It might have been an opening, but I didn't have the heart for talking. I pushed on through to my bedroom where I climbed onto the bed and lay there, shoes and all, staring up at the ceiling, getting sand on the bedspread, watching the shadows shape-shift.

He answered the phone as though he had been sitting beside it, waiting for it to ring.

"I did it," he said, "I quit my job."

"You what?"

"I wrote you. I wrote you I was going to."

I didn't remember reading this, but then, what had I actually read? I was silent.

"I bought a truck. I'm going to Alaska. "

"You're what?"

"Going to Alaska. I'm leaving tomorrow. That's why I've been calling. I wanted to talk to you before I left. I wanted to hear your voice. And I wanted you to know before I left."

"Does Mz. Hiller know?"

"This isn't about her."

I noticed he hadn't answered the question.

"Listen, I don't care if she goes." (This was not entirely true. I felt bad tempered the instant I said it. I wanted to thump him or kick him, jab him in the ribs with a sharp stick or stab a fork into his thigh. I wound the phone cord around my thumb until it turned white.)

He didn't say anything.

"You're joking, aren't you?"

"No. I handed in my letter of resignation."

"Really?"

"You told me you couldn't be here in school for your senior year if I was here too. And now I won't be."

I thought for a moment. I had said that.

I said, lamely, "But you were the Teacher of the Year."

He said nothing.

I tried again, still not believing him. "You're really quitting because I said to?"

"Absolutely. It's the right thing to do. I've rented out my place, packed up the truck, and I'm headed out."

"What are you going to do in Alaska?" I asked politely.

"Hike, see everything. I've always wanted to go." It was like talking to a stranger. Something was running underneath the conversation, something dark and cold. Or maybe I was just imagining Alaska, the thought of which made me shiver.

"Is Jason going to go with you?"

"No, he's got soccer camp. I don't have him in the summers anyway, remember? He's with his mother. His mother has him."

I knew that and had forgotten. He sounded weary, not as aggressive as he usually did on the subject of his ex-wife and the custody of his youngest son.

"What about a job? What are you going to do after Alaska?"

"I've applied to a number of good private schools to start either in the winter term or the following year."

He paused and then added, almost hopefully, "I won't be too far away." He said this as though it had something to do with me.

"I'm seeing someone," I blurted, but firmly, to set him straight somehow, to get him off my heels. "I'm in love."

He was quiet for a moment. Then, "That's great," he said, tenderly. He began to talk about how anyone who got to be with me—my future boyfriend or husband—was terribly lucky, that I was a gift, that he wished he could be that person but he knew that great love would come to me. He had gone down this road before, and I generally didn't listen while he was talking, which under other circumstances he would do while stroking my hand. He always managed to sound paternal and wistful all at once, which really creeped me out.

"Right," I said abruptly. "Well, it's a done deal now."

There was a long pause.

Then he said, a little quavery, "I know you can never love me as I love you," which made me cringe.

What is there to say to this? Who thinks it's a good idea to speak this way?

We sat in silence. Chester the cat pushed open the door to my room, sat down heavily on the braided rug, and began washing his white waterbed of a belly, vigorously, as if he had really let things go and needed to make up for lost time. He made small, reproachful, grooming growls, snatching at the fur with his teeth. His pink skin was shining through the fur.

"Okay then," I said eventually, attempting brightness and finality. "Have a safe trip."

The MP sighed and then cleared some phlegm from his throat. The noise was kind of disgusting, although I felt a little bad about being repulsed. Later I thought he might have been crying. But all he said then, after a minute, was, "Thank you."

I went out to find Titch, who was still squatting on the tile floor cleaning her brushes. Chester had joined her and was sprawled on the sunny tiles on his back now, all his legs spread out, underbelly completely exposed, in a vaguely obscene pose. I looked away from him.

"The MP is quitting," I said. "He's going to Alaska."

"Roger Peters is quitting teaching high school? For good?"

"He's leaving our neck of the woods anyway."

"Well, that's dramatic."

"I asked him to," I said, feeling a little sick. "I just didn't ever think he would actually do it."

She looked up at me, almost impressed. "No shit."

Later, in her basement, she would ask, with hesitation, "Did you really not care what happened with the MP?"

My head ached and I said, with difficulty, "It's not that I didn't care. I don't know. I thought I was out of it. I thought I was on to the thing that mattered."

"And now?" she asked.

"Now it seems really sad. Like maybe I should have known or something."

She rubbed her nose. "Yeah, I can see that," she said, finally.

CHAPTER 28

Sarah and I were both busy and preoccupied during the day, but we were spooned next to one another at night. I had pretty much recovered from the terrible visit to Hyannis, when, a few days later, over dinner out, I said, "What's the plan for the weekend?" and Sarah said, "Plan?" As if it were a word she had never heard before. As if I had invented it.

Then she said, "Oh right, sorry. I thought I'd go into the city and take care of some things. You have to be at work, right? And I have to meet with my agent on Sunday."

"She works on a Sunday?" I said, surprised, and just then, when I reached for the bill, she made an ugly face at me, sucking on her teeth, and I pulled my hand back. I felt like I'd been slapped.

We drove in silence toward Wellfleet until without warning she pulled right across Route 6 and turned down the Davidsons' sandy road.

I said, "Why are you taking me here?"

And she said, "Isn't that what we planned?"

"No," I said, taken aback, "we have no plan, remember?"

"Right," she said, smiling as though we were sharing a joke. But she kept right on driving through the undergrowth.

"Sarah?" I said. But she didn't answer.

She didn't talk to me again except to say, "Okay then, I'll call you," as she pulled up to the house.

I got out of the truck and shut the door, mechanically. I

watched her reverse, and drive away, the truck tires spitting gravel and sand. I felt a little stunned, a little fuzzy about the edges, a metallic humiliated taste in my mouth, almost as though I'd had too much to drink and gotten my signals crossed with a complete stranger.

When did you know? *Never. There was no moment that I knew.*
Also: *I could not have imagined it.*

I would have liked to talk to Titch about what was happening, but that wasn't possible anymore.

That same day that Sarah dropped me off in Truro so abruptly, I looked up late in the night and saw Titch standing in the doorway. The light was behind her so her face was in darkness. I realized that she was saying my name and I struggled to wake up. I thought for a disoriented moment that she had come to tell me something about one of the cats.

But it was nothing like that at all. Titch had to go home. Her mom's cancer had returned and she was going back into the hospital for surgery the very next day.

"Do you need a ride?" I asked, completely groggy. But she said no, tight-lipped. There was a cab coming to take her to the airport. She was leaving the car.

"Is Ruby going with you?"

"No. She's staying. I just talked to her. She'll come later if she needs to."

"Are you okay?" Saying this was a mistake. Her eyes welled for a moment and then the tears drained right back into their ducts and her pupils were dilated, hard black points.

"Are you coming back?" I asked, but she didn't say anything. She was as still and tense as a lightning rod. We sat in the living room in silence, punctuated only by the sound of Jack's claws shredding the couch.

"Don't forget about the plants or the birdseed," she said, finally, when the lights of the cab cut across the house, and, dragging her duffel bag after her, she went out into the night. She looked really small all of a sudden, walking away.

"Call me when you get there," I called after her, but she didn't turn around.

I told Sarah about Titch's mom and said, "It's just so sad, it's so wrong and sad." We were tucked into a sand dune on Ryder Beach the following evening, sitting on chilly, damp grey sand. I thought about how much I loved Lois with the waves of dark hair springing up from her forehead, and I could feel the drumbeat of dread in my pulse. But I was conscious too of being snug in my own well-being, unperturbed, of affecting sadness. I was so glad to have Sarah back after her strange departure the day before, to have so soon a pressing reason to cleave into her side, that I was almost light-headed with relief and gratitude.

Sarah said, lightly, kindly, "Grief comes to us all, Mary Margaret." Then she swung her knees over my outstretched legs and huddled in. We put our salty wet noses together like dogs. Her hair blew over me, stinging at the tips. There was no way not to feel safe and loved in that place. I asked for it, I wanted it, I gave over to it: the greatest state of grace I had ever known.

It felt like I should be at the Davidsons' more, now that Titch wasn't there full-time, and Sarah came over a few times, but she had to walk Biscuit, who couldn't visit because of the cats. And I knew she preferred staying at her apartment. I did too. Without Titch—and even though she hadn't really taken anything more than a suitcase of clothes with her—the Davidsons' house seemed both enlarged and empty, almost echoey. When I turned the television on for company, the reflection jumped in the glass door behind my bed. I had never noticed how much glass there was around the house, all the windows and skylights and the sliding glass doors I needed to lock in every room, all the ways to see into the house, its distressing exposure.

"Chester got out," I told Titch, when she called from home. Lois was still in the hospital.

I had watched him that morning, Chester the white cat, make a crazed lunge for a bird perched on the ledge of the porch. His full-body leap in the air made him look like a furry bungee jumper, the furious stretch, the hope and elation in it. My heart stretched its rubbery cord bounding up and out with him. I hoped he would take the bird, his first, maybe his only. He had slipped past my legs the day before, when I was standing with the sliding door open, staring into space, thinking about Sarah. Now I could not get him to come to the door of the house even with the promise of open cans of cat food.

"Good for him," Titch said tonelessly.

"I don't know if I can lure him back in," I said, mostly to keep talking. She didn't respond. "I'm kind of worried about him," I said. "Not to mention the Davidsons."

"It's your fault," she said eventually, "for taking him to the beach." But her heart wasn't in it.

I had forgotten. I had forgotten that the first weekend we came I insisted, as a lark, on taking Chester to the beach. He had never been out of the house before. We packed a picnic of cheese sandwiches and a little tuna fish for him, but he was too wretched to eat it and sat on the sand, tail lashing, trembling at the sight of the ocean.

"You gave him a taste for freedom," Titch added, sadly. "You know that right? You gave him a sense of a whole other world. He'll never know how to be happy indoors now."

"It's not looking good for Lois," my mother said, in her practical way, the following night. When I didn't say anything, she added, "I spoke with Randy. Lois is not responding well to the treatment. Some kind of secondary infection set in."

And: "You must be lonely out there without Titch."

It was lonely at the Davidsons'. I couldn't see how I could miss Titch since I hadn't been living with her, but it was strange in the house without her. After only two days the plants were listless, and Jack the cat was even more than usually on edge without Chester. He would walk back and forth in the kitchen, his nails clicking on the Mexican tiles, his tail twitching, his ears swiveling to and fro, crying incessantly. After I talked to my mother, I grabbed some clothes, fled the house, and drove to Sarah's.

"Is Lois going to make it?" Sarah asked, sympathetically, that night in bed, after I climbed in beside her. I couldn't really make sense of the question. The words bobbled in the air. My eyes swam.

But Lois wasn't the one who died. Instead I got another call.

here's been an accident," Titch said.

It was five o'clock in the afternoon, six days after Titch had gone home, the seventeenth of August, still hot out, the threat of thunderstorms hovering. There were only four days left of the workshop, we were deep in rehearsals. I was in Truro and I was running late. I was supposed to be meeting Sarah in Wellfleet for dinner before heading over to the rehearsal space. The sky rumbled ominously in the background just as Titch spoke. Her voice was uncharacteristically high and tremulous, piercing.

"Jason, Jason Peters, the MP's Jason was in an accident. He was in a really bad car accident, Nina. Amy Klein's mom hit him with her car at Ledyard Bridge and nobody knows where the MP is. Do you know? Because Jason was asking for his dad. When he woke up, he was asking. And Jason's mom doesn't know where his dad is. Nobody knows where the MP is. You've got to tell if you do. They have to find him. Amy's freaking out, her mom is sedated. Everyone is losing their minds here."

"Okay," I said, "okay."

I was shaking. I had just stepped out of the shower and my towel had slipped to my knees. I focused on pulling it back up and tucked the top in as firmly as I could. The phone fell off my shoulder onto the bed while I was doing this, but Titch never noticed because she was talking and talking. I could hear her muffled voice in the bedspread while I dug around in the pile of envelopes in the drawer by the bed and scrabbled through them. It smelled like singed hair in the room, like rank fear. My fingers were thick and stupid. I put the receiver back to my ear, but I couldn't focus on the post dates and the water from my hands and wet hair was making the letter paper pulpy and clumped together. Titch was talking nonstop, her voice dipping and shivering.

"He was swimming in the river, Jason, he was just swimming with Brian McNulty, and he just came up I guess and ran over the road to the boathouse, and Amy said that her mother just didn't see him at all until she ran right into him and he's been asking for his dad, when he was conscious he was asking for his dad and nobody could tell him anything and now he's back in the coma, but I thought you've got to know, right? I mean he told you, right?"

I had found the letter with the MP's itinerary, with numbers and dates lurching about on it. I gave Titch the motel numbers for the month. She repeated the numbers back urgently, snapping a little, like a manic operator, and started to say goodbye in a rush when I broke in.

"But, Titch, listen. Stop. *Titch*. This doesn't come from me, it can't come from me. Okay? This is important. I don't want it to come from me because why would I have this information? I can't be connected to him."

"Oh for Christ's sake, Nina," she burst out, "who cares? Jason could be dying. He's in a *coma*. He needs his dad. They don't know if he's ever going to wake up. What the hell is wrong with you? It's not always all about you."

Then with very deep hatred, nearly spitting, she said, *"Everything is not about you."* And she hung up, with a great bone-rattling bang.

I sat with the receiver between my knees until the buzzing came on that's so loud it broke through and then I put the receiver back in the cradle, super gently.

I did not think about Jason, about our long-ago one-time conversation on the bleachers, the blueness of his eyes, the sun illuminating the back of his intact head. I did not think about the impact of the car, the adrenaline that must have flooded Mrs. Klein's heart, the way she drove her foot down on the brake pedal when his shocked eyes locked with hers through the windshield. I did not think about the tires squealing or the sound of Jason's femur bone and pelvis snapping like dry tinder, his body bouncing to the pavement and then not moving. I did not think about Mrs. Klein stumbling out of her car, collapsing beside him on the road, her legs giving away; the terrible keening, the terrible silence.

I thought about Jason's voice, when it finally emerged, his wondering parched voice, asking for his father in the hospital. I thought about the MP finding out that Jason had asked for him, that he had asked for him when he woke up and that the MP had not been there, that the MP did not know that he was the one who was summoned, he was the one who was wanted.

I thought about calling the MP then and letting him know what had happened, except it seemed totally wrong for that news to come from me. It didn't seem like it had anything to do with me. I thought about how angry Titch was, how far away. And I was thinking about the MP far away too, somewhere out there in the Alaskan wilderness with his backpack on, eating his freeze-dried meals out of powder and water, not knowing, taking notes on the wildlife, looking at the birds through his binoculars, his son lying in a coma in the hospital, all the while not knowing. I was thinking about that precious, precious time before you know, before the piano falls from the sky on your head. Sitting on the edge of the bed, I held my breath and wished hard, I wished with all my might, that he was really happy right now, wherever he was, in his last minutes of not knowing.

Then I went in search of Sarah. She was at Luke's house, sitting at the kitchen table with a beer, peeling the label off the bottle and laughing. I saw her through the window first, and I stood there watching for a minute, feeling small and lost. It was getting dark and the birds were gathering in noisy clusters overhead, arguing, visiting, comparing notes on the day. Through the window, it seemed to me that Sarah was the source of all the heat and light in the room, that everything bright and inviting was emanating from her. It was chilly outside and my fingers were stiff. I thought, *I'll warm my hands by her.* When I came in nobody paused, the flow of talk continued unchecked. The Beatles were singing "Ticket to Ride." Luke gave me a giant affectionate smile, which bathed my heart. Then I slipped in beside Sarah on the high-backed bench and she curved into my side, not even looking in my direction, mid-conversation, threading her fingers through mine, miraculously anchoring me, shoring up my faltering self, the way she did that very first time and every other time she took my hand in hers. *Bravely and hand in hand.*

Jason didn't die, but he lost all movement from the waist down, which seemed almost worse somehow. I still think about him running across the green soccer field focused and keen in his white shorts, sweat on his forehead, serious and lovely, intent like only boys following a ball seem to be. I think about him more than I think about his father, if you want to know.

The MP never found out, because the MP was dead. It's possible that around the time I was wishing that his last few minutes would be undisturbed he might actually have been having his last few minutes. He never applied for any other jobs. He quit because someone threatened to turn him in. Not about me, although maybe in part because of the rumors about the girl before me. Or maybe he knew that was coming next. Mostly though, he had been embezzling money. (*What money? Embezzling from where?* Titch would say. *The teachers' retirement kitty? Madame Henderson's Montreal trip fund?*) He made it to Alaska and then he shot himself in the head. I kind of like to think it was on an ice floe, but the truth is that it happened in a ratty little motel room.

Titch called to tell me. I had spent the day struggling through our first run-through of *Three Sisters*, and there were a dizzying number of rehearsals and locations and people and lines and exits and entrances and props and cues to remember. She called the gallery to look for me, and then she called the main number during our dinner break. Ann found me outside and said there was a phone call. I was looking at scattered clusters of actors eating, lounging, talking, napping on the floor in the gallery, while Titch was telling me that the MP was dead, that he had killed himself. I felt the MP—who had never existed here in this space with these people, who I had cut loose, given the slip, who was supposed to be gone—I felt his death attempt to reassert his presence, to demand a place, to drag loss, and worse, into the room. I found myself carefully, methodically displacing what Titch was saying, picking up the ugly squarish package of it—like picking up a head itself on the stage, a prop piece decapitated head—and moving it to one side, to the wings. I did this so that the mountain of performance minutiae from the day—also my life— could stay center stage, could still take up its necessary active square footage in my head. I did this too so that the information could not attach itself to me, so that it had nothing to do with me.

I thanked Titch for calling; I said I had to go. Rehearsal was starting right back up, and I didn't say anything to anyone. I sat watching the fourth act, which I hadn't seen all the way through before, and in which I had nothing to do. Occasionally the thought—*the MP is dead, he killed himself*—would flicker past, but then my brain would kick in officiously, like a British policeman, a bobby swinging a nightstick saying briskly, *Move along, nothing to see here.*

I could never have imagined this ending for the MP. I was so sure of what I knew, but what did I know? *I could not have imagined it.* Tiny cold filaments of doubt crept through me. I tried to keep my attention captive to what was in the room at the moment.

Sarah was on book, sitting on a tall stool off to the side with one foot on the floor, and one foot hooked around a rung, mouthing along with the lines, her finger in the script, watching the actors. Periodically I would watch her watching the actors, but she was like a buoy bobbing hazily on the far horizon. I felt completely unconnected to her.

Everyone is hurtling forward on their own trajectories. You think it has something to do with you.

It might.

It probably doesn't.

I tried to focus on the actors, but I was equally removed from the story inexorably trudging forward in front of me. Except for one moment.

Geoffrey was playing Chebutykin, the old army captain, the old family friend who has known the sisters since birth, who was in love with their mother. I found myself drawn in by his generous anchoring presence, his openhearted tiredness and good humor. The girl who was playing Masha in this act asked him:

Did you love my mother?

And he said: *Very much.*

When Masha hesitated, Sarah prompted her next line: *Did she love you?*

Did she love you?

He paused.
That I can't remember.

That I can't remember. When he said that, I thought for a fleeting instant that I might cry, the way you sometimes think you might sneeze, but I waited, and it passed.

CHAPTER 30

O n top of everything else, the Davidsons had called to
say they were coming home early, they would be back
on Sunday, at which point I would have to be moved
out of their house.

"What are you going to do?" Titch asked me, soberly. I had
called to ask about sending her stuff and to follow up on the
plant situation, since I was afraid I had killed one of the spider
ferns. This was not long after the murky underwater conversation when she had called to tell me about the MP. I could tell
she thought I had called her back to talk about it. I could tell
she was waiting for me to react this time and when I didn't—I
still couldn't, it was like I had dipped into a well inside me
when she said *he's dead* and I had pulled up an empty
bucket—she and I had entered an even more alienated place
than before.

Now there were short questions and shorter answers.

"What about your mom?" Titch asked. "You know Kay
would be ecstatic to have you back."

"Yeah, I don't know. It's not like she came home for me," I
said, trying to cover the sliver of self-pity in my voice, "She
came home for her mother."

"How do you know that?" asked Titch, fighting irritation,
and, "Who cares? What does that matter anyway? She's home
now. Don't you want to spend some time with her?"

Too late I thought, *She's talking about Lois, she's thinking
about her mom, about not having enough time with her mom,*

but, "No," I had already blurted, and she said, "Well then you're a bigger idiot than I thought you were."

I was silent, realizing how she'd heard what I'd said, not knowing how to go back.

"What are you going to do then?" she asked again, curtly, after a pause.

"I don't know," I said, but I did know, I had the feeling of a plan forming underneath my rib cage, expanding. I would stay. I would stay with Sarah. I wouldn't go back. What was I going back to anyway? High school pettiness. My mother who was probably packing to leave for another continent right now. My grandmother. I did stop there. I thought about her wispy hair, the curve of her spine, the way she would pat my knee absently or squeak if I came up behind her suddenly. About the companionship of sitting together silently over early dinners of bread and butter sandwiches with the light fading, the warmth of the woodstove at our backs. But then I thought about how she could have that milky, otherworldly, patient look, that waiting for the spaceship *waiting to die* look, and, although this terrifying thought was unthinkable: I don't want to be there when she dies. I don't want to be alone with her when she dies. And I'll visit. Sarah will come with me. But Sarah was my home; Sarah was where I knew I wanted to be. *How are we going to live our lives? Bravely and hand in hand.* We could stay on the Cape and when it was time we would move to the city and she would go back to school and I would, what. Finish high school here, or in the city? And apply to colleges this fall? Or next year? Would I be allowed to do that? Here I paused again. But I clung to the burning light of Sarah at the middle of the thought, the absolute glowing certainty of her. The two of us together. *Coupled and inseparable.* The truth of it dazzled me. *You're my person.* And I thought, that's it. It's already done.

"I'm staying here," I said.

Titch paused.

"You can't," she said, sounding genuinely puzzled.

I didn't say anything. I felt like I could hear her tension crackling in the silence.

"Okay, what about school?" she said tightly. "You have to go to school. What about college? What about our applications? It's senior year, Nina."

"I know that. I'm only a semester away from enough credits to graduate. I can pick them up whenever," I said broadly, dismissively. I felt relieved and magnanimous. It was decided.

"Whenever? *Whenever?* What are you talking about?" Now Titch was getting really mad. She was snorting through her nose when she spoke.

But I didn't want to have the conversation anymore. I wanted to run to Sarah and tell her what I'd decided. I wanted to get out from under Titch and all her narrowness, her judgment, her thinking she knew me.

"I was going to do it anyway," I said, which I believed was true.

"What are you talking about?"

"I was going to New York with Sarah anyway after graduation."

Now it got dangerously quiet at Titch's end. Or maybe she was just shocked.

"She asked you?"

"Of course," I said, although actually we'd never talked about anything so specific. But if we were going to share our lives, what else would we do?

My mother called. "Is it true?" she asked, her voice stretched painfully tight.

I didn't say anything for a moment. Heat seized my scalp. I was terrified.

"Um," I started.

She hung up.

She called again. She was yelling and I immediately lost what she was saying as she was saying it, as though it went under a wave. Her anger was a huge, obliterating wall of noise. After several minutes she stopped yelling and began firing questions, which she clearly did not expect me to answer. The only difference was that her voice curved upward at the end. These I was mostly able to make out. Among them:

"How could you be so stupid?" "You were involved with this man?" "You know the police have called?" and, "What the hell were you thinking?"

"I can't come there right now to get you," she said eventually, in a pinched, determined, strangely self-righteous voice, "Because I have my hands full here. So you need to pull yourself together and we'll talk about this when you come home."

"I'm not coming home," I said. It was the first thing I'd said.

She started to laugh. She sounded genuinely, if crazily, amused.

"Listen," she said finally. "Listen, I don't know who this girl is, or what you think you are doing with her, but it's going to stop. I don't know what's going on with you, but you have school starting next month and you are coming home."

I couldn't speak. My throat was swollen shut. There was a dangerous pressure in my stomach, a vomiting pressure. I thought I might say things, I could feel them surging upward, I might say things we were careful not to say and I would not be able to take them back.

I did. I did say some of them.

"What about you?"

"What?" Her voice was soft and dangerous.

"You knew something was going on. You didn't even try to find out what it was. You knew I was lying to you when you came home, you said so to my face, but you didn't do anything. You're my *mother*. Aren't you supposed to do something?"

"You think the mess you've made here is my fault? Is that really what you want to say to me right now? You're old enough to be responsible for your own actions and you know it. What is going on with you? What in God's name is this about?"

"It's about my life. And I'm not coming home. I'm staying here."

"Where? On Cape Cod? Doing what exactly? Where are you going to live? What are you going to live on? Who do you think is paying for what you're doing right now?"

"I can get a job, I have a job."

"You don't have a *job*. That's not a job. You think this girl, whoever she is, you think she is going to support you? You're going to college, Nina. You have plans"—for a moment she sounded completely bewildered, unmoored, almost, distressingly, compassionate—"you've always had plans. Something's wrong, something's happened to you. None of this makes any sense."

"Well, obviously something's happened to me but you don't care about that. I don't think you've ever cared about that. You've never paid any attention to what's happening in my life."

That turned her right back around, although now her anger was shot through even more violently with incredulity and sarcasm, like this was all some kind of colossally bad joke.

"Oh, you want attention? Is this really how you would go about getting my attention? Well, good work, because you have it. And not just mine. Everyone's paying attention. The *police* are paying attention. The neighbors are paying attention. The whole *town* is paying attention. You must be very pleased."

She exhaled through her nose hard. My heartbeat was deafening.

"I haven't said anything to your grandmother," she said after a moment. "Not that she necessarily understands what

I'm saying to her anyway, I mean who knows I can't tell. But. I haven't said anything. She doesn't need to know any of this. She would be so disappointed in you. She would be crushed. I don't even think she would believe anything I told her about what you've been up to."

I couldn't speak. My mind was full of my grandmother's hands, the bumps and ridges, the hardened raised topographical map of veins, the way her palms were partly permanently cupped, more like paws than hands.

"You need to come home now," my mother said again, and this time her voice was tired.

"Are you even going to be there?" I asked, finally, nastily.

"Where else would I be?" she snapped. And then, weary, "Yes. I'm here for the foreseeable future."

When she hung up, I sat for a while. I realized I was gripping the phone fiercely on my lap. My fingers were so clenched they had begun to tremble. The shocked pulsing in my ears subsided. In its place was a gathering rage. I had to stab at the receiver and missed dialing the numbers a few times when my index finger buckled.

"How does she know that? Titch? How does she know?"

There was a very long pause, which told me what I needed to know, what I already knew.

"You told my mother. You told my *mother*?"

"No, I told Amy and she told her mom. I guess Amy's mom called your mother."

"You told *Amy Klein* about the MP? Everyone will know." She was silent. She knew it was true.

I was assailed by the smell of the harsh cleaning solvents in the claustrophobic carpet in the high school, the sensation of the institutional grey-flecked fibers flying upward toward my face as though I were falling. I saw the walls tilting in, the turning heads, the whispering.

"Titch," I said, hissing through my teeth. "How could you do that? How could you do that to me? And you told my mother about *Sarah*? What the hell is wrong with you? How could you tell her about Sarah? Why would you do that to me?"

"I'm sorry," she said eventually. "I wasn't thinking. Or I was mad. I don't know."

"I don't trust her," she said then suddenly, vehemently. "I don't know what's happened to you since Sarah came, I don't know who you are."

"Don't talk to me, don't talk to me *ever again*," I said violently and hung up. Then I burst into ragged noisy sobs. My cheeks were purple and swollen with effort and my scalp was burning hot. There was snot all over.

I had to go right to rehearsal, I was already late, and I wanted to catch Sarah, but everyone had gathered and the first scene of the second act was under way. Of course Sarah could tell something was wrong as soon as I walked into the room; she raised her eyebrows at me but I just shook my head. I sat looking around at everyone in the room, everyone going through their motions, everyone I had spent so much time with, thinking, *None of these people know me. None of these people know anything about my life.* It was not disturbing, only insistent and starkly true.

On break from the dress rehearsal, at the intermission, I huddled with Sarah in the stairwell of the art gallery, which smelled like rotting seaweed and bleach.

I said, "I'm not going home, I can't go home, I'm staying here with you."

Also (although I did not say this): I don't know where else to go. I don't know what else to do. And: *I cannot be out of your company.*

Sarah just stroked my hair methodically and didn't say anything until I stopped crying.

"It will work itself out," she said. "It will."

"We've got to go back in," she said, finally, not unkindly. She kissed the top of my head and stood up. "I've got to go back in at least. I can tell them you're not well, if you want," she offered, gazing down at me. But I followed her. Where else was I going to go?

"You're not very cheerful today, Masha," Shisha said when she walked up to me inside the gallery the following morning.

"Yeah," I said, unable to hold up my end by saying my lines in return.

"Wrong play," she said, grinning, "If it is a play. What's going on? Moscow got you down? Some trouble in paradise?"

"I can't talk about it." She sized me up.

"I really can't."

"Okay, come on. Quick trip to the pier."

We left the other students behind, everyone mingling and swapping notes from the rehearsal the night before, and slipped outside. She put her arm through mine, and listened.

I was jumpy and spent at the same time. By the time we had gotten home the night before, Sarah had gone instantly to sleep on her back in the bed, without even brushing her teeth, one arm flung up and over her face. But I couldn't sleep. I had sat on the wooden stairs that led down to the driveway and waited in the inky black for what seemed like hours, until I was stiff and cold. I don't know what I was waiting for, but I couldn't quiet my head.

"I did not see that coming," Shisha said. "Dark horse."

"But you can see that I can't go back home, right? Everyone knows everything now."

We sat in meditative silence for a moment. A seagull shrieked.

Then, "You're like a lesbian Lolita," she said and snorted her deep contagious snorting giggle. A weight took wing and flew off my chest. I got my airway back. I howled, she snorted and wheezed. We scared the hell out of the birds.

"I do know something about standing out," she added a while later. "Hello. Black girl from Oklahoma."

She said, "You're going to stay here then? For the rest of the summer?"

"Or longer," I said, bracing myself for her response. But she just smiled at me. "I hope you're happy," she said. "You're a funny one." She looked out across the water for a minute. "If you've got people who love you, you should go to them. They're going to get over it. But," she added, "if you wind up going to New York, with that one or without her, you should look me up."

I looked at her, wiping my nose on the back of my hand.

"Yeah, I'm moving there."

"Is Judith going too?"

But Shisha just smiled again in her lopsided, unrevealing way and shrugged, her large hands palm up to the sky. She stood up and brushed her bottom off.

"You be good now, you hear?" she said, so I said, Okay. I said thanks.

"It's been a pleasure," she said and snorted again.

Chapter 31

The final show of *Three Sisters* that Friday night did not feel like the culmination of the summer's work. It came and went very fast. That evening was like being trapped inside a kaleidoscope, the lights and whirling colors and dizzying speed of everything. The show itself was an awkward patchwork of scenes, with a handful of gorgeous moments and a lot of ragged ends. It hardly mattered anymore, whether the work we did was good or bad or indifferent, it had been suffused and surpassed by everything else going on for everyone—the emotions of the end of the summer and the pull between being present and preparing to leave, all these people dispersing to their other lives. For me the total uncertainty, the brand-spanking newness of whatever was coming now, right now, made me feel like I was holding very still at the center of a storm.

Some people's families came to watch the final performance, and like at graduations, their presence heightened the oddness, the distance between what we thought we knew of each other and other, maybe realer possibilities. There was too much beer, too much food, too much praise. Most people spent a lot of time hugging tearfully, even businesslike little Ann. Bill McNeil of course did not tear up, but even he made an appearance at the cast party after the performance of *Three Sisters*. Everyone stayed up until dawn that night and then packed, hungover. Sarah had to miss the party because she was heading into New York for the television pilot workshop that

began the next day. But I was glad in a funny way to be just
with everyone else, to go down to the beach before dawn with
all of Group 6 and some others, to put our feet in the water,
and make all kinds of promises about staying in touch that
probably no one would keep.

It was a relief too when everyone finally drove or bussed
away and quiet descended. The Thursday before I had cleaned
out bags of trash from the Davidsons', and Luke had finally
coaxed Chester back inside, where he sat dejectedly, watching
the birds busy at the feeders and watching me leave. I took my
stuff and moved into the apartment in Wellfleet for almost one
whole perfect month.

Sarah was going back and forth to New York a lot, between
the pilot workshop and various auditions, and sorting out her
status at Tisch, where she thought she might return for school,
maybe even in the spring semester. She seemed apprehensive
about work, although I told her time and again I was sure it
was going to be fine. I was so happy in the apartment, waiting
for her, walking on the beach, visiting with the guys. Luke had
a habit of walking out of his small house, standing in the yard
between his house and the apartments, and shouting up some
piece of information he thought we all might want to know,
like a town crier—*Interview with Al Pacino on NPR! Putting
on spaghetti for dinner, come and get it in ten minutes!*—and
then walking back into his house and letting the screen door
whine and slam behind him. I cooked and read and picked up
hours at work, which was easy to do because the season on the
Cape extended fully through Columbus Day. Eddy was happy
to have me and he said there would be other opportunities
through the winter if I wanted them.

The first day of senior year came and went. It was odd that
morning, disorienting, thinking about what was happening
there and about all those people, but I felt overwhelming relief
about not being there too. And it did feel like another life, not

mine, not for now. I had called my mother and left her the phone number at Sarah's so she could reach me if she needed to, but I hadn't talked to her and she didn't call. She wrote a short letter instead, with bits of news about the farm. She wrote that she expected me to come home when I was ready. The likelihood of this seemed remote, but I wasn't angry anymore. Now that I was really here—really living with Sarah—I felt safely over some hurdle.

Biscuit stayed mostly with Luke at his place, but when I wanted to play with her, I would whistle and she would come bounding out for a walk. She was excellent company. Except the last weekend in September when Sarah took Biscuit with her. She said Dan, her New York roommate, wanted to visit with her.

I was sitting in the kitchen when Sarah called.

That morning when I woke up, I thought, *Thank goodness I'll see Sarah tonight.* Thank goodness she is coming home tonight. I spent the whole day in happy preparation, cleaning up and shopping. I made vegetable soup and baked two loaves of whole wheat bread from the Tassajara bread book, licking the brown sugar and yeast and the sticky clumps of dough off my fingers. I was really happy in my last minutes of not knowing. It's painful to think about how happy I was, but there it is.

I thought dumb, happy, lazy, domestic thoughts.

I thought, *We need a proper breadboard.*

I thought, *Maybe I will scrub the bathtub. But it doesn't really need it yet.*

I thought, *I should get myself a pair of red union suit pajamas like Sarah's,* which I was wearing. Then I thought, *I don't need to, because I can always wear hers.*

When Sarah called, I was sitting at the table reading an old *New Yorker,* wearing her pajamas, and eating fresh bread with plenty of butter, one foot folded up under my bottom on the chair. Before I could say anything, she spoke, in a tone I had never heard, a measured, tender, regretful, terrible tone.

"Listen," she said, and all the books fell off the shelves. All the birds fell out of the sky.

"Listen," she said again while I sat transfixed with everything hurtling violently down around me. There was a powerful smell of sulfur, making it hard to breathe. My heart shrank to the size of a pin. Everything was electrified, dangerous, like before a huge thunderstorm. I thought to myself confusedly, *Whatever you do, don't touch the wire.*

"The thing is," she said. "The thing is I'm going to move back to New York."

She exhaled a hard breath. "I'm moving in with Marg."

"Marg?" I said. "Who's Marg?"

I think that's what I said. I might have said, "Marg who?" There was a deafening pounding in my head like hail hitting the roof of a car.

"Marg Hawthorne," she said softly.

"Marg Hawthorne?" I repeated. I couldn't remember who this was for a moment.

Then I remembered her in class. I heard her voice say meaningfully, *Raise the stakes. Raise the stakes.* I strung together what I knew on a very short string. Marg Hawthorne was a middle-aged casting director who lived in New York. Marg Hawthorne had the pouchy, soft cheeks of someone's mother. Marg Hawthorne had suggested Sarah audition for the pilot workshop in New York. Nicky had said, *It's a big deal if she likes you, she's very well connected.*

Marg Hawthorne had been kind to me. *She had been kind to me.* This last stung up and down, like nettles, and I broke out in a rash.

"What are you talking about?" I said to Sarah.

"I'm telling you what's happening because it's important that you know," she said gently.

Her gentleness cracked me wide open with molten rage and fear.

"I'm in love with her," she said.

"You can't be," I said, shaking, furious, certain, and desperate all at once, a disemboweled madman under torrential heavens, *"you're for me."*

I thought that was the final word on the subject. I didn't know there was any other response to *you're for me* except *yes, I am.* I thought those were the magic words that woke her from whatever strange spell she was under. They had been magic words, but now they were drained suddenly, completely, and forever of all their power. And so were we. It's hard when you don't know something's irrevocable until it is.

After that conversation, we didn't speak again. So it was the final word on the subject, but not in any way I could have imagined.

When we got off the phone that night in September, I didn't move until late the following day. I was running a fever. All night I thought she would have to appear, she would be coming in the door at any minute, *now*, right now. Or *now*. I calculated the driving time slowly, excruciatingly, repeatedly. The time to walk to the parked truck, the drive, eyes glazed, strained, determined, out of the city, the bad radio stations, the cold coffee, the relentless street lights boring into her skull, the need to get to me, my need pulling her out of New York, through Rhode Island, around the roundabouts, over the bridge, the lights flashing yellow all night long, Route 6, the first salt air coming in through the windows, the one-lane traffic, passing by Orleans, turning left at PJ's, in the long cool whispering night, the car whistling over the gravel pulling onto the oyster shells in the driveway, the door closing, her feet coming up the steps, running up the steps, she would come running up the steps, she was running up the steps, I could hear it: she was coming. All night long I was still sure.

Or the phone would ring and she would say, *Oh my love, I didn't mean it.*

Any minute. There would be her voice. The voice I knew. Any minute.

Oh my love. I'm for you. Oh my love.

That night was longer than all the nighttimes in my life put together. I was delusional, heartsick, crashing into things, shivering from fever, lost. I couldn't stop thinking about how I had no place to go. All night long I thought, *She will come,* she will throw me a lifeline, she won't leave me here in the wilderness. (*Mine enemy's dog, though he had bit me, should have stood that night against my fire.*) I got up at some point to go to the bathroom, tried to look into the mirror over the sink, and didn't recognize myself. (*Was this a face?*) I tried to pour a glass of water but my hands were shaking too hard and I fell over sideways, banging my hip hard on the toilet lid. I couldn't see any point in moving, so I lay face planted on the bathroom mat for the rest of that long darkness. I could feel the pulse in my neck on the floor. It beat out words to me, tunelessly like robotic Morse code. Some diction exercises. *Red leather yellow leather*, for instance. *Toy boat, toy boat, toy boat.* But also, *Make it stop, make it stop.* And *please please please please.* And of course the permanent scalding one-two call and response of my heartbeat, *I'm in love with her, You can't be, I'm in love with her, You can't be, I'm in love with her, You can't be.* Call and response, a game we liked to play.

I was there all the rest of the next day until about 5 o'clock. I went out then, finally, in a haze, unwashed, stumbling around in the twilight. I wound up sitting on the steps of the town hall with the kids playing on their skateboards whisking along the middle of Main Street. They made me feel about a hundred years old. The town seemed deserted, filled with strangers, now that all the other actors had left for their own homes. I couldn't face talking to Luke yet, or anyone who actually knew me, but I thought the darkness closing in again might swallow me whole. I was a little terrified. I was having some trouble breathing and my neck and hip hurt. Eventually, I found my way to Eddy, and he sat with me on the steps of the pier and smoked and listened.

"She's hustling," Eddy said after I told him. He said this not meanly, but as though it was a known truth.

"She says she's in love," I said. I was curled over like a sick field mouse, my head drooping pathetically between my knees.

"Well, she's not in love. Some people are like that," he said. "Some people are parasites. Some people stand on their own two feet. But she doesn't. She never has and she never will. She's hustling."

"But she told me she's in love."

"Everyone needs to survive," Eddy said patiently.

He ground out his cigarette on the concrete and looked at me kindly.

"You too," he said. "You too."

"And you," I said, hopefully.

He continued to look at me kindly, without wavering, but something—dismay, bleakness—crept in around the edges.

Luke said I was welcome to stay as long as I liked. I didn't go to find him, but five days after the phone call, I saw his shadow outside the screen door and I went over in my pajamas and stood on the other side of the screen, my head hanging down from something—the double-barreled weight of humiliation and sadness. I reeked of dried sweat, despair, unwashed cotton, and sticky grief. I could tell he knew. I hated that Sarah had told him. Then I thought for one wild surging hopeful minute that maybe he was checking up on me because she'd called to say she was worried if I was okay. That was not the case. It would never be the case. But I asked anyway, trembling like a fool, which made his sweet face crumple with reluctance. *No, she didn't ask about you.* I could tell already that it would take me an ungodly long time to learn not to ask if she had, not to force people to disappoint me. I could not stop trying to find any opening to say her name, to plead for recognition, to beg for any scrap of her, to nose out any invisible crumb of hope on the floor. That morning Luke jammed his hands in his pockets helplessly and said, *Look, why don't you come on over for blueberry muffins.* So I put on my jeans, carried my battered shamed heart next door, and took what I could get. They were good muffins.

Three days later, after I had wobbled back to work and tried to act like a normal person, I came home to find that all of Sarah's things were gone. When I walked in the door, I saw her old gardening hat had been taken off the hook on the wall. My breathing accelerated and I crisscrossed the apartment, hunting in every corner like a dog. I thought maybe she'd been there; I thought I could smell her in the air; I thought there would be a note; I thought there had to be something, some evidence, something other than even more absence and removal. Finally I dropped down on the kitchen chair, just slammed by dizziness and sadness. Her shirts were gone from the drawer, even her pillow from the bed. How could she look at the bed and not remember? Did she know I would be out? Could she have looked at me and still walked away? How could something and someone vanish so fast?

But it was Luke who had come to collect her things—the very little she had left behind. Sarah had asked Luke to come pick up her things and send them to her. Out of some respect or embarrassment, he did this when I was at work so in that moment when I got home, I was sent reeling from a sensation of seismic shuddering deep underground, a tectonic and molecular rearrangement. Something was being taken, piece by piece, an edifice being demolished. There was so little to collect that anyone else walking in would not have seen the difference, but to me the sink had been wrenched out of the wall, the floorboards ripped up, the furniture overturned, the walls pulled down. Again.

Every day that Sarah made no effort to reach me, to take back what she said, to take me back, even to hear my voice, to know if I was still alive or okay, every single one of those blank days opened my chest—a flap of skin that turns out to be as easy to push aside as a curtain—to reveal the wound, the cavity, the loss in red, like an angry stupid painful wet mouth throbbing gaping *gaping* in dumb astonishment that she has done this, is doing this. Every day, one after another, she made no effort.

Every day I tried to lay a poultice around the edges, to smooth it and hold my heart in place, cup the cavity. I would actually lay my hands down on my chest on my bare skin and say, *You are still here, your heart is still in your body there are so many things, maybe everything that she can't take away from you.* But I didn't believe it. I would think only *I want my heart back I want back everything she's taken from me* and just like that I would be shredded again, undone. Every day I tried to stitch this dumb wound up it would pop open, sometimes just leaking around the seams, sometimes totally ripped apart, running, squelchy, raw. These long, horrifying, gutted days kept piling up, one after another, a heap of days, flat as pancakes.

I bet on the wrong horse. I put all my eggs in one basket. My grandmother couldn't have said enough about what a bad idea that was. She couldn't have said anything that would ever have persuaded me not to do it.

When I was younger, starting right after my father left, I used to do a lot of checking to try and catch myself off guard, to test what the real state of things was, to see if I was okay, and to see if I was prepared for the unimaginable. For example, I had a game in which I'd be walking along a busy street and if a truck began lumbering up behind me and I could feel it bearing down on me, I'd pretend that it was going to swerve off the road and hit me *boom* and I'd be dead and then I'd ask myself urgently would that be okay? Would it be okay if right now *right this instant* with no warning I was run over? Was I ready? Did I have regrets? Were there things I wished I'd said or done before I died? And I'd wait to see what the response was that leapt up in my head as the truck went roaring by and the pins and needles in my feet settled. Usually I thought it was a bad idea to die and sometimes I'd even have jolted articulate feelings about why, but mostly my subconscious was unmoved and my brain became deliberately insultingly slow to respond. It was about as effective as trying to hit yourself in the knee with one of those reflex hammers, or attempting to tickle yourself.

What I didn't know then was that the trick of conjuring the fear of impact from a truck was also about the fear of colliding with another person, someone who had mattered to me. For a long time I envisioned the scene of meeting my father again, inventing where and how that would happen. I pictured it when I was bored or sorry for myself. But this is different, and incalculably worse, because I know Sarah, I chose Sarah. The thing is, losing someone you love can be worse than having that person outright die because you always know—I will always know—she is out there, living, carrying on in her life, day to day, place to place, and I can't believe that having collided once, with the force that we did, that we aren't on a collision course even now, that in some magnetized way we won't eventually have to be pulled together again. So my childhood make-believe has become thinking *what will it be like when I see Sarah*, when she crosses my path, when I accidentally turn a corner, *boom*, and there she is? Who will she be with and what will she look like? What will I do or say? Will I be ready?

Is it possible for me to be ready, to suit up, for this moment? Is there enough armor in the world? That anticipation is the equivalent of trying to prepare for the trauma of being mowed down by a truck. Incomprehensibly, painfully, relentlessly, I can't stop looking for the crash and dreading it all at once.

All the while I can't stop asking the same stupid question again and again, which amounts to this: how do you solve a problem like Sarah? I have asked anyone who would talk to me. I have asked people who didn't know me. I have asked people who were sick of talking to me. I have particularly asked people who were sick of talking to me but would still talk to me. *How do you solve a problem like Sarah?* And as far as I can tell the answer is: you don't. Eventually you drop it like a hot potato, like nothing you want to lug around for another ever-loving minute; you cut loose its gnawing tether and let it sink into the ocean abyss; you let it sail up over the rooftops like the red balloon until this time it pops and you watch it explode, satisfyingly; its wings of wax melt by the sun and you think loudly, *Well, thank god for that*! All I have wanted finally was to get that monkey off my back, that sand out of my craw, that stitch out of my side; to obliterate that stabbing migraine pain behind my left eye that brought me to my knees like a downed wrestler begging *begging* for some moment when everything wasn't bubbling poison in the blood.

I said out loud, under my breath, howling, in the car, in the pillow, in the bright sun, in the company of friends, alone, and even once horrifyingly in a crowded bagel shop, flat out loud: *Make it stop, make it stop make it stop make it stop, please make it stop*, like a mantra, as though saying it would make it true. As though all those people that day waiting in line to pay for their bags of bagels in Orleans—all frozen or turning to look at me so that I realized suddenly that I was crying out loud, that I was begging the very air for help, that I had crossed some line of containment, that I was out of bounds, out of line, out of control—as though all those regular people going about their regular days could do anything other than simply recoil, or feel grateful, deep in their bowels, that they were not at that moment in an uncontrolled grip of despair.

It used to be that someone else's misfortune was always an accident I was driving by on the highway too, something to stare at from behind the safety of sealed car windows, until the day that it's you standing on the hard concrete with messy unreality in front of you, the cold wind, the curious uncaring eyes rolling past. *Grief comes to us all, Mary Margaret.*

No one can do anything about this. Because there's no comprehending this feeling, there's no *solving* her, there's only knowing that someday the claws of this will have to retract a little, and someday sometime long after that, sometime in my life, someday, she will finally *finally* be dead and gone, deadweight released.

My mother sent me a second letter, and then a third. She did not know what had happened with Sarah. She did not mention my coming home or the beginning of the school year, but in the third letter she did mention that my grandmother had been to see her doctor. I picked up the phone and called.

"Can I talk to her?" I asked.

"Yes, of course, but she's not going to be able to hear you."

"She's not wearing her hearing aids?"

"No. I bought her new ones and she stored them in the refrigerator. I think it's safe to say that she doesn't have any plans to wear them ever again."

"Well, would you put her on the phone for just a minute anyway?"

There was short rustle and then I heard the wrenchingly lovely sound of my grandmother's emphysema breathing.

"Hello, Gamma," I whispered. Since she couldn't hear me anyway, whispering somehow seemed like the right thing to do.

Besides it was all I was capable of suddenly. "It's Nina. I just want you to know that I know running away never solved anything. Also, I miss you." I paused. "Also, you were right about everything."

I stopped again for a moment, listening. "Also, Gamma, I promise I am going to come home to see you as soon as I can. I'm working on it."

There was no change in her breathing, but I felt better.

Then my grandmother coughed and said, "Nina? Is that you, Nina?" Her voice was scratchy, but not weak. She coughed again.

I shouted, "Yes! Yes, it's me."

"It is I," she corrected me.

"It is I."

"Well. It's a real pleasure to hear your voice, lambie. I'm going to hand you back to your mother now, alright?"

"Okay!" I waited but couldn't hear anything. "Mom?"

"I'm here."

We were quiet.

"Is she going to die?"

"We're all going to die," my mother said. She heaved a short impatient sigh. "Doctor Mueller says she's as strong as a horse. She didn't say your grandmother is as stubborn as a mule, but that would have been an even more accurate assessment. So yes, she could live another twenty years or she could die tomorrow, like anyone. I think it's going to be awhile." There was a pause. "Either way, she could use your company."

"Sarah left," I said. "I don't think she's coming back."

My mother breathed a very long slow even breath.

"Well," she said. There was another even longer pause, during which I steeled myself against her pity and desperately hoped for it at the same time.

"Well," she said again. "We could both use your company."

"How am I going to live my life?" I asked Luke once after Sarah was gone. He just smiled at me and shrugged. "How does anyone?" he asked. Which was not what I wanted to hear.

About a month and a half after the last conversation with Sarah, on one overcast unseasonably cold late fall day, I went outside to empty the compost bowl, and all of a sudden the sun revealed itself. I closed my eyes hard, my face bathed in that warmth, until there were purple and black spiky crystals on the backs of my eyelids, and for a tiny, fleeting instant in the sunshine I wanted to stretch my toes in delight and my skin was warmed, alive. I thought about my mother, her worry and her anger, her finally being home and maybe even staying, and about my grandmother, her kind, gnarled hands, and about the farm, about the smells and sounds. That's not where I went first though.

Chapter 32

Wh hen I pulled into Titch's driveway, it was four
o'clock in the afternoon. Her house looked the way
it had always looked, with its modern shape, like
three stacked wooden blocks, two on the bottom, one over-
hanging on top. Everything was misted over, dampness dripping from the hemlocks that draped over the gravel. I almost
drove right around the circle in front and headed back out
again, but I didn't. I was so beaten, and tired and stiff from the
driving, that I pretty much limped to her doorway. I saw her
from the chest up through the window, moving about at the
kitchen counter, about three seconds before she saw me. She
was feeding the golden retrievers, standing at the sink adding
hot water to the kibble in their shiny metal dishes. My heart
was sputtering with anxiety, my stomach a hard knob of
despair. She blinked when she saw me, turned her back to put
the dishes down, and disappeared.

"Does anyone know you're back?" Titch asked. She didn't
seem surprised to see me but she didn't move toward me
either, just stood there holding the door, her right foot drawn
up slightly and pressed against her left calf, like a stork, or a
ballerina at rest.

"No." We looked at each other and then at the same instant
we squinted and looked away. "Can I come in?" I asked
abruptly. My teeth felt gritty.

She didn't say anything, just looked at me.

"How's your mom?" I asked.

There was a silence. She was staring stonily at the bridge of my nose. She looked skinnier even than usual, shrunken up in her clothes, her wrists spiny, her fingers all bone gripping the door. There were big purple loops under her eyes. The part in her hair, where a winding path of scalp showed, looked strangely vulnerable. Behind her in the hall I could see the outline of what might have been an oxygen tank, a looming metal canister on wheels, coils of plastic tubing, medical, forbidding.

"I know I should have come," I started to say. I wanted to say something about letting her down, about her mom, about how I knew I had abandoned her, about how I knew she had been all alone and afraid this past month and I had left her there, about how Sarah had abandoned me, about the whole summer and everything that had come before, but there was a giant jagged glittery rock in my throat. I was choked and stripped and so sad I thought I might topple over. *If she be traitor, why so am I.*

"Okay," I said finally, helplessly, instead. I couldn't swallow. One of the dogs, done with dinner, stuck its muzzle around her thigh and looked out at me with passing interest.

"She's at the hospital," Titch said at last, not giving an inch.

"But she's okay? I mean she's going to be okay?"

"For now," she said and turned away, and then over her shoulder she added, "Come around to the basement."

When I didn't move, she said, "I'll meet you down there," and closed the door.

I went around the side of the house and let myself in the sliding doors to the basement. It smelled moldy and familiar. I could hear the pounding of some music on the rock station in the room above us. I heard Titch yell something and a lower voice responding. In a couple of minutes she came thudding down the carpeted stairs.

"It's just Randy," she said when she came into the room,

dismissing her stepfather. We looked at each other again and finally she said, "Does anyone know you're here?"

"No."

"When did you get back?"

"Right now."

"Are you going back to school?"

"I don't know."

"Are you going to New York?" (This, carefully, not looking at me.)

"I don't think so."

"Are you going to stay?"

"I don't know."

She made a face, pulling the corner of her lip up, and then rubbed her nose with her right index knuckle violently, making the cartilage squeak. It was a familiar gesture. I watched her.

"I was doing some homework," she said, finally. I waited. She grimaced up at the ceiling, in the direction of the water stains over my head. "I guess you can hang out here for right now. If you want."

"You're a complicated animal," I said, so relieved suddenly that I thought I might throw up right there on the shag carpet with its damp curling edges.

"Yes," Titch said, flatly, unforgiving, "but I'm worth it."

How many times can one person break your heart?

Sarah would send me a note eventually, from New York, where she was living with Marg Hawthorne. In the note she said that she would be in love with me forever.

All my life, I will not know what that could possibly mean. You are either hand in hand, or you are not.

She was on my side. *Whatever I'm for.* And then she wasn't. *I'm for you.*

That's betrayal, however you slice it, whatever else you can say.

That Sarah doesn't want or need me or care, that she didn't choose me, is like having a long thin sword in my chest. Like a good two feet of flat skinny blade sticking out of my chest, so that movement—just walking or standing up even—makes that protruding blade twang and reverberate through my heart and all the way through my guts. Eventually I'm sure I'll adjust to it, I'll move around with the unconscious knowledge that I'm carrying a thin sword in my chest. But now, I can be going along and forget that I am stuck with this blade and then I turn and *thwack* it will hit something hard and *boing boing* there are shudders on shudders on heartache, all my muscles shocked, jumping, jangled.

"I've been thinking about how hard it was for you when your dad left," my mother said to me when I called and told her I was planning to leave the Cape. She didn't directly address the question of where I was going, or say anything about Sarah—in fact I don't think she ever said Sarah's name—but she was speaking to me more easily now.

"It was so sad for you when he left. You missed your dad," she said, "of course you did. You have probably been feeling that loss all this time, carrying it around with you."

Without thinking I said, "No, *you* were sad because he left, you were sad about him, but I mean I didn't really miss him. How could I miss him? I didn't even really know him. But I missed you then. I was sad about you."

She was quiet.

"I think Mother is a little better," she said, finally. "She's been out walking with me in the woods, and she's keeping close watch on the birds. You were right about the Jello. She eats custard too, which is even better because of the eggs.

I'm not very good at making it, but she doesn't seem to mind. She seems to want a lot of sweet things, which is funny, because she never liked sugar before. But why shouldn't she have it?"

"Yeah," I said, "it's not like she has her own teeth to worry about anymore."

"You have given my parents a lot of joy," my mother said, ignoring this. She spoke more firmly now, her voice back underneath her. "I think you have given them a focus and an outlet and tremendous joy. I didn't have that relationship with them. We had a harder time. So without you, you know, they would never have had that. You anchored my father, even when he was drifting away. He loved you so much, I think he stayed himself and I even think he stayed here as long as he could for you. And I think it must have been such a relief for him that you did not expect him to be anyone other than who he was—you did not *want* him to be anyone other than who he was—even at the end. You have been a great gift to them."

I had hot tears pooling in my eye sockets. I sniffed loudly, before I could stop myself.

"I have talked to your teachers," she went on. "You know you only have a semester's worth of credits left and they say you can finish them in the spring if you want to. Or even next year. Although I think you might just want to get back in there and get it over with. Everything that's happened this year will be old news before you know it, it will all die down. It's the nature of a small town like this one; there's always someone else to gossip about. And, Nina, once you are done with school, you are done. I know it feels like a circle of hell, but once you are out, you are out, and you never have to go back. You should graduate this year, get on out into the world. You've worked hard for this, and you need to go to college sooner or later. Go sooner. You don't want to throw it away.

And listen, I can tell you, I can *promise* you, that some endings really are only for the best."

For an instant she sounded almost a little forlorn. Something in her voice made me remember that she had been in the same high school, that she had also lost my father and her father, and that there must be other endings too about which I knew nothing.

We were silent for a while, but it was a good kind of silence.

"I would have killed that teacher if he hadn't done it himself," she said finally, thoughtfully. And it made me laugh out loud, without my meaning to at all.

"Or at least kicked his ass," I said.

"Or at least kicked his ass," she agreed.

In the end, I tell Titch everything I can in the basement. She listens.

When I finally come to a stop, she is quiet for a minute. Then she says, "Don't take this the wrong way. Because I'm not saying you should be grateful, exactly. Except, you know, maybe you should? A little bit? Or at least. Nina. Not many people know what it's like to have something like that."

"But I don't," I say despairingly. "I don't have it. She says she's in love with someone else."

"Well. Yes," Titch says. "Yes, she says that now."

"Do you still have stuff of Sarah's?" she asks then. "You should make a funeral pyre."

I have the headshot of Sarah in my bag and I hand that over to her. There are other bits and pieces in the car, letters, cards, scribbled notes, sweaters, T-shirts, jeans, books, a wrap, pictures, photos of the two of us running about like idiots on the beach, mixtapes covered in her beloved curvy handwriting, her jaunty *y*'s, gifts from small to large, decorative thimbles to a mossy green suede bag, everything freighted. First comes love, then detritus. I am not ready to rake it all up, to look at the crazy sad pile of it. Maybe in another eight months, or a year, I'll be ready to gather everything up in a large garbage bag, noose the neck with a yellow plastic tie, and throw it out. Or burn it, if that's not too dramatic. But not yet. I can't do it yet.

Titch studies the headshot critically for a minute, her head tilted at an angle. I lean in, unable not to look at the picture. There is the black-and-white sweetness of Sarah's mouth, curved, pursed, sloping, the heart-shaped cheek, the stark pale eyes. There is my predictable lurching pain.

Titch, frowning at the photograph, says, "Something's missing."

I look at her, confused.

"Strength of character maybe," she adds, and looks up, grinning at me so quickly that I almost miss it. "Or maybe integrity," she says musingly. "Something small like that."

She hands the headshot back, this time with her blessed, twitchy smile.

Something unknots in my chest. Kindness is what does it, kindness is to blame. I rub my face hard, covering my eyes, but when I take my hands down there is snot and wet all over them. I am shuddering, my chest seizing and heaving in great bumpy waves. I try to mop up with the tail of my shirt, the backs of my hands, and my sleeves.

Titch is visibly wincing. She hates emotional displays, even the threat of them. She grabs a dusty box of Kleenex from the top of the VCR, throws it at me, eyes averted, and goes back to her book.

"I'm serious about burning that," she says, without looking up. Her hair falls over her face.

Earlier after I'd said I didn't know if I wanted to go back to school, or home or New York, Titch had asked, "Well, where do you want to be then?" not exactly testy, but brisk, in the manner of old that suggested from time to time how very much

I got on her nerves. It was her tone of *no nonsense*, as my grandmother would say, approvingly.

Well, where do you want to be?

I think about that now.

It reminds me of the time at summer camp four years and ten lifetimes ago when the counselors asked us to imagine where we would want to be during nuclear war. You know, if the president slipped up and hit the wrong button, which everyone I knew seemed to think was fairly likely. Grown-ups I knew gave betting odds on that, and they weren't good odds. It seemed like a kind of morbid party game. Someone might say, *He won't do it, he has children himself*, but then if you looked at Ron Jr. and Patty, that wasn't encouraging, that wasn't going to make you think oh *right* they would be enough somehow to stop the all-out devastation of the world as we knew it. Who wanted the future of humanity to hang on that sad pair? Someone else might say in a grimly jovial way, *So what do you think? Is this the year?* Like the president was going to hit a homer and he was batting for the other team. The apocalyptic team. The death team. The planet incinerator team. All the *would he* or *wouldn't he* conversation was mind-bogglingly depressing, paralyzing.

It was the same thing with *The Day After*, that awful television movie about nuclear war. We had to watch it as a homework assignment for school and discuss it in class. The television network gave out viewers' guides that were supposed to prepare us for the graphic scenes of horror and destruction, radiation burns and the end of civilization. There were hotlines opened on the day the movie aired with the 800 number at the bottom of the screen so you could call in and talk to a counselor, who presumably would soothe your now frantic fears about nuclear winter. At the same time, censors reportedly forced ABC to cut a scene in which a child woke up screaming from a nightmare about nuclear holocaust. It was hard to square these things. Were we supposed to be afraid or reassured, or afraid and then reassured, or what?

The word was that President Reagan wept when he saw the movie. All that ever stuck in my mind was the ad that ran repeatedly, showing the mushroom flash going off, *poof*, obliterating the word *Apocalypse* on the television screen, and then a horse who was galloping through a field away from the explosion suddenly became nothing but bones, a skeleton that instantly disintegrated into dust.

Titch went around in the week before it was going to be shown on television solemnly repeating some version of the movie's tagline, which was *The End of the Familiar, the Beginning of the End.* When something wasn't going well in class she'd intone, *It's the End of the Familiar, the Beginning of the End.* This should have been funny, but actually it bummed me out. I hated seeing that horse's bones. I can still see them on the back of my eyelids, to this day. Why did the horse have to die?

At summer camp, we were supposed to describe in great detail the most beautiful, restful place we could imagine being. A place that was safe, a place that was home. The idea was that then we could visualize ourselves there whenever we got anxious about nuclear war, or, I guess, in the event of the actual nuclear war. I can still hear the kind, encouraging tones of the woman counselor—I think her name was Mary—who had an overbite and a crazy long, dirty blonde hippie braid tied with limp green string. I can hear her say coaxingly, *Where do you feel happy and loved? Where do you feel calm? Where do you feel you are truly at home?* And for a while the more I tried to locate this place—*Where the hell was it? Where* did *I feel happy and calm? Where did I feel loved and at home? Did such a place even exist?*—the more freaked out I got, like why were they so sure that we needed to visualize this place? What did they know? What were the odds, anyway? And why wasn't there anywhere that I felt this way?

Eventually this is what I came up with:

Once walking up to the barn early, early in the morning during lambing season, when it was bitterly cold and my nose ran, there were delicate crackling sheets of ice over the puddles in the road and I jumped on every one, shattering them. I was walking between the majestic bulk of my grandfather, his big steamy breath leading the way, and the elegant stem of my grandmother, and what I remember is that they both stopped and waited patiently while I crunched the ice. There was no talk of *coming along now*, only the happy satisfying crash and tinkle of those hundreds of fragile panes of glass. The winter light was grey and bleak on the road, with black looming trees, but the barn's warm darkness was comforting. The patiently chewing sheep heads turned in our direction, stirring in the hay. The sound of the tins of grain being opened—a screeching of metal on metal, the hollow drum of reverberation—would start a different kind of rustle in the barn. One after another the sheep would call until everyone was joining in the full-throttled *baaing* breakfast chorus. Occasionally the sounds of deep stomach gurgles mixed in, or a loud wet satisfied sheep belch. My grandmother, moving gracefully and efficiently, broke the layered inches of ice in the water buckets, banging the stretched and distorted black rubber tubs against the fence or on the frozen ground. My grandfather handed me flakes of hay to parcel out in the snowy barnyard, and to stuff into the feeders. Weak sunlight came out to light the ground in patches. I let my forehead rest against the splintery slats of the hayrack, breathing in that prickly sweet smell mingled with all the good warm animal smells of wool, lanolin, grain, manure.

That's where I'd be.

And on this day in the moldy basement, I think: right here, right here where I am with Titch. That too.

I feel emptied out, subdued. I look over at Titch, slouched over her book. I stand up.

"Where are we going?" she asks, folding down the page. And stretches her arms upward to join me.

The End

ABOUT THE AUTHOR

Tamsen Wolff is a professor in Princeton University's English Department, where she specializes in modern and contemporary drama, voice, directing, and dramaturgy. She has published essays in numerous journals, and is the author of *Mendel's Theatre: Heredity, Eugenics, and Early Twentieth-Century American Drama*. *Juno's Swans* is her first novel.